Saved for Something More

By Sandra McKee
and Kyle Grob

Copyright © 2012 Sandra McKee, Kyle Grob

Cover art: Anita Stewart
Authors photographer: Dominic Frascella

All rights reserved.
ISBN: 147528215X
ISBN 13: 9781475282153

ACKNOWLEDGEMENTS

The authors would like to thank the many open and supportive people who shared stories and information about the world of motorcycles and about the faith-filled people who ride them.

We are grateful to Gloria Spencer for her manuscript editing assistance in the early stages of this project and to Sandy and Amanda Stahl for their encouragement and input as critical readers.

Anita Stewart's professionalism and inspired creative efforts on the cover gave this book a visual presence we are very proud of.

Finally, we wish to thank the CreateSpace publication staff for their efforts on our book's behalf.

༺༻

FROM SANDRA

This project has had many starts and stops over the years, but it's always been a path of heart and I am grateful to my son, Kyle for this journey we have shared.

FROM KYLE

I would like to thank my mother for her wisdom, inspiration, acceptance and guidance.

PREFACE

*A*t the time my husband and I split up, my oldest son and I were not close. He was always more attached to his dad and had chosen to live with him when we separated. I knew I had to do something and do it right away to open the door for an ongoing relationship with Kyle. So, we went on a Mother-son retreat to the beach. On the way home we used a somewhat primitive laptop(it was 1998) that I had bought, and we roughed in the characters and the story during the four-hour drive. The idea originally came from a speaker Kyle had heard in church, a motorcycle minister. After the plot outline and characters were created, meetings and phone calls filled in the gaps as not only the book's story, but Kyle's and my story, unfolded. We wrote a new and loving relationship that we now both treasure.

Though divorce generally tears a family apart, in this case a mother and son project actually created a new and stronger relationship. We may not be able to control what happens to us, but we can choose how we go forward from a life-changing event. Experiences that a parent and child share weave the tapestry of relationships that last forever.

Throughout this book the elements of adventure and moral complexity serve as settings for redemption and conversion themes. In addition the reader receives the message, "Bidden or Unbidden, God is Present." Not everyone who comes to God's service comes willingly; some require a push. The characters in this story are no different.

<u>Saved for Something More,</u> though certainly inspirational, isn't a story about religion. It's a story about how

people of faith behave in a sometimes dangerous and oftentimes confusing world. They say the true test of character is the choices people make when no one is looking. We have, it is hoped, given you a peek into the private lives of devout people as they wrestle with life's challenges.

CHAPTER 1

The ancient blue Cadillac chugged and hissed. Smoke belched from its rear, puffs of surrender to mechanical coma. A metallic grinding death knell signaled the final shudder.

Crystal threw open the door, jumped out and slammed her hand down on the hood. She drew a deep breath and assessed her situation. As far as she could see in both directions, fences bordered expansive pastures that held yellow and white Chianina cattle. Their look of vague curiosity at her predicament angered her further. Ahead, she saw only large round hay bales and a rusting 1950s tractor.

The other direction held a bit more promise. Phil's Diner, a small white concrete block building, sat atop the hill about a mile away—a tough walk, all uphill, but doable.

Standing with hands on hips, she addressed the car. "I can't believe you've done this to me again, out here in the middle of nowhere. Well, what do you have to say for yourself?" It only hissed in response, as steam rose like horns from the hood.

She shaded her eyes and checked both directions hoping for a passing motorist but today no one was out on Parson's road except Crystal. Lifting her purse out of the car, she placed the strap resignedly over her shoulder. As an afterthought, she reached in and took out a large-brimmed straw hat with giant pink flowers on the band. *"Remember how easily you burn, Crystal. That's why God made hats."* Her mother's words of caution came back to her. Faint freckles on her pale skin contrasted with dark hair that framed a fine-boned face set off by deep blue eyes.

She adjusted her hat and straightened her already perfectly arranged clothes, muttering to herself. "Well, Crystal, a little walk might do you some good today." Not altogether convinced of its benefits, she nonetheless set off in the late August sun toward the white building.

Twenty minutes later she approached Phil's diner. Parked outside the familiar white block building, though, were fifteen large road-type motorcycles. They were mostly Harley Davidsons with a few custom bikes, but what worried Crystal, who didn't know motorcycles, was what she had heard enough about bikers to be frightened. Glad to avoid a meeting, she was relieved the pay phone outside was working. Through the open door she could hear loud laughter and occasional shouts as one or the other missed a shot at the single pool table Phil Woods had inside. With a slight shudder, she walked around the bikes and approached the pay phone.

"...I will fear no evil...thy rod and thy staff...." She recited softly under her breath. At the phone, however, she had another setback. "Oh, no. I don't have a quarter!"

Anxiously foraging through her purse, she didn't notice the man stand up at the end of the row of motorcycles.

HE HAD BEEN WORKING on his vintage Indian bike, but was distracted by the woman's mutterings. Curious, he watched her from his vantage point. He studied her statuesque shape from her refined ankles that showed beneath her flowered summer dress all the way up to her face now contorted in frustration and dismay. The corners of his eyes crinkled in an amused smile.

"Nice hat," he called as he approached her. She looked up sharply in surprise. The man, slightly taller than her own 5'10" height, stepped over to her. Lean but looking slightly top-heavy in his bulky leather jacket, he wore a black leather head wrap, which topped the unbroken darkness of the boots, leather pants and black tee shirt. Yet his smiling green eyes presented a look that was intimidating but at the same time boyish.

Though he had startled her, her desperate state and his friendly manner made her let her guard down momentarily. She studied him for a full second or two.

"Uh, what did you say?" she asked, regaining her composure.

"I said, 'Nice hat,'" he repeated with a grin.

She responded hesitantly, "Nice, uh, jacket." *I can't believe I'm talking to this hoodlum!*

He studied her again and felt his neck begin to turn red, reacting to her profound loveliness. *I can't believe I'm talking to this straight.* They looked at each other awkwardly for a few seconds. Then two of the other riders came out of the diner.

"Hey, Duke, what'cha got there, a lady?" one of them heckled then broke out in raucous laughter.

His disarmed moment passed, and he replied coolly, "Yeah, and she seems to be all alone. Maybe she needs our help. Ya' think?"

"Sure, our favorite thing is helping out the ladies," laughed an especially large and lethal-looking man laden with chains and tattoos. "I think she'd look great on my back seat." He cocked his head a bit as he ran his eyes slowly up and down, while sneering at her through a thick beard that extended halfway down the front of his torso.

Sensing the potential for trouble, Duke stepped in. "Oh no, Grunt, I saw her first. I'll take her out on a real bike. You'll just have to wait your turn."

As Crystal's face turned pale and real fear began to creep into her visage, Duke reached out and gently took her hand saying in quiet tones, "Don't worry, you'll be okay. Where do you need to go?"

His careful touch and the soft timbre of his voice reassured her, but her hand still shook. Wavering, she answered, "My car is broken down, and I need to get to Faith Church about two miles from here."

Just then the owner of the diner came out. "Miss Crystal, is there something wrong here?" He surveyed the bikers beginning to crowd around her.

Relieved at the interruption, she called to Phil Woods, the guardian of one of her students, and though a generation older than herself, a good friend. "Oh, Phil, my car broke down."

"You boys just move on back inside now and play a game of pool while I take Miss Crystal here where she needs to go," Phil suggested carefully.

Duke glanced at Phil then over at the men who were watching from the stairs. Slowly, he released her hand and backed away. Still training his eyes on her face, he called over his shoulder, "Yeah, Grunt, I haven't whipped up on you at pool in a while. How 'bout best two out of three?"

The large man studied Crystal, then answered Duke, "Okay, but I think you'll be sorry."

Duke glanced back briefly at Crystal who had turned away and was walking toward Woods. With a quick sideways smile he said, "Yeah, I probably will be."

He went into the diner with the big man and didn't see Crystal as she cast a surreptitious look at his back.

"CHILDREN, NOW WE WILL do the flower scene," Crystal instructed her charges as they moved around the stage. Directing a play with children was not an easy task to begin with, and the fact that they were all handicapped in some way made it even tougher. "Joey, will you help Angela to her place? Remember the signs I taught you?"

"Yes, ma'am," Joey responded. He wheeled his chair toward a small girl with curly brown hair playing with the paper flowers that were scenery for the play. Gently, he touched her arm and she looked up at him. He formed the words of Crystal's directions with signs and other hand gestures. Angela nodded and followed Joey to her spot.

Phil Woods, who had given Crystal a ride from the diner, lovingly watched his foster son, Joey. Crystal spoke to him as the children organized props for the play. "Thanks for your help today, Phil. You're a real friend."

After the rehearsal he asked her, "Did those biker hoodlums frighten you today?"

"You know, it's funny. I was afraid at first, but that one guy, the tall young one, seemed like he was trying to be nice."

"Don't be fooled by his kind, Crystal. I serve 'em because I have to and it keeps the peace but I don't trust any of 'em. They don't live by our rules. They aren't like us."

She thought about that for a moment. "Yes, I guess you're right. Thanks again."

"Anytime." He smiled then added, "Oh, by the way, there's a motorcycle rally just down the road in Greenville, so there'll probably be a lot of those guys around here for a while. You be careful."

"I will."

She paused. *What is it the Bible tells us about those who are different? I thought it was that we shouldn't judge, but I guess a woman does have to be cautious.*

"HEY MAN, IT'S YOUR shot. Where's your head at?" Grunt called Duke back from his daydreaming.

"Oh, I was just thinking," he responded.

"You know, you do way too much of that. Just play pool." Grunt took a shot then straightened.

"I was just wondering—"

"Wonderin' huh?" Grunt raised his eyebrows and grinned. "Wonderin' about the honey at the phone?"

"Watch your mouth!" Duke snapped.

"Whoa!" Grunt's surprised look faded to a curious one as he studied Duke for a moment. "Oh, I get it. You think you'd like to get to know her, do you?" he said mockingly, leaning on the pool cue. "Let me tell you about that kind. They dress in their nice dresses, go to their nice jobs and their nice homes and their nice families, and they ain't interested in us except as one of them rebellious fantasies, they call it."

"What? Are you a shrink now? We're going to have to start calling you Dr. Grunt."

"Let's just say you ought to stick to your own kind. They do."

"Maybe. She was just—right."

"What do you mean, right?" Grunt snorted.

"I don't know. She even looked good in that stupid hat."

"Uh-oh! The dude's lost it now. A pretty face and he's all soft and squishy."

"Drop it!" Duke said sharply. "Just play pool."

"THANKS FOR THE RIDE home, Phil. I'll get the car later." Crystal smiled and waved as Phil drove off. She opened the screen door then let it close again. With a thoughtful look, she removed her straw hat and picked at the flowers on it absently then walked over to the porch swing. As she sat, she placed the hat in her lap and smoothed her dress. The swing creaked deliberately forward and back, that groaning sound of chain hook against galvanized eye.

That's me, always coming back to the same place. God, can I ask you something? I'm truly grateful for my wonderful family, my job and for Phil. Yes, I'm even grateful for my old car. She chuckled to herself. *But why am I so restless? I stay close to home, do my job, stick to my path. Is that all you want me for? Is there nothing more?* Looking down, she sighed softly, picked up the hat from her lap and stopped the swing. She stood and gazed off down the road for a moment before she went into the house. Just as the door closed behind her, a lone motorcycle topped the hill in the distance.

CHAPTER 2

Crystal waited outside the judge's chambers. She had accompanied Phil to renew his petition to adopt Joey. As the door opened, she rose expectantly but sank back to the edge of the chair when she saw Phil's face.

"How'd it go?" she asked softly.

Phil shook his head. "Said he didn't want an old bachelor to have Joey permanent." He grumbled, "Social services report was good but he wanted to, as he put it, 'leave the door open' for a couple to adopt him."

Crystal touched him gently on the arm. "Don't be upset, Phil. They just don't understand what a special relationship you two have." She smiled then added lightly, "I'll bet if you were married the judge would look at things differently."

Phil cocked his head at her and raised one eyebrow thoughtfully for a second. "Yeah, maybe you're right." Then he forced a chuckle and hastily added, "Maybe I'll get me one of those mail order wives I heard about on TV."

"Phil Woods!" Crystal looked at him in feigned shock. "Shame on you!" They both laughed.

As they walked out of the building together, Phil offered, "Thanks for coming with me today. It meant a lot to have your moral support."

"Don't think a thing about it. You know there isn't anything I wouldn't do for you and Joey." She took his hand and squeezed it for just a second, then released it.

DUKE STOOD UP AND stretched. Stiff from crouching to work on the meticulously detailed Indian motorcycle, he swung his arms and arched his back. He typically rose earlier than the rest of the bikers he rode with. Mornings were his time for the daily maintenance the old bike required.

A 1953 Indian Chief, it was perfectly refurbished in every detail with the trademark red fenders and gas tank. The black leather seat had a silver-studded fringe around it. Duke sat back and admired the powerful and distinctive machine. Finally, he put his tools into the saddlebags, threw his leg over the bike, started it and revved the 1300cc motor. Liking the sound, he pointed the wheel away from the rising sun and rumbled out the driveway of the motel. He eased off the gas, savoring the ride. *It doesn't get any better than this.*

For the first few miles he rode at an easy pace then inched the throttle up. Shifting into a higher gear, he pressed the powerful motor. The road was flat and it was still too early for much traffic. The speedometer needle moved further and further. Made for high speeds, the engine settled into a resonant rumble as it continued to accelerate. The wind on his face egged him on, resisting his advances yet yielding to the force of man and machine.

As a car appeared in the distance he looked down, noticed his speed and began slowing. But when he passed the car going in the opposite direction he was still doing better than eighty.

"DID YOU SEE THAT?" Joey cried excitedly and craned his neck around to watch it disappear behind them. "What a bike!"

"Humph," Phil grunted his disapproval. "Those bikers think they can run the roads at any speed. At this hour too, with kids on the roads on their way to school. Bet that one's been out all night doing God only knows what." Phil paused as if waiting for affirmation from Crystal. He didn't get it.

It was him. I know it. The hair on her neck prickled, and her stomach jumped. She, too, had turned to watch the biker.

"What Phil? Did you say something?" She smiled sweetly as she turned her attention back to the interior of the car. "I was thinking of something else."

"Oh, never mind," Phil grumbled. "I'll just be glad when that motorcycle rally is over and those guys move on."

"Wow, cool," Joey repeated to himself.

Crystal's day began early. The handicapped children arrived at the school before the others so as not to make her students have to navigate through the crowds of rushing bodies when the first bell rang. Phil helped Joey unload his wheelchair and handed him his book bag.

"Thanks for the ride, Phil." She waved cheerily. "I hope the mechanic can fix my car one more time. This isn't a good time for me to have to buy another car."

"I'm sure they can take care of it—again," he laughed. Crystal's car was a well-known source of amusement and to find her standing by it on some road or other was a generally expected happenstance.

"But it's got character, and integrity, and class," she had once explained to Phil. "It was my grandfather's. I remember good times in that car."

He shook his head and smiled to himself as he called goodbye to Joey and drove off.

"Good morning, Tim." Crystal greeted the expressionless boy who walked right past her and went to a book on the shelf. He walked to his seat, laid down his book bag, opened the book and turned the pages in a ritualistic pattern, smoothing each page at the seam and scanning each line with his finger.

"Hello, Angela. That's—a pretty—dress." Crystal enunciated carefully while she signed the words to the smiling, curly-haired girl.

Then she saw Victor's head bobbing up and down in his familiar uneven gait. Crutches and braces allowed him to walk, though in a labored manner. He stopped as he approached. Carefully supporting himself, he extended one hand that held two plant bulbs.

"Plant dese." He managed to get the words out with difficulty, but confidently.

"Yes, we will. And this spring, they will bloom into beautiful, strong plants. Just like you." She tousled his hair as he went by her.

He stopped and turned, looking at her quizzically. "I not a plant."

Crystal laughed, remembering why she had majored in special education to begin with; the children had disarmed her with their unaffected truth and vibrant view of life. In spite of the Herculean efforts required by almost all of her students to perform their school activities, each one brightened her day in some significant way.

As the rest arrived, Crystal spoke to each one and reminded them of the assignment for the day. Christine arrived last. Though not handicapped, she was adopted from Romania and knew almost no English. Crystal agreed to take Christine in the special education class so she could get the attention and remedial work she needed while she learned the language.

The compassionate teacher surveyed the group with all their diverse needs and started the day, as she did every day, with a silent prayer. *God, help me this day to add to each child's life in the way that child needs. Oh, and if it's not asking too much, could you give my old car one more chance at life?* She smiled to herself, hoping the last part wasn't blasphemous.

"All right, children, this morning we'll start off with the state song and the pledge of allegiance. Your learning activity packets are on your desks. Please sit down."

CHAPTER 3

At the end of the day, Crystal waited outside the school. Heat caused the asphalt to send up shimmering water images and blurred the lines of the road. Sweat ran down her eyebrows and she pushed her hair back from her eyes. Even the occasional breeze didn't help in the hot southern sun.

Where IS Phil? I'm going to melt into a greasy spot right here on the sidewalk.

She removed her hat and fanned herself briefly, then looked up at the gas station across the street. After checking for traffic, she walked over to the store.

In a few minutes she came out with a soft drink. "Thanks, Jenny. See you later," she called over her shoulder.

She stepped down from the door. A motorcyclist rumbled up suddenly, startling her and nearly causing her to spill her drink. She glared at him for a second then crossed quickly in front of the bike.

"Sorry," he offered with a tentative smile. "I didn't see you."

She looked up as she passed, just long enough to see his smile. *Those white teeth. It's him again.* With irritation, she felt her face flush. "It's okay. No harm done."

She turned her head hurriedly to hide the beginning of a flirty smile that crept involuntarily onto her own face. Shoulders back and eyes straight ahead, she strode to the other side of the road with the no-funny-business attitude all southern girls are taught to use when accosted.

He really is cute. She shuddered a moment at the thought and chastised herself for even looking at him. *Oh, I sound like a teenager. But he doesn't seem like those other seedy-looking guys I saw at Phil's.* She felt him staring at her. She was at the same time both apprehensive and flattered. *What was that Phil said about bikers? I wonder if he carries a gun.* With her back to him, she took the luxury of an unguarded, schoolgirl grin.

DUKE WATCHED HER BACK. While he pumped the gas he thought, *What is it that gets me so about her? Grunt's right. She's not my kind and I'm not hers. But there's something about her—*

He put up the hose and went inside the store to pay. She cast a careful glance at the store then looked away when he came out and threw his leg over the bike. After he'd put his sunglasses back on he stole a look across the street without turning his head. Firing the throttle he roared out of the drive, off down the road.

Crystal, gazing after him, didn't notice the pickup truck zigzagging erratically toward her from the other direction. When she finally saw it, she froze.

In the rearview mirror, Duke saw the truck heading toward the curb where she stood. He spun the bike around. "Look out!" he yelled.

She blinked and jumped back, falling just out of the path of the truck. As it hit the curb, the driver jerked the wheel and the truck lurched back to the roadway.

Never slowing, the old pickup continued its wandering in Duke's direction. He swerved to get out of its way but it passed close enough that he slammed the hood with his fist.

Revving his engine, he reached Crystal in seconds. She sat on the sidewalk, her hair half pinned up, half fallen down, trying to examine a bleeding elbow. He dismounted and, squatting beside her, removed his dark glasses. "You okay?"

"I—I think so."

He offered her his hand. "Here, I'll help you."

She looked up at him, shading her eyes from the glare of the sun.

A little dazed, she took his hand. Even through his leather glove it felt warm, firm and strong. He lifted her to her feet. She surveyed her clothes for signs of damage. "Thank you," she said softly.

"Doesn't look like a good day to be on foot," he observed good-naturedly with a boyish grin. "Can I give you a lift somewhere?"

At that moment, Phil drove up. Seeing Crystal's hand in Duke's, he jumped out of the car. "What's happened? Are you all right?" He turned to Duke with a scathing look. "And what are you doing?"

Duke, taken by surprise, self-consciously dropped her hand. Then he set his jaw at Phil's attack.

"Billy Nyson—" Crystal stammered.

Phil hustled Crystal to his car, still running with the door standing open. A bit stunned from her near miss, she obediently submitted to Phil's directions.

Duke followed her with his eyes as they got into the car. He bent over, picked up the straw sun hat she'd forgotten and studied it for a few seconds. After the car sped away, he put it in the saddlebag on his bike.

Crystal turned around to look. "Wait, I don't think I thanked him."

"Don't worry about it," Phil muttered. "What happened anyway?

"Billy Nyson nearly ran me down. Must have been drunk again."

"Do you think you should stop by and see the doctor?"

"No, it's just a scrape, but I think I tore my dress." She looked around her on the seat. "And my hat. I left my hat."

"Let it go. You need to get that arm taken care of," Phil insisted.

She was quiet the rest of the way home. With a mixture of shock, relief and a feeling she couldn't quite identify, she replayed the scene in her mind. Rubbing her palm, she remembered the feel of his glove. His smile hung in her mind as well. *Who is this guy?*

"DRINK UP EVERYBODY! TODAY'S my birthday so the drinks are on me!"

Duke held up a glass and saluted the crowd at the table. The rally was in its third day. The campground was full, mostly with Harley Davidson hogs of various vintages and custom designs. Phil Woods' diner was the only place in the area that served food and beer so bikers gathered there each night.

Grunt stood up, rocking slightly. After he righted himself, the giant man raised his glass and sloshed a little on the coarse-looking tattooed blond woman beside him. She didn't seem to notice.

"Listen up, all you puppies."

Everyone laughed at Grunt's feigned formality. "It is my duty to announce that the kid's finally a man. He's turning twenty-one today."

Everyone hooted and whistled. Grunt motioned for quiet. Duke laughed along with the others at Grunt's play-acting. "So after today he don't have to have a note from mommy and daddy to stay out late."

Grunt roared and slapped Duke on the back, causing guffaws of laughter to fill the place.

The vacant-looking blonde stirred from her stupor and laughed with the others then stood up and staggered over to Duke. He had stopped laughing and was staring into his beer. She put her arm around him and drew her body close. "And I'm going to give him a reason to stay out past his bedtime." Then she pressed her face into his.

He pulled back and forced a smile. "Yeah, Dolores here and me are going out. Don't wait up."

Grunt howled in laughter again and slapped Duke on the back. With the woman hanging around his neck, Duke moved toward the door. Outside, he pulled away from her and, with a scowl, strode over to his bike.

"Where ya' goin' honey? I thought we was gonna' have some fun."

"Beat it," he snapped. "I'm takin' a ride." He fired the Indian's motor and peeled out of the parking lot, spraying gravel behind him.

"What's your problem?" the bewildered woman called after him.

Duke bore down on the throttle and went quickly through the gears. As he buried the speedometer needle, the wind blew the tears that burned his eyes. He set his jaw and blinked to fight them back but it was no use. All the pain came back.

He remembered the phone call. "I'm sorry to have to tell you this, but your parents are missing." It was Pastor Clegg. "The military overthrew the government in a countrywide coup. The village where your parents were is occupied by troops and several of our people have been killed. We don't know for sure about your parents; they won't let us in to recover the bodies."

The man had paused, waiting for a response. Hearing none, he continued.

"I'm sorry. Don't give up hope. We don't know for sure what's happened to them. They could have escaped. They are good and devout people. I'm sure God is looking after them."

"Yeah, like he looked after the ones that were killed?" Duke had responded.

"I'll let you know as soon as we hear anything. All we can do now is to pray."

Eventually, through another mission group and Red Cross negotiators, some of the bodies of the church team who had died in Guatemala were recovered. His parents' bodies were not among them.

"We're sorry. They only let us go in once. We didn't see any sign of your folks."

Several people had come over to the house to offer support. "Don't give up hope. God works in his own way, and we must accept his will."

He had stayed for the funerals of the other missionaries and had yielded to the ministrations of the church members for meals and such. Then, exactly two weeks after the first phone call, he went to the garage, took the cover off the old Indian motorcycle he and his father had painstakingly rebuilt, climbed on it and rode out. No goodbyes, no note, nothing.

That had been three years ago. The boy, merely eighteen at the time, had grown up.

HE SQUINCHED HIS EYES and wiped them with a gloved hand while the other tightened on the throttle. He shouted to the wind. "They were fools. And so was I." He shook his fist at the sky. "God, I will never, ever forgive you!" Ticking away miles in fractions of minutes, he barreled down the highway.

CHAPTER 4

Two months had passed since the motorcycle rally ended with no sign of the mysterious young man on the "cool" bike. The day after her near miss with the drunk driver, Crystal had received a note at school. "Hope you're okay. Try to stay out of traffic," it said. She had thanked Phil for the note then discovered he hadn't written it.

"I wonder—" she said aloud, sitting on the front porch swing. She remembered the strong hand that had picked her up.

"Crystal, honey," her mother called, "the phone's for you. I think it's Phil Woods."

"Okay, Mom." Inside, she picked up the phone. "Hello? Oh, hi Phil. Yes, I'll meet you there. What's this about? You sound so serious. Is something wrong? Okay, see you later. Bye."

"Was that Phil?"

"Yes, and he says he has something very important to discuss with me. He sounded awfully serious."

"What do you think it is?" Not waiting for a response from Crystal, she continued, "He's such a nice man. And that little Joey's a real dear. It's a shame they won't let Phil adopt him; he loves him so much. Anyway, what time are you meeting him?"

"In an hour. Wants me to meet him at Shea's on the River. Said he had to close up the diner first and wouldn't have time to come by and get me to make a 7:30 reservation. Very strange."

"Oh, well, it's a nice place. I'm sure you'll have a good time. I never have to worry about you with Phil. I know he takes good care of you."

Oh, Mama, are you ever going to think of me as grown up? She turned to go up the stairs to the room she had lived in since childhood. *Am I ever going to think of me as grown up?*

CRYSTAL SCANNED THE MENU—AGAIN. Phil arrived out of breath. "Sorry I'm late. Someone came in just as I was closing."

He paused when he noticed her staring at him.

"Phil, why are you so dressed up?" She studied his suit, white shirt and tie. "I don't believe I've ever seen you in a suit except at church."

"Let's order," he said hurriedly, taking the chair opposite her.

All through dinner Crystal noticed that Phil was unusually fidgety. By the time dessert arrived, Crystal's curiosity had gotten the better of her. "Okay Phil, what's going on? What is so important that you're wearing a suit?"

"Crystal, I've been thinking," Phil blurted. "You know, about Joey and what that judge said." He took a deep breath. "And, well, I believe that if I was—married—you know, mom and home and all that—the judge would grant me an adoption. What do you think?" He concluded with a huff and gazed at her, wide-eyed.

"Goodness, Phil." She clasped her hands in front of her. "I guess that would probably work, but who are you thinking about? You hadn't mentioned that you were seeing anyone."

"That's what I wanted to talk to you about, Crystal. See, you're awfully good with Joey, and we're good friends and I was wondering—uh, hoping that—well, here." Phil shoved a small, velvet box toward her.

Crystal stared. She asked cautiously, "Phil, what is this?"

"I wanted to do it right."

"Do what right?"

"I want—uh—will you—would you consider—marrying me?"

Still not touching the box, Crystal's mouth opened to speak, but no words came out.

"Joey loves you, and I—"

Crystal still had not spoken. She slowly reached for the box and turned it over in her fingers.

Phil pushed on. "I know you don't really love me, not in the marrying kind of way, but this is for Joey. I know you care for him. We wouldn't have to be really married, I mean—you know." Phil blushed, but continued like a man with a mission. "You could have your own room and—"

"Phil, I don't know what to say."

"It would give Joey a chance for a home, a real home. He deserves that. Would you at least think about it?" Phil summoned a strained smile that did nothing to break the tension. "I'd treat you well, Crystal, you know that. You wouldn't want for anything. I could even get you a new car."

Crystal slowly opened the box and looked down at the ring, an emerald cut diamond with baguettes on each side. Phil reached across the table, took her hand and looked at her earnestly. "Please think about it. We could be a family."

She looked back at Phil, her dear friend, her frequent guardian angel. Instead of the definite answer that was making its way to her mouth, she stopped short of an on-the-spot refusal. "Phil, this is sudden and unexpected. But I will honor your request by thinking about it."

She closed the jewelry box and put it in her purse.

"Thank you, Crystal. That's all I have the right to ask."

She stood to leave, avoiding eye contact with Phil who was looking for any sign of encouragement. She walked to her car, leaving Phil still standing at the table.

Crystal drove home slowly. After pulling into the driveway, she sat in the darkness. Reaching into her purse, she removed the small, velvet box, rolled it over in her hand then opened it. The ring shone as if it had its own source of light. *It is beautiful. Phil was sweet to go to so much trouble. He's right. Joey is a wonderful child and deserves a family. Phil's a good man.* She sighed and touched the ring.

How many guys are going to come along in this town? She sighed again, heavily this time, and looked down the highway. *What other chance will I have for marriage and family?* A tear escaped the corner of her eye before she realized it was there. *Still, I had always dreamed there would be more. Just a dream, I guess.*

With another heavy sigh she put the ring on her finger then went into the house.

CHAPTER 5

"Is this the motorcycle crack-up?" A young orderly approached the nurse who was wheeling an unconscious patient.

The regional medical center, thirty-five miles from Crystal's small town, had a relatively sophisticated trauma center so accident victims were taken there.

"Yes, we're moving him to the neuro unit. He's still in a coma."

"I heard about it. They found him walking along the road but the cop said he looked like a corpse."

"Strange thing is his bike ended up at the bottom of a gully. How did he climb that hill with a broken hip, a concussion and massive internal injuries?"

"Maybe he had help," a voice commented. A short, muscular man with a ponytail took the patient's hand and held it for a second.

TWO WEEKS LATER THE young patient still lay in the sunny but sterile hospital room.

"Daniel, Daniel, you need to wake up now."

He heard a soft, female voice off in the distance. He tried to focus on it but felt as if his body were separate from him.

Mom? Is that you? His feeble attempt at an answer just came out like a faint groan.

"You say he's moving more? As severe as his injuries are it's probably just as well he's not fully conscious. But I want him to come around soon. We need to see what effects that head injury had on his motor skills. I don't know how he made it; got to be a tough young man there. Have you found any family yet?"

"No, ma'am. The address on his driver's license is not current, the police officer said."

"Well, at least it looks like we won't have to notify next of kin. It appears Mr. Davis is going to be with us a while longer." The doctor checked the bandages one last time. "Keep trying to get him to come around."

FINALLY, NEARLY A MONTH from the day of his arrival at the hospital, the man in the mirror looked back but with no face he recognized. His broken jaw was still swollen and the red marks of thirty-six stitches held the skin of his cheek together. Strawberry blond hair was growing around a second closed gash in the top of his head. His eyes traced the healing incision line from mid-chest to just below his waist. *Don't know why they didn't just put in a zipper while they were at it.*

"Hello, I'm Doctor Zath." Surprised, Duke turned quickly toward the voice. "I worked on your jaw when you came in and wanted to check on how my work turned out."

"When do I get to eat real food?" Duke mumbled in return.

"Looks like you're healing well. Soon, I think."

"This is pretty ugly. Will it get better?"

"Well, you gouged a piece out of your cheek when your jaw broke. You'll heal but there will still be a pretty noticeable scar."

"Great."

"I would think a man your age might consider a beard." The doctor pointed toward the mirror while Duke studied his swollen face. He rubbed the stubble that was starting to emerge and nodded thoughtfully.

That afternoon, he was moved to the Agape Center, a rehabilitation hospital. He had just settled into his bed when the inhalation therapist came in. "You're not going to make me breathe into that little thing with the balls are you? That hurts like h—"

"Oops, we don't use language like that around here," the therapist jumped in. "This is a Christian facility and everyone would appreciate it if you would respect the sensibilities of those around you."

"What? You mean I've fallen into a bunch of do-gooders? Next thing I know someone will be tryin' to save me."

At that moment, a man walked in. He was about 5'7" tall, square-jawed and narrow-hipped, his brown hair pulled back into a ponytail. Overly muscular for his size, he looked like a miniature Mr. Universe. Brown eyes so dark the pupils were barely discernable peered at Duke, not in a challenging way, but not passively either.

"Hello," the man began, "I'm—"

"Oh, let me guess. The local preacher calling on the poor and infirm, right?"

The man's easy smile showed no trace of offense at Duke's attitude. "No, actually, I'm Casper Penmartin, the physical therapist here, and the thing I intend to save you from is a lifetime of walking with a limp. That is, if you cooperate with me."

A little chagrined, the young man replied, "Yeah, sure. What have I got to lose? I ain't goin' nowhere just now anyway." Then he grinned a little. "Casper?"

"Yeah, I know, the ghost and all that. But it's a family name and you'll just have to get over it. I have. Now, you and I have work to do. You might as well start recovering right away. Here." He set a folded aluminum framework beside the bed. "Use this walker to get down to the therapy room. You've had some nerve damage in addition to the hip replacement and you're going to have to reeducate your body for walking."

"Walker? Hey, I'm not using this. These things are for old people—"

"—And for people having balance and control problems as a result of injury." Casper finished the patient's sentence and grabbed him as he came off the bed and was teetering for a fall.

This guy's like a rock! Duke thought. Casper supported him only a second then shoved the walker in front of him.

"Now, let's understand each other. I'm not your crutch or your cane or your mommy. But if you listen to me and do as I say, you'll get your mobility back. Until then, use this."

A little wide-eyed at this stranger's direct manner, the wobbly man put first one hand then the other on the walker and straightened. Casper pushed the door open and turned back to his patient. "Okay, time to get moving. Take small steps at first. The main thing now is left, right, left, right in some sort of rhythm."

Casper looked on as Duke struggled a few steps. The inhalation therapist winced in sympathy and moved to help him. With his head down in intense concentration on making his unwilling legs move, he barely noticed Casper waving her away.

As Duke labored out the door, one carefully placed step at a time, Casper kept talking. "C'mon, we've got a lot of work to do if you're going to get out of here anytime soon. It won't be easy but we can progress as fast as you're willing. Just remember no one can do this for you." Casper turned slightly back into the room and gave a thumbs-up and a wink to the therapist. She smiled knowingly and returned the gesture.

AT CRYSTAL'S CHURCH, PASTOR Reasons stepped away from the pulpit and walked out into the congregation. A tall, stout man, he had a warm smile that softened the formidable appearance of the dark robes of his faith. He was silver-haired and round-faced with a handkerchief in his hand to wipe his ever-perspiring forehead.

"I want to open the announcements of church business with some wonderful news. Phil Woods and Crystal Harper are engaged to be married." He walked toward the row where Phil, Crystal and Joey sat. "Most of you know Phil, owner of Phil's Diner, and some of you have children that Crystal has taught." He extended a hand in a sweeping motion. "Would you two stand so everyone can know you?"

Crystal stood but blushed and looked sheepishly at the floor. Phil smiled broadly as he rose. He glanced at Crystal and his face tightened a little. Then he waved tentatively as they both sat down.

"Lovely couple, don't you think?" Pastor Reasons remarked. The congregation applauded. "They haven't set a date yet, but we all look forward to the wedding. Right, Joey?" He leaned down to the boy in the wheelchair.

Joey stretched toward the lapel microphone. "We're going to be a family," he beamed. Crystal smiled briefly at everyone, patted Joey on the hand and returned her attention to the hymnal.

They're all looking as if they wonder why we're doing this. Well, who cares what they think? Phil is a good man and Joey is wonderful. I know I'm doing the right thing.

After the service Pastor Reasons called Crystal aside. "You have my warmest wishes, my dear." He took her hand between his two large minister's hands, held it firmly and looked her earnestly in the face. "I am so fond of both of you."

"Thank you, Reverend," she replied softly. She turned to walk to the car.

"Oh, Crystal, I almost forgot. A rehabilitation center I know of has some state funds for educational activities. I thought you might like to go over and meet with them to see if you could use some of the money in your programs."

"Well, yes, I'd love to talk to them. Do you have a name I should contact?"

"Let's see. It's something to do with ghosts. Spectre? No." He paused and scratched his head, perplexed. Crystal gazed at him expectantly. "Oh, yes, yes, I have it now. Casper something. That's it." He sighed. "Anyway, you go meet him."

"I will, thank you." She replied.

"WHAT'S 'GAGED' MEAN, MS. Crystal?" Victor stopped his work and looked up at the teacher as she bent over him.

"You mean, EN-gaged, Victor?"

"Well, you know. What's it mean?" he insisted.

"It means a man and woman are thinking of getting married and they spend some time seeing what that feels like."

"When you married, you goin' have babies? My sister says married people have babies."

Crystal felt her cheeks burn. "We'll see. You need to get back to work now, Victor." Crystal straightened up. She looked over at Joey working at his place. *I guess I hadn't really considered that.* She walked back to her desk and sat down. *Joey will be with us. That's enough.* She looked out the window down the familiar rural highway.

MONDAY AFTER THE CHILDREN had gone Crystal called the Agape Center in Forest City.

"This is Crystal Harper. Is there a Mr. Casper—?" She paused.

"Penmartin, Casper Penmartin," the voice at the other end filled in. "He's director of physical therapy here. Who may I say is calling?"

"I'm Crystal Harper. Robert Reasons, the minister at my church, mentioned some educational funds that I should talk to Ca—uh, Mr. Penmartin—about."

"Oh yes. I'll page him."

"Thanks." Crystal studied the engagement ring on her finger while she waited.

"Ms. Harper? This is Casper Penmartin. Bob Reasons tells me you have some trouble with funding over there at the school and the state has just given us some money that we're not sure how to spend. I know that sounds ridiculous but we are a therapy and rehabilitation center here and the money must be used specifically for education programs for physically handicapped children. Guess they thought we'd figure out what to do. Can you help us?"

Crystal was taken aback by his almost brusque manner. She stared blankly at the phone, silent for several seconds.

"Ms. Harper?"

"Uh, sorry. It's just that we have so much trouble with money that—"

"Yeah, we do too, and now the blasted state is telling us how to spend what they give us. We're funded mostly by churches and a private foundation. But since we're the only rehab center for the area I guess they figure they have to do something for the folks around here. I'm busier'n Aunt Tilley at a white sale but would Thursday work for you?"

Still startled by his hurried and directive manner, she stammered, "I—I think Thursday would work. Yes."

"Take Highway 19 to the third four-way stop after the county line. Turn right and you'll see us about three quarters of a mile down on the left. It's an old mental hospital we've converted and refurbished. Sometimes I wonder if you don't still have to be a little crazy to work here. All righty, see you Thursday. About five? Goodbye now."

The phone had already clicked by the time Crystal got out a soft, "Goodbye." *Whew! Well, I'd probably meet with Atilla the Hun if I thought he could help my kids. Sure would be nice not to have to worry about money for field trips or extras.*

She 'humphed' softly to herself.

THURSDAY AFTERNOON, CRYSTAL LEFT straight from school and drove to Forest City. Following Casper's directions she drove to an old brick one-story building with bars on the windows. A tall, deteriorating chain link fence surrounded the immaculately tended grounds. Even the fresh paint didn't disguise the obvious former use of the place. As she pulled into the parking area, she passed a large formidable looking man on a loud motorcycle. He stared right at her for a second then turned away to look for traffic before he roared out onto the highway. She shuddered as he went by. *That guy looks familiar. Where—?* She thought a moment then shook her head. *Doesn't matter. Now, let's meet this ghost fellow.*

"WELCOME, MS. HARPER!"

Crystal studied Casper Penmartin, noting first his height, which was several inches less than her own, and his athletic build. He shook her hand firmly and she found herself instantly comfortable with this warm, energetic man.

"Thank you for thinking about our program," she began. "We're always looking for ways to meet the children's needs."

"Well, we know about that here. All our patients need so much. Many don't have anywhere to go when they leave here. But they're all God's; it's our job to figure out how to help them." He directed her down a hall to the right as he talked. "Let me show you around our facility." He told her about the center, its constant funding problems, the success stories, the occasional failures.

Crystal listened, fascinated. "What brought you to choose this type of work?" she asked.

He paused thoughtfully for a second then smiled. "It isn't a choice. This is what I do, who I am. I don't question it. What I do contributes to the quality of someone's life everyday. Who could ask for more?"

Crystal laughed. "Mr. Penmartin, I agree completely." *I like this man,* she thought. *He accepts his service just like breathing.*

When they reached an office door he motioned her inside. "Come on, I'll show you the grant papers and we can begin to work on some programs." They pored over the papers, made notes, discussed alternatives. Finally, Casper looked at the clock and stood up. "Crystal, I have a therapy session. Before you head out you might enjoy meeting this patient.

He's a real tough guy. Shoulda' died from his injuries, the doctors said, but apparently no one could convince him."

Not waiting for her assent, Casper guided her out of the office and continued to talk. She had to hurry to keep up with his brisk walk. Crystal smiled as he directed her. *I'll bet nobody tells this guy no—ever.*

They entered a large room that looked like a small gymnasium. Weight machines of various sorts lined the walls. In the far corner was a whirlpool. A young man came through the door walking slowly and leaning heavily on a cane. His appearance startled her. He was thin—not in a lean and fit way—like someone who hadn't eaten well in a long time. Movement appeared to be painful as well as difficult. His face drew her attention, though. A short, reddish-blond beard covered his lower jaw and his hair was cut as short as the beard. He seemed focused on the effort of walking. As he approached, she heard, "Left, right, left, right—"

"Daniel," Casper said, "I'd like you to meet someone."

The sound broke the man's concentration and he jerked to an unsteady halt. He looked up from his laborious steps. Momentarily, he wrinkled his brow when he saw Crystal.

Sensing his awkwardness, she smiled quickly. "I'm Crystal Harper." She extended her hand then noticing the cane in his right hand, withdrew it. "Mr. Penmartin and I are working on a funding project together."

"Not much fun about this guy's projects, I've noticed," the stone-faced man commented dryly.

Crystal peered at him for a second not knowing if he had misunderstood or was making a joke. Seeing just a hint of a smile forming, she laughed lightly. "Yes, I can see that about him," she responded. "Look, you guys have work to do here. I'll be going." She pulled the door open then called to Casper, "I'll write up those modules we talked about and the occupational therapy objectives. See you next week." Then as an afterthought she turned back briefly. "Nice to meet you, Daniel."

BENT OVER THE WEIGHT machine, Casper cut his eyes sideways and caught his patient watching her go.

"What?" The younger man snapped. He looked like a child caught cautiously regarding the cookie jar.

"Nothing," Casper shrugged, grinning. "Let's get to work."

CHAPTER 6

A week later, Crystal returned. "Mr. Penmartin please," she addressed the receptionist.

"Oh, he's in the therapy room working with a patient. He's expecting you and said to send you on down. End of the hall, right then right again. Room C."

"Thank you," she called as she walked.

Penmartin's unmistakable voice carried out into the hall.

"Come on. My five-year-old nephew can do more reps than that. Besides, you're bionic now, so let's see some weights move."

"Hello, Mr. Penmartin, the receptionist told me—"

"Yes, yes, Daniel and I are just finishing up here. Let's all go get something to drink." Crystal glanced questioningly at Penmartin's charge.

"Yes, sir," the young man mockingly acquiesced. Then to Crystal, he added, "It's useless to resist."

"What?"

"It's useless to resist—the force—you know, Star Wars, Darth Vader and all that?" Crystal giggled.

"Actually, though, I think he looks more like Yoda. What do you think?"

"All right, all right, enough already. Last one to the coffee shop has to buy." Penmartin disappeared out the door.

Awkwardly, Crystal turned to offer. "Do you need help?"

"Not really," he answered. "I would appreciate it if you'd walk with me, though, since Penmartin has run off—just in case."

"Oh, yes, of course."

"Ladies first." He held the door for her.

After several minutes, Crystal and Duke arrived at the coffee shop. Penmartin looked at his watch. "You two go ahead and chat. I have to take care of something. Crystal, stop by my office in a bit and we'll go over that proposal." Then, before either could speak, he strode out the door.

"Well, I guess it's just us," Duke offered. "It'll be nice to talk to someone from the outside."

They got their drinks from the fountain and took a table by the windows. After making small talk for a while, Crystal asked what had happened to him.

"I don't remember anything." He looked outside for a long moment. "The doctors told me an off-duty cop found me walking along the road and took me to the hospital. I woke up three weeks later with four broken ribs, a slice out of my face, a metal hip to replace one that got crushed and stitches up the front of me like Frankenstein.

Crystal stared wide-eyed at him. "How long have you been here?"

"Gee, I don't know. Days are all pretty much the same."

"Doesn't anyone visit you?" She knew she was prying, but she hoped it might pass as casual conversation.

"Well, there's G—," he began then caught himself. "Uh, a buddy of mine stops in when he's in town."

"No family?"

"There isn't anyone else, not really. My parents are dead."

"Oh, I'm sorry." Crystal looked at him sympathetically.

"Yeah, well, no big thing. It was several years ago. I'm over it," he responded with a nonchalance that seemed carefully contrived. But a dark sadness came over him. Uncomfortable, she hurried to change the subject.

"Can I ask you a favor?"

"Sure, that's what I'm here for." The coldness remained.

She dropped her eyes, chagrined at this new treatment then stood up to leave. "Never mind. It'd be too much trouble. Sorry I brought it up."

He hurried to stand and touched her hand as she was turning away from him. "I'm sorry. Guess I've been locked up in here too long." A sincere contrition in his eyes conveyed a real apology. But there was something else. The touch of his hand on hers felt embarrassingly natural. She froze for a second, recording the moment. She remembered someone whose touch had felt that way.

She looked down at his hand on hers. His face reddened slightly and he released her. She slowly withdrew her hand.

"What was it you wanted to ask me?"

"Uhm—" She hesitated then pushed on quickly. "—Could my children write to you?" She studied him for a reaction. "They need the practice and you would have something to read."

He raised an eyebrow and cleared his throat. "You have children?"

"My students," she smiled. "I teach special education. Penmartin is helping me with funding. It's why I've been coming over here lately."

"Aw, I thought it was to see me." The light cockiness returned with the confident smile. His relaxed and disarming manner let her know this time it was okay to laugh at his joke. "Actually, writing to the kids would help my therapy. The last three fingers on my right hand are numb. They work okay, I just can't feel anything. Penmartin tells me I need to use the hand as much as possible. And it's getting boring around here."

"Good." Crystal turned again to leave then sheepishly turned back to him. "Excuse me, but I don't know your whole name."

"Davis, Daniel Davis. And yours?"

"Crystal Harper, for now anyway."

"What does that mean?"

"Well, I'm engaged to be married," Crystal answered softly.

"That didn't sound very enthusiastic for a woman in love. When's the happy event?"

"We haven't set a date yet. We're still—uh—working out details. You know, family schedules, work, that kind of thing."

"Well, the guy had better step up to the plate soon or someone else may come in and sweep you off your feet. Anyway, congratulations. And of course I'll answer the kids' letters. Will you be bringing them?"

"I hadn't thought about it. Um, yes, I guess I could. Mr. Penmartin and I have a few more details to work out so I'll be back at least once more."

He stood up, put his hands in his pockets. "Good. See you then."

"PHIL, I'M GOING TO a conference in Jackson, Mississippi at the end of the month. Mr. Penmartin says I need to begin using the grant money in case the state has a budget cut. I've been asked to present a workshop on my use of drama with handicapped children. It's an honor but they don't pay anything."

"That's wonderful, Crystal. But how are you going to get there?" Phil chuckled. "I don't believe that old car of yours would make it."

"Okay, no jabs at my car." She shook her finger at him. "In fact, I'm taking the train over. My old college roommate lives there and she'll meet me. I'm staying a couple of extra days to spend time with her so I'll be gone a whole week."

"I don't know about that," Phil said. "My 'intended' running off for a whole week." He smiled and kissed her on the cheek.

She returned his smile quickly then turned away. "I'll see you later. I have to go. The substitute will need detailed lesson plans and I have a lot of work to do." As she went out the door of the diner, she called, "You and Joey find yourselves something to do while I'm gone and don't get into any trouble."

"Okay, we'll see if Rev. Reasons has any projects going. That ought to keep us busy. He's always into something."

She laughed out loud. "Yes, he is. Be careful though, you never know what he's up to."

"Bye, Crystal," Joey called from the yard where he was playing. Phil walked outside and waved to Crystal as she left.

Phil turned to the boy. "You know how much I love her, Joey?"

"This much?" He stretched his arms as wide as he could.

"Yes, and then some." Phil put his arm around Joey.

LOOKING INTO HER REARVIEW mirror, Crystal regarded them. *I'm really lucky to have those two. When we're a family, I'll finally have my place. Maybe then I'll feel settled.*

THE FIRST WEEKEND CRYSTAL was gone, Phil worked in the yard, stripped and waxed the floor in the diner and took Joey to the park. It seemed he couldn't find enough things to do with the time on his hands. Finally, Sunday arrived. He and Joey dressed in their church clothes and arrived early.

"Well, how are you two doing?" Reverend Reasons asked. "I hear Crystal's away this week."

"We miss her—a lot," Joey volunteered, and Phil nodded.

During the announcements, the Reverend made a request. "As you know, our congregation helps support Agape Center, a rehabilitation hospital. This time they are not asking us for money but for a home. One of the patients is ready to leave the hospital but he has no family and is not quite ready to strike out on his own yet. They've asked if anyone here could take this person in for a time." A muffled ripple of conversation passed over the crowd. Someone raised a hand.

"How long?"

"As I understand it, a month would be the commitment, along with a little help with job-hunting and general starting over. This young man has survived a terrible accident and nearly died. Apparently, God has saved him for something more, so the least we can do is to help him along a little."

Another hand rose tentatively. "He can come and stay with me and Joey, Reverend," Phil volunteered.

"Thank you, Phil, but what about your upcoming marriage?"

"Oh, we're probably going to wait 'til the end of the term so Crystal can have some time off and that's a ways away yet. I got that big old house, plenty of room, and it's just us fellas there, me and Joey. I think it'll work out real fine," Phil closed matter-of-factly and sat down.

"Good, Phil. I'll call the director tomorrow and tell him. He'll get in touch with you on the details."

The minister continued with the service while Phil whispered to Joey. "Crystal told us to find something to keep us occupied and out of trouble, didn't she? Won't she be glad to hear about this?"

MONDAY MORNING, PHIL ANSWERED the phone.

"This Phil Woods?"

"Yes, it is. What can I do for you?"

"I'm Casper Penmartin, director of the Agape Rehabilitation Center. Reverend Reasons gave me your name. Said you volunteered to provide a step home for one of our patients."

"I did," Phil confirmed.

"Why don't you come over and meet the young man? There's a bit you should know about him before you decide."

"Okay, my diner is closed this afternoon. I guess Joey and me could ride over."

"Good, then it's set. See you this afternoon."

Casper Penmartin hung up the phone, drummed his fingers on the desk a moment, then pushed back his chair resolutely. "Well, Daniel Davis. Now comes the really hard part."

CHAPTER 7

"So, Duke, you bustin' out'a here?"

A robust, bearded biker sat across the table and peered at the younger, frowning man in a flannel shirt and jeans. The big man leaned back on the worn couch and threw one arm across the back.

Duke turned the bottled water around and around in his hand.

"I don't know, Grunt. They tell me I'm moving in with some old guy and his kid." He paused. "What I'd really like is to just ride out and forget this whole thing."

"It ain't gonna' happen, kid. Reggie's still trying to put your bike back together, but there's not much she can do. Those parts are pretty scarce. It ain't like they're makin' any more of 'em. She did say there's some guy in Atlanta that's an expert on Indians. He might be at the swap meet coming up next month."

"That'd be great if I could make a connection with him. But I gotta' get some cash or it won't do any good. And I can't do that in here."

"So what you gonna' do?"

"I'm not sure." He paused, troubled for a moment. Then, he brightened suddenly. "Grunt, there's somethin' I gotta' tell ya'. You remember that girl?"

"Girl? What girl? What're you talking about now?"

"Remember? The one at the phone? At that diner, with the hat?"

"Oh yeah, the one that was 'right.'" Grunt mocked him with his own words. "What about her?"

"I met her again. Here."

"No way, man. Who you think you're foolin'? That kind don't hang around with—"

"She doesn't know anything about me. Penmartin introduced me as Daniel Davis. She hasn't got a clue."

The big man looked at him incredulously.

"No, see? The hair, the beard? She doesn't know."

"Who does she think you are?"

"Just a poor guy who's had a rough time." Duke cocked his head. "And don't you screw it up."

"Who me? Wouldn't think of it." Grunt slapped the table as he stood to leave. "I can't wait to see how you play this one." He reached across and grabbed Duke's hand in a solidarity handshake. "Hang tight, man. See ya' around."

A CAR PULLED INTO the driveway of the center. Standing in the window, Duke watched a man get out of the car and walk around, opening the door on the other side. He went to the trunk, deftly unfolded a wheelchair and pushed it around to the open door. Moving the chair close to the car, he waited while a boy shifted himself into the chair, careful to allow the child to do it himself.

He studied the man and boy. *That coulda' been me, stuck in a wheelchair. I think I'd 'a rather died.* The man and boy smiled and talked as they went up the ramp into the building.

Duke sighed and turned carefully, placing considerable weight on the cane he held, bracing his other hand on the wall. Slowly, he made his way to the elevator.

"AH, MR. WOODS. PHIL is it? "Casper Penmartin extended a strong handshake in greeting. "And who is this?"

"My foster child, Joey."

"Hello Joey." Penmartin smiled and shook Joey's hand also. "You two come on in. We'll talk, then I'll get Daniel and you all can get acquainted."

"—AND THAT'S PRETTY MUCH all I know. They put his body back together in the county hospital then sent him to us for the next part—putting the rest of his life back together. We've gone as far as we can here but he needs more."

"I see." Phil looked down at the floor then over at Joey. "We want to help, but I ain't trained for none such as that. There's some exercises me and Joey do for his legs and back but—"

"No one expects you to do anything that we can do here," Penmartin said. "He'll come to us for his physical therapy once a week. Would you be able to bring him over?"

"I reckon."

The director studied Phil for a moment then Joey's smiling face. "Mr. Woods, more than therapy, this young man needs to find the answers to some tough questions. He's been a while without family and I think you two taking him into your home will help him sort things out."

"I guess he's been through a lot," Phil ventured.

"Yes, he has, but it runs deeper than his accident. There's an emptiness, a coldness in him. But it's not a heartlessness." He paused thoughtfully a moment. "It's more of a sadness so deep, so excruciating that he has to use anger to keep it covered. His injuries from the crash will heal. This other—well, I hope you can help us, and him, out on that."

"What can I do?" Phil was beginning to squirm in his chair. "I'm no counselor. Maybe he should be in a halfway house or something."

"Mr. Woods, you can back out if you want to. But you have an opportunity to help give a young man his life back. We can talk the talk but it takes real spiritual conviction to walk the walk." Penmartin rose and moved toward the door. "I'll leave you two to talk about this. I'll be back in a few minutes. Think about it, will you?"

PHIL TURNED TO JOEY. "Well, Joey, my man, what'cha think? This may be tougher than we signed on for."

Joey looked at Phil with a wrinkled brow. "Nobody can do anything to fix my legs, but you've made me happy. Maybe, if he's just sad, we could—you know—fix it."

Phil smiled and roughed the boy's hair. "Okay, but if this blows up in our faces, it's your fault."

Joey laughed.

Saved for Something More 53

WALKING DOWN THE PATH of an old estate, Crystal stopped to watch the pecan harvesting in progress. A giant machine moved up to each tree and shook it, causing the pecans to fall into huge sheets.

"That lets us get them before the squirrels do," explained Debby.

Crystal studied her friend. There was a satisfied calm in every aspect of her demeanor whether she was feeding ducks at the pond or explaining the latest renovations in the antebellum home she and her husband were restoring.

"Debby, you seem so happy. Who would have guessed the most ambitious business major at Mississippi State would end up—here?" Crystal gestured to take in the surroundings.

"Well, my life with Jim makes sense to me. Not to my mother, of course, who thinks I should be living closer to her. Then there's the other thing."

"You mean, Jim's being so much older?"

"Yes. It doesn't look that likely on paper but it works for us. He understands what it means to be passionate about life and about someone beside himself. She smiled fondly as she spoke of him.

"I can see that and I envy you."

"But Phil's asked you to marry him, right?"

"Yes," Crystal answered softly.

"What is it? You believe he loves you, don't you?"

"Yes, I can see it in his eyes and in everything he does when he is with me but—"

Debby stepped in front of Crystal and looked her straight in the face. "But?" She crossed her arms, waiting.

"I don't know." Crystal squirmed and cast her eyes downward, trying to hide from the penetrating gaze of her friend. "Phil's wonderful to me. And I love Joey. And he should have a family. And—"

Debby bobbed in front of her averted look. "So what's bothering you?"

Heaving a quick sigh, Crystal looked up and blurted, "All right! I don't love him." Tears sprang to her eyes and escaped before she could stop them. "I don't love this man who would do anything in the world for me, who's devoted and solid and—"

By now, she was sobbing. Debby wrapped her with strong arms and stroked her hair, letting sympathetic tears fall unbridled.

"It's okay, honey. It's okay."

Finally, Crystal pulled back, still sniffling. "Debby, what am I going to do? I have to marry him. I said I would. It's been announced in church."

"Sit down, Crystal, and I'll tell you what I think." Debby motioned toward the base of a giant pecan tree. "I've known you a lot of years, since we were kids. I love you and I think you know that."

Crystal, still looking down, nodded slowly.

"I can't stand the thought of my dearest friend in a loveless marriage even if it is for a good reason. God meant us to find a spiritual partner. And you will, Crystal, but when it's the right time and the right person. You can't get married just because someone else wants you to."

Crystal smiled weakly at her friend.

"So," Debby slapped her knees as if shifting gears, "you have to tell me, is there someone else?"

Crystal's wet cheeks suddenly felt glowing. "No."

"Nice try, toots. Now remember whom you're talking to. Come on, out with it. You can tell me. Who's going to hear but the pecans? And they'll be pie soon." They both giggled.

With schoolgirl excitement, Crystal told Debby about her chance meetings with the biker she couldn't forget and about all that was stirring inside her.

"Well, what happened then?" Debby pressed eagerly.

"He disappeared."

She lifted her eyebrows with incredulity. "You mean, you never saw him again?"

"No—" Crystal stared thoughtfully into the pecan grove. "But there's this other guy I met. I don't know, he reminds me of—"

"Hmm," Debby prompted when Crystal fell silent.

"I don't know anything about him really except that he was in a terrible accident and that there's a desolation, some kind of pain about him that touches me. Yet he has a dry sense of humor, too."

Debby grasped her knees and rocked a little. "Go on, go on."

Crystal's felt her eyes smiling. "It's just that he—"

Debby stepped in. "—makes you smile when you don't particularly feel like smiling, makes the hair on your arms stand up and makes the room seem twenty degrees warmer when he talks to you?" They both giggled.

DURING THE LONG TRAIN trip home, Crystal replayed their conversation and felt the same sweet warmth again. But remorse, reason and resolve all played in her thoughts. *Okay, I know I have to do something. Dear God, can you help me decide? Can you show me the right thing to do and the right way to do it?* She stared out the window listening for a voice through the rhythmic roar.

WEDNESDAY MORNING DUKE LOOKED one last time out across the grounds of the Agape center. *This is sure the right place to be leaving—a lunatic asylum. But I wonder if it's not going to be crazier out there.*

Casper Penmartin entered the room, interrupting. "Daniel, Phil Woods and his foster son will be here in a few minutes, but I'd like to talk with you. Sit down."

Duke still didn't understand why he always did exactly as this man said. It just seemed natural. With a combination of aversion and gratitude, he looked at the intense taskmaster who had put him through the excruciating ordeal of the past few months.

"I told you your first day here I wasn't going to try to convert you or beat you over the head with any religious sticks, and I've stuck to it."

Penmartin paused briefly as the young man laughed.

"But there is one thing you need to think about as you leave."

"What? Why this happened to me so I won't do it again?"

The sarcastic edge to the man's voice seemed to roll off Penmartin. "No, I know you think God has dealt you a bad hand, and it's not just this last little adventure that's caused that. We've all got our demons, son. But let me tell you, God isn't one of 'em." He paused before continuing.

Duke bristled a little.

"The question isn't, 'Why did this happen?' What you should be asking is, 'Why did I survive?'"

Penmartin's sharp eyes felt as if they were boring holes through the layers of emotional insulation around Duke.

"Each of us has something to contribute—a reason and an opportunity to make our lives count. God may very well have something important for you to do to make this world of ours or the people in it better."

Duke's eyes widened but he kept silent.

"You've been through a lot; I understand that. But, where you've been isn't nearly as important as where you're going. You choose how you travel your path. You can set markers and make a difference along the way or just shuffle dust with your feet. Think about it."

The intercom broke in, "Mr. Penmartin, are you in there?"

"Yes, what is it?"

"Mr. Woods is here."

"Thanks. We'll be right down," he answered in the general direction of the speaker on the wall, but he never removed his gaze from the young man's face. "Time to go, Daniel. Take it easy. Remember—left, right, left, right—move forward and keep the rhythm. Kinda' like dancin' eh?"

Penmartin bobbed his shoulders and stepped out to some unheard music, chanting, "Boom, sha boom, boom-boom, sha boom."

Duke shook his head and chuckled as he grabbed a small canvas bag in one hand and a cane in the other.

CHAPTER 8

"Daniel, you got to try this cheesecake Ms. Walters brought around to the diner," Phil offered a bit too brightly. "She wants me to sell her pies to my customers instead of the ones I buy from the distributor and she left this one as a sample."

"Yeah, Mr. Daniel. She makes real good pies. Go ahead, I love the cheesecake," Joey encouraged happily.

The guest, who had ignored Phil's offer initially, cut an eye toward Joey then smiled just slightly at the persistent and cheerful boy. "He makes a good case. Yeah—" then after a second's pause, "—please."

Out of the corner of his eye, Duke caught Phil winking at Joey and giving him the thumbs-up.

After they had finished the dessert Duke struggled to stand with his cane in one hand and the plate in the other hand. The plastic dish slipped and fell back to the table with a clatter.

Before he could even react, Joey wheeled to his side. "Let me get that, Mr. Daniel. Don't worry. I drop stuff all the time. It's okay—it doesn't break."

Duke frowned.

"No, really. See?" Joey picked up the plate and dropped it again. It bounced. Then he picked up Phil's plate and dropped it on the table with a clatter.

The somber young man softened then laughed involuntarily. Turning to Phil he asked, "Is he always like this?"

"Pretty much. Only sometimes we drop other things, like young'uns." Phil growled playfully and scooped Joey into his arms. He cradled the gleefully screeching child, spun around two or three times and deposited the boy back into his chair.

Duke watched them, warmed by the display. But then his demeanor darkened again. *They're lucky.* He turned away, leaning on the cane as he made his way out into the living room.

Phil and Joey stopped their play. When he'd passed through the doorway Duke heard Joey whisper, "I thought we were getting somewhere with him. Remember, the man said he was sad. But he smiled for a minute. I saw him."

"Maybe."

"Maybe he misses his family."

"Could be. You need to get on to bed now. It's later than you usually stay up. Let's go."

Joey urged, "Will you talk to him and help him not be so sad?"

AFTER A HALF HOUR of bedtime rituals with Joey, Phil eased, smiling, into the living room where their guest sat watching the television. "Hope we weren't too rowdy for you. People who aren't used to kids sometimes take offense at the noise."

"No big deal. I'm just not into that gig," Duke responded flatly, never taking his eyes from the television. He pressed the remote a few times. "Never anything good on."

Phil studied him. "No, there isn't." He sat on the edge of the sofa and clasped his hands together with forearms resting across his knees. "What about a girlfriend? Surely a young fella' like you's got a girl somewhere."

The young man's tone suddenly brightened. "No girlfriend, really." He paused thoughtfully. "But there's this girl I met at the rehab center. She's a real fox—but not trashy—refined, sort of. We've only talked a few times but I think she goes for me, too."

A shocked expression flew over Phil's face. "Really?" After a tense moment, he added, "I've got a girl, too. She's great with Joey even though she's not his mom. Real nice and pretty. A great person. Everybody thinks highly of her. Me and Joey just love her to death. We're getting married sometime toward the end of the year."

Daniel listened to the not eloquent but certainly heartfelt way Phil talked about this woman. *Loves her to death. He's so clear on his feelings. I don't know what I feel. Except that I look forward to seeing her—but when? How?* He was still puzzling over this question when a voice interrupted from the porch.

"Phil? You still up?"

"Is that you, Hon?" Phil jumped up. "Come on in. There's someone here I want you to meet."

CRYSTAL LAID HER PURSE on the table as she passed the kitchen. Phil stood grinning like an awkward boy.

"Welcome back! Come in. This here is D—" Phil motioned toward the visitor who rose slowly and turned toward the doorway. Crystal's smile faded into confusion when she recognized her Daniel right there in Phil's living room. She froze and her eyes widened. She stopped so suddenly that she lost her footing and fell headlong toward the two men.

They both yelled at once and leaped to help her up. Phil moved more quickly and got to her side first with Duke right behind. Each holding an arm to steady her, Phil and he looked at each other. Crystal struggled to regain her stance, looking back and forth at each of them with a questioning expression on her face.

As if she didn't feel awkward enough, things got worse. Crystal's thrashing upset Duke's precarious balance and he dropped her arm to catch himself. She buckled at the unexpected loss of support and fell toward the younger man yet again. Phil grabbed her waist. Duke crashed backward across the overstuffed chair. Crystal's ankle crumpled under her and she cried out in pain.

Finally, everyone recovered. The men helped the stunned young woman to the sofa. "I'll go get some ice for that ankle," Phil offered solicitously. "It'll swell pretty fast if it's sprained. Daniel, can you stay by her for a minute?"

"Sure. Be glad to," he grinned.

When Phil had left the room, Crystal stammered, "What—? How—? When—?"

"Shhhh." Duke held up his hand and continued quietly, "He's letting me stay here for awhile. Penmartin set it up."

Just then Phil called from the other room. "Oh, Crystal, that's Daniel Davis. He's staying with Joey and me for awhile."

"Thanks, Phil. We've met," she called back thinly.

"Is this the guy you're engaged to?" He whispered huskily. "This old guy?"

Crystal bristled. She was about to retort when Phil returned to the room.

"What did you say, Honey? I didn't hear you." Phil stooped to apply the ice to Crystal's ankle.

Duke frowned and shook his head.

"Uh, I said he introduced himself already." She winced in instant remorse at the untruth. Phil misread the reaction.

"Oh, does that hurt? I hope it's not sprained." He examined the ankle with concern. "Crystal, this is starting to swell. You'd better put it up on something. Here, this stool should help."

"Thank you." Crystal smiled at Phil who moved the stool closer. Over Phil's back, she saw her Daniel grinning from across the room.

"MR. DANIEL, WAKE UP," Joey called gaily as he wheeled into the sleeping guest's room. "Everybody's up but you. C'mon"

Duke groaned and rolled over. "Go away. It's too early." He threw a pillow at Joey, who caught it and persisted in his mission.

"No, it isn't. The sun's been up for two hours. You're missing the day!"

"Okay, okay. I'm up," he mumbled. *Anybody but you, kid, and I'd strangle 'em.* Amused at Joey's infectious good spirits, he rolled over and sat up, squinting at the sun through the open curtains.

Unsteady with the early morning, the young man stumbled into the kitchen wearing an old T-shirt and cut-off jeans and reached for the coffeepot. Still bleary-eyed, he didn't acknowledge Phil when he bustled into the room.

"We're heading out to church. Why don't you come along?"

"Nah, I'm just gonna' hang out here—now that the morning rooster's gotten me out of bed." He shot a playfully accusing look at Joey, who laughed gleefully.

"Today's Friendship Sunday," Phil offered, "and there's a potluck picnic afterwards. Rev. Reasons tries to keep it short on picnic days. And you may not know it but you've ended up in a town where some of the best cooks in the state live. It'll be worth the trip." He paused expectantly.

"Oh, wouldn't want to miss that." Duke straightened and put his hand on the small of his back.

The sarcasm brought a frown from Phil but Joey called brightly from the doorway, "C'mon, Mr. Daniel. It'll be fun. Mrs. Mooney cooks the best fried chicken."

Stirring his coffee, Duke responded, "Hmmm."

"Crystal always brings macaroni and cheese," Joey continued undaunted. "It's good."

Perking up a little, Duke turned toward Joey. "She does, does she?"

"Oh yes, and I'm sure she would love it if you would come."

After a second's pause, Duke picked up his cane and walked toward Joey, roughing his hair. "Hang on then and I'll get ready."

Phil smiled.

AFTER THE SERVICE, PHIL and Duke walked slowly out of the church. Joey raced ahead. "C'mon! They're setting up the food!"

Duke smiled at Joey's antics. "You're right—I guess he is always like that."

"You ain't been around kids much, have you?" Phil commented more than asked.

"No, but Joey's a trip. He gets under your skin quick."

"Well, he's all boy, that's for sure."

"What's his story?"

"Joey came into the church home after his mother died from cancer. They don't know anything about his father. When I met Joey, he was just like he is now. All his troubles, and even being left with no one like he was, none of that showed on him. That afternoon I filled out papers to be his foster parent and soon afterward he came to live with me."

Duke watched Phil closely. The man never took his eyes off Joey, and there was a softness about his face as he looked lovingly toward the boy.

"So, how does Crystal fit into all this?"

"When she and I get married, the courts will let me adopt Joey and we'll be a family. Joey deserves that." Phil looked over at Duke. "Maybe you and that lady-friend of yours will get married someday and have a family of your own."

Crystal, with her back to the two men, was talking to Joey. Duke leaned on his cane. "You go ahead, Phil. I'm going to sit down for a minute and take a load off." He eased onto one of the wooden slat benches along the walkway.

"You okay?"

"Sure, no problem. Just a little stiff."

"I see. Do you want me to have Crystal bring you a plate?"

"Nah, don't bother. I'll be fine." He gestured toward Joey. "Go on."

At that moment Crystal turned and saw them. She waved tentatively then looked down for a second. Phil smiled broadly and waved back, quickening his steps in her direction. Duke observed the scene then looked away. Crystal glanced in his direction but he pretended not to notice.

"Say, aren't you Daniel from the lion's den?"

Rev. Reasons' greeting caught Phil's guest off guard. He started then answered, "What did you say?"

"Oh, that's just my way of remembering your name. Daniel in the lion's den. You're staying with Phil Woods, right?"

Duke puzzled over this strange greeting as the rotund minister pushed in beside him on the bench.

"That's right."

Reasons extended his hand and Duke reluctantly shook it.

"Good to have you." The minister pumped his arm. "I'm Bob Reasons, the minister here. I wanted to tell you, someone donated an old truck to the church and it needs some fixing. Maybe if you're interested, you could look at it."

"Sure—I guess." Duke still felt a little overwhelmed by this whirlwind of a man.

"Great! Call the office tomorrow morning and I'll get you the key. Gotta' run now. Wonderful to talk with you!" He hurried on toward the picnic tables, offering a jocular greeting and lively handshake to everyone along the way.

Crystal walked up and smiled sweetly. "Aren't you hungry?"

"No, not really," he replied without emotion.

"Would you like to join Phil and Joey and me? You still look like you could use a few good meals."

"I'll get something after while." He studied her as she waved at Joey. "He's a tough kid." He stopped for a minute. "So—that's the guy you're marrying. Seems okay."

"Yes. But that's a ways off yet." Crystal looked at him intently, seeking something in his face.

He met her look briefly. "Your ankle okay?" *She feels something, too. I know it.*

"Yes, it's fine." Laughing, she added, "That was kind of comical the other night."

He interrupted and looked away. "Probably a good thing."

"What? What's a good thing?"

"You getting married. Good for everybody." He took his cane and shifted his position to stand.

"Yeah, well, I guess I will get something to eat." He moved away from Crystal's gaze and stared purposefully toward the tables. "Where's this Mrs. Mooney and her chicken?"

He caught a glint of disappointment on her face. As she walked beside him up the hill, both were quiet.

CHAPTER 9

"Okay, ten more reps and we'll quit."

The twice weekly trip to the Agape Center for therapy returned Duke to the hands of his benevolent torturer. Grimacing and grunting with pain and effort, he pressed on the weight machine with his arms.

"Seven, eight, nine—"

"Say, how's it going?"

"It hurts like—"

Penmartin pointed a chiding finger at him, "Ah, ah, ah. Language. We value suffering in silence around here." He smiled at his patient's scowl then went on conversationally, "What's going on? Are you meeting people? Have you seen any more of that Crystal woman?"

"Not much, no. And she's engaged."

Penmartin grinned mischievously. "I know that. She just seemed like a nice person for you to, uh, talk to."

The young man stopped his exercises and looked hard at Penmartin. "She's engaged to the guy I'm staying with," he said in an accusing tone. "He's got that handicapped kid and they're going to adopt him."

Penmartin sobered. "Oh, I see."

"Yeah, well, no loss." Duke rose from the weight machine and wiped his sweating face with a towel. "She's not my type anyway."

"DEBBY, I DON'T KNOW what to do now." Crystal swung her arms wildly at the phone as if her friend were in the room. "It's all so awkward. He seems so indifferent, uninterested. How could I have presumed—"

"Whoa. Slow down," said the voice at the other end of the line.

"Sunday he said the strangest thing. He said, 'It's good you're marrying Phil. Good for everybody.'"

"Hmmm. I'm sorry."

"Debby! This isn't helping. What am I going to do about Phil?"

"If Daniel weren't in the picture, could you honestly say you care enough for Phil to marry him?"

Crystal was silent, wrestling with the question. When she finally spoke, it was barely a whisper. "No, but—"

"No buts, Crystal. You have to tell him. Whatever might or might not happen between you and this guy is another issue. If you respect Phil, you owe it to him to be honest. And you owe it to yourself."

Crystal hung up slowly. She walked out to the porch and sat in the old swing. Rocking back and forth, she fidgeted with the engagement ring on her finger. After a time she stood up and gazed down the long highway. She let out a despondent sigh. Looking down at her hand, she admired the ring perched there. After turning it several more times, she went back into the house.

"HERE'S YOUR TOOLS. THEY were still in your saddlebags. Nobody ripped 'em off. But it'll take more than tools to get this reject from a demolition derby running." Grunt kicked the tires of the '76 Chevy pickup spray-painted bright green except for one gray primed fender on the left front. The hood lay on the ground next to it and Duke stood on the bumper peering at the engine.

"You don't get it, man. I gotta' blow this pop stand."

Grunt eyed the truck skeptically. "You ain't goin' far in this rag even if you can get it to turn over. Anyway, what's the rush? Your life's a piece o' cake here. And then there's that—"

Duke cut in before Grunt could finish. "Until I get wheels I can't get a job. And 'til I get a job I can't get my bike fixed. And 'til I get my bike fixed I'm stuck in this po-dunk town. Last Sunday they dragged me to a picnic. C'mon, you know that's not me."

"Whatever you say."

"Yeah. Oh, did you talk to Reggie about that job?"

"She says she can only pay you contract—a percent on the bikes you fix. And she found a motor for you but the guy wants $2500 for it."

Duke stopped working for a second and sighed. "Then I guess I'm stuck here awhile. Hand me that socket wrench, will ya'?"

Grunt leaned on the hood as Duke resolutely tinkered with the old truck.

"CRYSTAL, HONEY, YOU'VE BEEN moping around here ever since you got back from your trip." Ann handed her daughter a glass of iced tea and sat down in the big oak rocking chair on the porch. A graceful, refined woman with perfect hair and make-up, she had the same fair skin as Crystal. Her dark hair showed only a few hints of gray.

"Sweetheart, how about if we go into the city and look at dresses? You can pick out the colors for—" She continued in animated chatter.

Crystal looked at her but became lost in her own thoughts. *Oh Mama, you just don't get it.*

"—And we'll check at the Woman's Club for the reception. It's such a lovely old place. It just oozes charm and class. When are you two going to set a date so we can get started with the planning?"

Crystal sighed. "I don't know Mama. Phil's busy remodeling the diner and there's so much going on with the students and this new grant from the state. I'm just too tired to think about it now."

"Bless your heart. Maybe after you and Phil get married you won't have to work."

Crystal eyed her mother sideways and raised an eyebrow in disapproval, but then softened. *I can't expect you to understand.* "We'll see," she responded vacantly.

"HEY PHIL, CRYSTAL KNOW you're going to redo the house?" Bob, the tile man, called from the corner where he was placing the last of the new flooring in the diner.

"No," Phil chuckled in amusement. "I've had her looking at samples for the last month. She thinks they're for the diner. I had to have the floor redone here so she wouldn't get suspicious." He smiled again. "Yeah, is she going to be surprised! Now don't forget—it's all got to be done next weekend. I'm taking her to Charlotte to meet my sister and we'll be gone over Saturday night. You sure you can get both the kitchen and the guest bedroom finished?"

"Yeah, my brother in law's coming to help me and he's got a couple of boys he's training in his business."

"You got the paint now? That special color mix she liked?"

"I already picked it up from the builder's supply. Say, why you fixin' that guestroom up so? Don't reckon you'll be needin' it too soon." Bob gave Phil a knowing wink.

"Uh," Phil stammered, then recovered, "you know how women are. They need their own place where they can do their women things."

Bob nodded thoughtfully. "Oh, yeah, women things."

"AS SOON AS THE play's over we'll take off to my sister's. I've got the car loaded already." Phil seemed unusually animated.

"Phil, what are you so happy about? I don't believe I've ever seen you like this. What's going on?" Crystal puzzled.

"Oh, I'm just looking forward to getting away. You know, you've been a little edgy ever since you got back from that conference. The rest will do you good."

"Maybe so." A troubled look slid across Crystal's face. But it didn't last long; the children were arriving in their costumes. As the auditorium filled, Crystal looked out between the curtains. She felt a quick rush when her Daniel walked in. She watched him make his way down to the third row.

Joey wheeled up behind her. "Can I see?" She pulled the curtain aside just enough for him to peek at the growing crowd. "Look, Miss Crystal, there's Mr. Daniel! He said he would come."

"Do you like Mr. Daniel, Joey?"

"Yes. He used to be sad but we're getting him all better. See? He's smiling now." Joey pointed around the edge of the curtain and the late arrival's thumbs-up.

After a few minutes the play started. Christine and Angela came out onto the stage. Angela giggled a little as she waved to her mom and dad in the audience. Christine's hair was pulled back in barrettes and she stood very straight in her blue and white dress. In carefully memorized syllables, Christine welcomed everyone and introduced the play while Angela signed her words to the audience.

Crystal took a deep breath and the curtain opened.

"CONGRATULATIONS, HONEY. EXCEPT FOR Joey rolling across Jordan's foot while he played the violin it all went pretty well, don't you think?" Phil beamed and lifted Joey out of his wheelchair to hug him.

"Where's Mr. Daniel?" Joey turned around in Phil's arms to survey the thinning audience.

"Right here, Wheels. You were great! Everybody thought that thing with the violin kid was planned. And that look you flashed the audience afterward!" Duke fake-punched Joey in the arm. "You ought to be a comedian."

Phil hurriedly returned Joey to his chair. "Well, we'd better get going if we want to be there before eleven. Let's go, Crystal."

"Yeah, you guys have a good time. I'll keep an eye on everything, though I'm thinking of renting out Joey's room to monkeys while you're gone." Joey's friend winked, making him giggle.

"Daniel, you'll watch that, uh, situation we talked about, won't you?" Phil asked, sounding vague.

"Oh, sure. And is it okay if I bring the truck over and work on it in the driveway?"

"No problem. While you're at it, why don't you look at Crystal's car? It should be due for belts and an oil change by now." Phil laughed. "I know this little girl doesn't do any of that stuff."

"Sure."

"Thank you." Crystal smiled warmly but not at Phil.

"Yeah, okay. Now get going. Have fun." He avoided Crystal's eyes and waved to Joey. He noticed her smile fade as she turned to go. "You jerk," he growled to himself.

All the way home his thoughts nagged him.

I know I owe the old guy, and the kid's cool. But when she smiles at me like that— I've got to get out of his house so I won't have to see her so much. He first pounded the steering wheel with his fist in frustration, then paused. *Maybe he's not right for her.*

REGGIE'S CYCLE REPAIR WAS in a converted gas station. The tanks had been taken out long ago but the old ESSO sign remained. "Reminds me of when I was a kid," she explained to anyone who asked.

First thing every morning Reggie and her helper rolled out the bikes that were for sale and parked them in a line out front. All were Harleys; several were customs with stylized renderings of flags, eagles, snakes or women on the gas tanks. Duke stopped to admire a bright blue and white panhead with a chopped front end.

A woman with a small flag tattooed on her left cheekbone joined him. "Pretty, ain't it?" Reggie was about 5'2" tall and had inch-long green hair. She stood next to a leather-seated bike that seemed to blend with her leather fringe-trimmed jacket. When she slipped it off, Duke noticed a larger tattoo on her forearm of a woman on a motorcycle with the writing, "Hear me roar." She extended her hand, "Grunt told me you'd be by. Duke, is it?"

"Yeah, uh," he paused. "Fine-looking piece of machinery, boss, but how's it run?" He asked.

"Just came in last night. The guy seemed a little tweaked out but the title was in his name. Nice finish. Like he kept it inside." She laughed. "But he looked more like he slept outside."

Reggie climbed on the bike, pulled the keys from her pocket and expertly kick-started the motor. "What d'ya think?"

Duke listened. "Got a timing problem but it may not be a big deal. Let's bring it in and take a look."

As they rolled the bike into the shop Reggie continued, "While we're talking about timing problems, I understand you've got a thing for a woman who's supposed to be marrying someone else."

Duke raised his eyebrows and stopped in his tracks. "What are you talking about?" He felt his reddening face betray him.

"It's okay. Grunt told me. Don't worry, your secret's safe."

"What does he think I—?"

"He thinks you need lookin' after." She sized him up. "I believe he may be right. C'mon, let's get to work."

Duke stood there, stunned for a second or two. Then he shook his head and followed Reggie into the shop where the day's motorcycle problems awaited him.

CHAPTER 10

On the long trip back from Charlotte Joey fell asleep in the back seat, exhausted from the weekend's play with Phil's nieces and nephews. They had rigged a safety rope across the small backyard swimming pool so Joey, clad in a life jacket, could play in the water with the other children. By the end of the weekend he was waterlogged and suffering a mild case of swimmer's ear but he was happy.

"Joey really had a good time, didn't he?" Crystal commented, looking over the seat at the angelic face.

"Yeah, too much fun. He may sleep a week. Now, though, I'm afraid I'm going to have to buy him a pool." Phil never took his eyes off the road, but he smiled broadly.

"You're probably right."

"What about you? Did you enjoy yourself?" Phil cut his eyes sideways briefly.

"Yes, it was nice. Your sister really makes a person feel at home."

"Well, we're big into the home and family stuff. Christmas and New Years look like a family reunion.

I'm glad Joey's getting to see all that." He reached over and squeezed Crystal's hand. "And you, too."

She gave him a brief, strained smile. Phil looked puzzled but said nothing. While he turned the radio on, she took out a book and started reading.

In an hour they were nearing home. Crystal closed her book and took a deep breath. "Phil, I need to talk with you about something. "

"Sure, Hon, but can you hold on a little while? I've got a surprise for you."

"Okay, I guess it can wait." She folded her hands in her lap and looked out the window.

They turned into Phil's driveway. "Well, here we are. Just another minute 'til the surprise. Wake up Joey. We're home." As soon as they parked, Phil went to the trunk and took out the wheelchair. Still groggy from his long nap, Joey rubbed his eyes and Phil quickly placed him in the chair. "C'mon, Crystal."

"Phil, what—?" Crystal questioned.

Phil took Joey inside first and went toward the back of the house. "Follow us. You'll see." The two went into the kitchen and turned around at the doorway to face Crystal. "Come on in. Here's the surprise!" Phil beamed as he backed away from the door and motioned her to come in.

Crystal took a step inside and looked around the room. The old white cabinet fronts had been replaced with new oak doors and brass hardware. A ceramic-top stove with a microwave oven mounted above it had taken the place of the old counter top unit and oven. On the shiny vinyl flooring sat a huge white refrigerator with double doors. An oak pedestal table and chairs filled the far corner.

New wallpaper and paint took the place of the old paneling.

As she turned, surveying the whole room, Crystal rested her hand on the polished brass light switch plate.

"Well, what d'ya think?" Joey asked excitedly.

"No, don't answer yet," Phil interrupted. "You have to go upstairs first. C'mon Joey." Phil scooped up the boy from his chair and hurried past Crystal who followed them, slowly climbing the stairs.

"You can come in now," Joey invited from across the room with glee in his voice.

She walked into the first room at the top of the stairs. New pale pink carpet spread before them. Rose-hued blouson curtains accented flowered wallpaper and a vase of fresh roses reflected in the mirror of a rattan vanity with matching chair. A walnut daybed with coverlet and pillows to coordinate with the walls sat on the right. On the left, a narrow white chest with seven drawers stood next to a new sewing machine. A picture of a woman walking in a garden hung on the wall opposite the door.

Crystal noticed Phil's furrowed brow, awaiting her response but Joey's eagerness jumped ahead of Phil's concern. "Well, do you like it?"

She paused for a moment, and her carefully chosen words came out slowly. "I think it looks like someone went to an awful lot of trouble." She smiled at Joey. "Did you do all this?"

Joey giggled. "No, Mr. Bob did it."

"Well, it certainly is lovely," she concluded. "Sweetie, don't you need to go to the bathroom after that long trip?"

"Yeah," Joey answered, swung from the bench he was sitting on an plopped into the small, lightweight chair always kept upstairs. "I'll be right back." He left Phil and Crystal alone in the room.

"Do ya' like it? We wanted you to feel at home here; not like you were living with two guys." Phil smiled, nervously.

She walked to the vanity without saying anything and dragged her fingers lightly across it looking into the mirror. Then she set her jaw and turned back to Phil.

"I think it's sweet that you went to all this trouble, but—"

"But what? I mean, you know, this is just a start. You can change anything you like once we—"

"Phil, I can't marry you," she blurted.

Phil froze. For several seconds neither said anything. "What? I—"

"I'm grateful for all you've done for me, and I adore Joey, but when it gets right down to it, I don't love you in that way. I'm so sorry. I thought I could but I just can't picture myself—"

"You can stop right there," Phil interjected. "I understand. You don't have to explain."

"I should never have—" Crystal searched for words to ease the blow. "Please know that I never intended to hurt you."

"Never mind me." Phil's face blazed. "I thought you wanted Joey to have a home."

"I do. And I'll do whatever I can to see that he gets one—but I can't do this." Crystal looked down at the diamond ring on her hand and pulled it off her finger. She extended it slowly toward Phil.

A voice called from downstairs. "Hey, you guys back already? Guess what? I got a job and an apart—" Duke stopped as he looked at the two sad people at the top of the stairs. "—ment." He looked first at Phil then at Crystal. "What's going on?"

"Nothing. I was just leaving. Phil, tell Joey goodbye for me, will you? I'll pick up my bags tomorrow." Crystal dropped the ring in Phil's shirt pocket as he had not moved to take it from her.

Did I just see what I think I saw? The heartened young man watched her hurry down the stairs and rush past him out the door. He looked at Phil for confirmation.

"What?" Phil said vacantly.

Hesitantly, Duke said, "I got a job and now I can move into an apartment and get out of your hair." He smiled slightly.

"No rush you movin' out. It's gonna' be just me and Joey," Phil responded sadly.

"What?"

"Never mind. I got to talk to Joey."

"Okay, I'll just get the last of my things and leave the key on the table." Duke started downstairs. "And thanks, man, thanks for everything."

"Sure," Phil answered flatly and sat down on the day bed. He looked around the new room and put his head in his hands.

"CRYSTAL. CRYSTAL, HONEY, WHAT'S wrong? Are you hurt? What's happened?" Ann stood at the car door and peered in at her daughter crying there.

She answered in the hiccoughing talk of tears, "Phil—and—I—broke up."

"I'm shocked! How could he do that to you? And I thought—"

"No." Crystal spoke emphatically now. "I did it. I couldn't marry him. The kitchen—the new room—and now Joey won't—oooooh." She began sobbing again.

"Crystal, what are you saying? I don't understand."

"He remodeled the house. He was so proud. I walked in, and I knew I couldn't— with him." Her sobbing subsided to moist cheeks and periodic sniffles.

Her mother retorted, "Crystal, what's gotten into you? Phil is a wonderful man. Any girl would be lucky to have him."

Stunned by her mother's reaction, Crystal jumped up and strode indignantly toward the house.

"Well, I can't believe it. What will everyone think?" Ann called after Crystal. The words stung her just before she slammed the door behind her.

DUKE HAD A MILLION thoughts going through his head on the way to his new place. *Did I see her give the ring back? Yes, I'm sure I did. The old guy was shook. She must have.* A smile pulled up the corners of his mouth and his eyes crinkled. He punched the air with his fist and said exuberantly, "Yes!"

CHAPTER 11

The classroom at East Gold Elementary was a familiar haven for Crystal. It was here she often came to think. Getting out of the house early kept her from having to talk to her mother who was in quite a state. About 7a.m. the principal came by and looked in.

"What're you doing here this early?" he asked with a surprised look on his face.

"Oh, I was catching up on my individualized educational plans. Ever since the conference, I've been behind."

"Yes, I know it's a lot of work with your group. But since you're here, Crystal, we might as well talk." He came in and leaned back on the table by her desk. "The board is looking at cutting funding again. There's talk of mainstreaming your kids and hiring paraprofessionals to fill in the gaps."

Crystal's mouth dropped open. "How can that be? The federal government has specific—"

"Now, let's not get all excited. We've been through this before. Your presentation at the conference impressed them. But you might want to do a little more paper-gathering and public relations to show the impact of your program. They understand documentation and public opinion." He stood to leave. "I wouldn't worry too much. They're just talking. They do that a lot."

I'm a teacher—who may not be teaching next year. Haven't I got enough to deal with already?

She put down her pen and sat back in her chair.

THE END OF THE day finally arrived for a tired Crystal. Not only was she physically exhausted but mentally worn out as well. So much so that she didn't notice the piece of paper under the wiper blade of her car. Climbing in, she plopped down on the seat, distracted, not looking up until she took out her keys to start the car. Then she saw the paper and stepped out to retrieve it.

"What's this? Some kind of advertising flyer?" she muttered as she snatched it from the glass. She was about to crumple it when she noticed her name handwritten on the front. Curious, she opened the note.

Hi. You headed out so fast last Sunday that I didn't get to tell you I looked at your car. The brakes are okay and I changed the oil but it's going to need a tune-up pretty soon. Let me know when you want to do it and I'll work on it for you. My phone will be hooked up in a day or two. I'll give you the number so you can call when you need me to change the plugs.
Your mechanic,
Daniel

Her eyebrows rose and cautious delight warmed her face. Her fatigue seemed to have disappeared as she hopped back into the car. She started up and drove out of the school parking lot. The upturned corners of her mouth spread into a grin.

THE NEXT DAY AFTER school she drove to the Agape Center. She needed to talk to Casper Penmartin.

"Hello, Miss Harper," Penmartin greeted her with surprise. "I didn't think we were to meet again until next month. What's up?"

Crystal's sober demeanor caused Penmartin to go immediately to his desk chair. "Mr. Penmartin, I'd like to have the rest of the grant money right away if you could arrange it."

"I guess that's possible. I'll have to speed up the check requests but I think we can do it. Why do you want it now?"

"Let's just say that I want this school year to be a memorable one for the students and I'll need all the money at once to make that happen. Will you help?"

Her supplicating look was so intense that he sat back in his chair, regarding her. "Of course, but I'd like to get back to my original question. What's up?"

"There are changes in the works at school and I want to ensure that my children don't get lost in the shuffle." She unconsciously reached over to her left hand to touch the ring that wasn't there.

Penmartin caught the gesture. He stood up and came around the desk. As he neared her chair he reached for her hand which she extended expecting a handshake. He held it as he spoke. "I guess it's in God's plan for both our lives to look out for those who otherwise might get lost in the shuffle." His kind and earnest manner disarmed her.

"Yes, if we don't get lost ourselves in the process," she responded somewhat sadly.

Penmartin released her hand and abruptly switched gears. "Speaking of lost souls, how is our Mr. Davis doing? Isn't he staying with a friend of yours?" He folded his arms across his chest and leaned back against the desk as he scrutinized her.

Crystal broke eye contact momentarily; her cheeks flushed a bit and just the faintest smile appeared as she responded, somewhat more brightly than before, "Actually, he's moved into a place of his own, I've heard. And I believe he has a job now." She hesitated a moment, regaining composure. "But Phil or Dr. Reasons would know more about that. Why don't you ask one of them? Or Daniel? Doesn't he come here to see you still?"

"Yes, yes he does, but not as often. He handles most of his exercises at home now." He uncrossed his arms and moved toward the door as she stood. "But if you do happen to run into him, would you ask him to call me and let me know how to reach him now? It would help me out a lot."

"Certainly," she answered as she headed out the door. "If I run into him."

AFTER SHE LEFT PENMARTIN returned to his seat and rocked back in it then swung around for a view out the window. He watched Crystal walk toward her car. "Hmm," he muttered thoughtfully.

JOEY CAME INTO CLASS late on Tuesday. "Good Morning, Joey," Crystal greeted him. "We missed you Monday."

He didn't answer but went straight to the shelves and took his lapboard. Finally, he settled down with his schoolbook opened on the lapboard desk and stared at it. Crystal walked over to him and laid her hand gently on his shoulder. "Joey, I'll be glad to help you catch up. And I have some good news I want to share with the class." Joey still didn't respond. Crystal paused for a few seconds waiting then turned toward the other students.

"Would everyone come sit around this table with me, please? I have something important to tell all of you." Angela and Victor were first to the table. Christine went over to Tim and told him to come, too. Jordan put down the math cube he was working with and sat in the chair closest to Crystal. Joey remained at his place. Crystal looked at him sadly for a few seconds then brightened as she addressed the children. "Class I have an announcement to make."

"Miss Crystal, what's a 'nouncement?" Victor asked immediately.

"It means, Victor, that I'm going to tell you something. Something I think you'll all like." The students began to smile and fidget.

Crystal continued excitedly, "Have all of you been to the Christmas parade they have every year in the county seat?"

"Oh yes, Miss Crystal," Jordan blurted out. "My daddy takes me. Are we all going to the parade?"

"Well, Jordan, we're going to do something better than go to the parade." She paused to savor the rapt attention of the children. "We're going to build a float and be IN the parade!"

The children squealed and clapped with excitement. For the next half hour the children blurted out ideas for the float. The class was so loud that when the principal walked past he stopped in to see what was going on.

"Miss Crystal, are you holding a pep rally in here?" He pretended gruffness then smiled at the children.

"We were just discussing the float for the Christmas parade. We have plenty of creative minds in here so it ought to be something special the whole school will be proud of." She beamed. *Finally, a real project and a way to showcase what these students are capable of. That ought to get the school board's attention.*

"Well, I look forward to seeing the float and all of you in the parade the day after Thanksgiving," he said and gave them a thumbs-up. That set them off and the roar began again. Crystal laughed out loud then spent the next hour trying to quiet them.

SATURDAY MORNING SHE PULLED into the driveway of an old garage with a small apartment over it. Blinds with missing slats hung at the windows. The whole building looked freshly painted, though, and was free from the remains of cars that usually surround garages. Instead of getting out of the car immediately she tapped the horn twice and watched the door. Within seconds, a smiling man with short strawberry blond hair and a slightly uneven gait walked out of the garage and over to the car.

"Do you think this is full service, ma'am?" He teased.

"I—I wasn't sure I was in the right place." *Listen to me,* she thought. *I sound like a kid who doesn't know what to say. Crystal, get a grip.*

His smile widened as he motioned for her to drive through the open doorway. When she turned off the motor he told her, "Pop the hood. I've got the plugs already so this shouldn't take too long. Why don't you get out and help?"

She sprang from the car laughing. "Me? I've always just taken this to a mechanic. I couldn't—"

"Sure you could. C'mon. I don't think the world order will be disrupted if you replace a few spark plugs."

His encouragement put her at ease. *He thinks I can work on my own car? I would've never thought it—but he did. Hmmm.* As he laid out the tools and explained each to her she watched and listened with the same wonder her students exhibit when they observe a butterfly breaking out of a cocoon.

"What intimidates most people is that they can't do stuff on their cars with the usual tools around the house. But if you buy the right ones you save more than enough to pay for them in a year. See?" He picked up a long, chrome piece and showed it to her. "This is a spark plug socket wrench. It's made like a regular socket wrench at the end to fit the spark plug, and this extension lets you reach down past all the wires and hoses to get to the plugs. Without this tool the job's a real pain." He walked over to her car and raised the hood. "Watch."

She leaned over the fender and peered down to where he pointed then intently observed him attach the wrench and unscrew a spark plug.

"And there it is. See how easy?"

He showed her the plug he had removed and indicated the location of the others. Then he handed her the wrench. "Your turn." She nodded in understanding.

Crystal grasped the tool gingerly, examining it from end to end. Awkwardly, she leaned into the engine area and looked for the spark plug. After some head-bobbing to get a clear view she said, "Oh, I see it. There it is!"

Duke laughed at her gleeful reaction. "Yes, now extend the wrench down to it and fit it over the end of the plug."

The first two attempts were misses but finally she secured the tool and looked at him. "Now what?"

"Rotate the handle until the spark plug comes out."

Her hair fell into her face as she bent down. She shook it back a few times in exasperation.

"It feels like it's loose. What do I do now?"

"Just lift it out. The plug stays in the end of the wrench."

"It won't fall out?"

"Nope."

Crystal eased the wrench out as if she were raising a fragile china cup then turned it up and looked at the plug. A triumphant smile spread across her face.

He stepped beside her and reached to shake her hand. "Congratulations! You did it. See? Not so hard."

"Yes I did, didn't I? I didn't know—I didn't think— That was great!"

"I'm glad you enjoyed it. Now you have six more to go."

She continued to grin excitedly as she examined the fouled plug. "I can't believe I'm doing this." She giggled, laid the old plug down and went back to the engine.

Duke busied himself around the garage looking over from time to time to check her progress. Crystal was apparently lost in her task and didn't seem to notice.

By the end of the morning they had finished the tune-up and rotated the tires. "A woman needs to know how to change a tire. Can't always count on someone to be around," he had explained as he handed her the jack.

Finally, they stopped for lunch. "Is it noon already?" a tired Crystal asked. By now her hair was tied back with a shoestring and only a few loose strands fell around her face. She had put on coveralls to protect her clothes but as she looked down at her hands covered with black grease she asked, "How do you get this off?"

"What? You don't want to wear it around all day to show everyone how competent you are?" he teased.

"Competent. Hmm." She savored the word. "I like the sound of that." She smiled with satisfaction. He grinned in return while tossing her a rag and a jar of hand degreaser. She caught both.

CHAPTER 12

That afternoon Crystal bounced into her house. A shoestring still tied up her hair and a smudge of grease remained on her cheek.

"Crystal, is that you, honey?" her mother called.

"Yes, I'm in the kitchen. Do we have any hand degreaser?"

"Do we have any what?" When Ann entered the kitchen, Crystal was poking through the contents of the cabinet under the sink.

"Hand degreaser. You know, the stuff you use to get car grease off your skin."

"No, honey, I don't think so. But why ever would you want that?"

At that moment, Crystal turned around.

"What on earth happened to you?"

"Nothing, Mama. Daniel and I worked on my car this morning. He lent me some coveralls to keep the grease off my clothes but I got some on my face."

"You did what? And who is Daniel?"

"He's the guy who's been living with Phil. You know, the one Dr. Reasons told everyone about from the Agape Center. He's actually a great mechanic. He taught me how to do a tune-up and rotate my tires."

By now Crystal had moved to the refrigerator and taken out a bottle of water. She unscrewed the cap, took a big swig then looked right at her mother. "Did you know that tires wear out twice as fast if you don't keep the right pressure in them and they aren't rotated regularly? Have you checked yours lately?"

Not waiting for an answer, Crystal breezed past her mother and out of the kitchen.

"I—I—guess not," Ann stammered after Crystal. She, too, turned to go out of the kitchen. "And who is this Daniel?"

SUNDAY CRYSTAL LOOKED AROUND for Phil and Joey at church but didn't find them. She noticed many of the church people staring at her and whispering which began to make her uncomfortable. At the end of the service many of the members spoke politely. "Crystal dear," Mrs. White asked in a syrupy sweet voice, "we heard about what happened between you and Phil. He's such a lovely man and seems so hurt." She patted Crystal's hand. "But I'm sure you had your reasons. If you want to talk, just call me. I'm a good listener."

—and gossiper, Crystal added mentally. *Why am I being treated like the bad person here? I made a mistake and now I've corrected it. Can't they see that?*

Just then Dr. Reasons approached and put his arm around her shoulders, moving her out of the stream of people leaving the church.

"All this will blow over in time. Don't worry. You're a fine person, Crystal, and I know it's been as rough on you as it has on Phil." He paused and stood beside her. "Why don't you take this afternoon and do something you enjoy? Take it easy. I myself find a good game of bowling to be very relaxing. You might try that."

As he walked away, she chuckled out loud. *Bowling? Did he say I should go bowling? You never know what that man's going to say.* Looking around her at the trees tinged in fall colors she felt more at peace and thought about what she could do that would be fun. Then she blushed, remembering what a good time she'd had working on her car with Daniel. *I feel bad for Phil. But I enjoy being around Daniel. He doesn't treat me like some fragile little girl. Around him I feel—competent.*

Crystal sighed resolutely and headed for her car. She smiled when she saw a note under the wiper blade. Instead of reading it immediately she tucked it into her purse and drove away from the church. At home, after she'd changed out of her church clothes and put on a sweater and jeans, she went out to the porch swing and unfolded the note.

Hi Crystal,

Just following up to see if we did okay yesterday and the old car is still running. You were great. If you ever decide to change careers, you may have a future in auto maintenance. Hope you're having a good day. Call if you need anything.

Your assistant mechanic,

Daniel

She read it several times, chuckling to herself. For many minutes she sat back in the swing and stared thoughtfully into the distance. Finally she got up and went inside, grabbed her purse and headed back toward the door. "Mama, I'm going out for awhile," she called.

"Okay dear. Where are you going?"

"Bowling."

"Bowling?" her mother asked the closing door.

BY THE NEXT TUESDAY Joey was still withdrawn. Crystal had tried talking to him but each day he had left right after school and she hadn't been able to get him alone. Finally she decided on another approach.

She drove by the garage apartment where her Daniel lived. When she pulled into the driveway he stuck his head out the upstairs window.

"Well, hello. Back for another class in auto repair?" he called to her.

"Not exactly. I have a favor to ask. May I come up?"

"No, the decorator hasn't finished yet," he laughed. "I'll come down."

She watched him slowly navigating the steps, remembering the months he had spent in therapy. When he finally got to the bottom, she observed, "Looks like you're getting around a lot better."

"Oh yeah, I'll be doing roller derby by next month." His sarcasm, like his limp, was less severe than before. When he was finally down he leaned on his cane with casual awkwardness. "What can I do for you?"

He wore jeans and a black T-shirt with 'Reggie's Cycles' across the front. For a moment she stared. *Something about him reminds me of—*

"Well? Are you going to tell me or just send it by mental telepathy?"

She blinked then stammered, "Uh—Daniel, do you still see Joey any since you moved?"

"Sure. I went over last night and stayed with the kid while Phil worked. "

"You baby-sit?" Crystal chuckled.

As he studied her face she smiled pleasantly then averted her eyes and put her hand to the pendant around her neck, sliding it back and forth absently.

"Sometimes we play games or watch TV, but last night we just hung out. Why?"

"Joey won't talk to me and I've got to fix that."

"Yeah, he's pretty weird about the whole thing."

"Can you help?"

"Well," he hesitated, "I'd like to but what can I do?"

"I don't know. I just thought—maybe you could think of something to get him talking to me."

"What about that float you're doing with the class? Don't you work on that together?"

"No, he's started riding the bus after school. Phil doesn't pick him up anymore."

"Well, would it help if I stayed after school with Joey to work on the float? I'm off on Wednesdays. Maybe if I was around he would loosen up."

"You know, we could really use your help. The plans for the float were taking shape just fine but then we realized we didn't know how to lay it out safely for the weight of the children."

"What is the float exactly?"

"'Children Are a Work of Art' is the theme, and—"

The two talked for more than an hour. She brought out a drawing of the design of the float. He stood over her as she sat on the step explaining the plans. Occasionally, he would reach over her shoulder, take the pen and add something. Her enthusiasm at each contribution elicited a broad smile.

CRYSTAL LEANED BACK IN her chair after she'd finished the day's business. The bell rang and soon several parents arrived to pick up their children and herd them out to the shed where the float trailer stood.

"Here is the drawing of how it will look and the list of what we'll need," Crystal announced over the confusion. "There's also a work schedule. If everyone would please sign up for something it would really help."

Crystal guided Joey over to the sign-up boards. "Okay, Joey. What would you like to help with? We have painting and making wire letters still left. Does either one of those appeal to you?"

"What's 'peal'?"

"It's appeal. It means what you would like."

Joey looked at the board thoughtfully. "Well, I think making the letters uh-peals to me."

Crystal laughed at Joey's exacting diction. She hugged him, which made him perk up a little. After a half-hour of discussion and planning, the parents began to leave with their children. Finally all had gone except Joey.

"Well Joey, looks like Mr. Daniel didn't make it to pick you up. Would you like me to take you home?" Crystal asked.

"If it's not too much trouble. Could you take me to the diner?"

Crystal thought a moment. *What will I say to Phil? I don't want an uncomfortable situation in front of Joey. But then, I have to see him sometime.*

"Sure Joey. I'd be glad to. Let's head out to my car. I believe it's warm enough today to put the top down."

"Yeah!" Joey pushed ahead of Crystal as they crossed the parking lot. She was glad to see a little of his old spark.

Though they didn't say much on the way, the quiet wasn't an uncomfortable one. Finally Joey spoke. "Miss Crystal, can I ask you something?"

She took a deep breath. "Yes, of course."

"Phil says you aren't gonna' come live with us."

"That's right."

"Will you stop bein' my teacher, too?" Joey looked down. "Cause I don't want you to."

"Oh no, Joey. I'll still be your teacher." Crystal laid her hand on Joey's arm reassuringly.

When he looked up, the old brightness had returned.

THE TWO PULLED INTO the drive in front of the diner. Crystal got out and lifted the wheelchair from the back seat. The two talked and laughed while she opened the chair and helped Joey into it. Once Joey was settled, Crystal moved to the back of the chair, grasped the handles and took a deep breath, eyeing the door of the diner.

When they entered, Phil had his back toward the door. "Joey, is that—?" He started to turn then stopped when he saw Crystal. His face froze for a second.

"Hi Phil. I—uh—brought Joey. Daniel didn't—"

"Oh, thanks."

There was an awkward moment of silence. "We were working on the float, and Joey volunteered to do the letters." Crystal said too cheerfully.

"Letters?"

"Yes, we're going to use small tissue paper bits stuffed in some kind of wire to spell out our theme. Do you have any ideas how this will need to be done?" Crystal moved toward a stool at the counter then sat down. "I brought the rough drawing of what we're trying to make. Look." She pulled a sheet of paper from her purse and unfolded it on the counter. Phil walked over and studied it.

With his eyes still on the paper in front of him, he said, "Sure, me and Joey'll be able to do that." He finally looked up at Crystal's face. "You can count on our support."

"Good," she said smartly and walked toward the door. "Bye, Joey. Bye, Phil."

"Bye." Both Joey and Phil waved at her, and both were grinning.

CHAPTER 13

The next day after school Crystal was heading home when a honking horn behind her caught her attention. In the rearview mirror she saw Daniel's truck with him gesturing for her to pull over. As she eased the car off the road into a clear space, he pulled in behind her. He got out of his truck smiling boyishly and tapped on her window.

She folded her arms as if in disgust and, for a second, just glared at him. He mouthed the word, "Please" and pressed his hands together in penitence. Finally, she rolled the window down just a little, pretending to pout. "You've got a lot of nerve showing your face around me. I can't believe you stood up Joey like that. It was—"

"Yeah, I know, thoughtless, irresponsible and all that. But I really have a good reason. How about we head over to the burger what-cha-ma-call-it and you can yell at me there?"

She opened the window all the way and gave him an incredulous look. "You're kidding, right?"

He put his forearms on the open window frame and leaned in, peering at her at eye level. "C'mon," he begged. "I know it's got to be tempting. Think of it. Me across from you contrite and apologetic, you sitting there upright and indignant. It'll be great." The hopeful request had progressed to playful insistence.

"All right," she sighed, trying to project a stern demeanor through the growing amusement she felt. "But understand. The only reason I'm agreeing to this is because I believe you owe Joey and me an explanation and an apology."

"No problem. See you there. I'll follow." He turned to go to his truck then suddenly reversed and leaned down again. "Unless, of course, you want to ride with me." She feigned a jab at him and he cackled in gleeful laughter. "Just askin'," he said throwing up his hands in mock confusion and jogging back to his truck.

FIVE MINUTES LATER THEY arrived at the hamburger grill. They found themselves pretty much alone in the place.

"Pick a table," He gestured grandly, "any table."

Crystal surveyed the dining area. "Over there." She pointed to a corner booth out of sight of the road.

"Fine," he agreed and motioned for her to walk ahead.

After they sat down she immediately began the tirade. "Daniel, just what did you think you were—"

He put up his hand to stop her as he looked at the menu on the wall. "I can't plead for forgiveness on an empty stomach. And besides, you need your strength to really let me know how terrible I am."

Crystal sat with her teeth clenched and arms folded, back pressed stiffly against the booth. He pressed the button for the intercom.

"May I take your order?"

"Yes, I'll have a burger with fries and a vanilla milkshake," he answered, then turned to Crystal. "Do you want a milkshake, too?"

"Well, I would—"

"Okay, two milkshakes please, and plenty of ketchup."

"Large or small?" the intercom box rattled.

He looked at Crystal and shrugged his shoulders in an exaggerated gesture. "I didn't know there was large or small ketchup." A chuckle broke through her calculated seriousness.

"Large or small milkshakes, sir?"

"Oops." He raised his eyebrows. Then to the intercom he responded, "Large."

"Thank you."

"Sure, anytime." Then he turned back to Crystal. "Before you get fully wound up here, tell me this. Did you get to talk to Joey?"

"Why, yes, I did."

"See, my brilliant plan worked." He peered intently into her face as if her answer were the most important piece of news he would hear that day. "Everything okay then?"

"As a matter of fact, on the way to Phil's we talked and it turned out he was mostly worried about whether I would still be his teacher since Phil and I weren't going to be married. Can you believe it?"

"Kids are amazing, aren't they? Wouldn't it be nice if us adults were as easy to please?"

"We adults?"

"You correcting my grammar, too, now?"

"No, I was correcting your reference to yourself as an adult." Crystal held a serious face long enough to cause him to just begin a frown. She burst out laughing followed by his uncomfortable snicker.

"Okay, you got me." He lowered his head for an instant then looked up more seriously. "Look, Wednesday Reggie sent me on a road call and I had to go. I'm sorry. Sounds like it turned out okay though. Maybe even better than the original plan."

Off-balance from his shift in tone, she paused before she spoke. "Well, except for one thing."

"What?"

"I ran into Phil."

"Ouch. What was that like?"

"Well, it was awkward and uncomfortable. Then we both loosened up and had at least a pleasant conversation."

"Did you heart-to-heart talk or just not rip each other's throats out?" He watched her frown.

"We didn't have a heart-to-heart or do the ripping thing either. We just exchanged a few sentences, which was more than I expected, considering everything." She stopped as a pained look came over her face.

He started to reach over to touch her hand in reassurance but withdrew it before she looked back at him. *You can talk to me. I want to know everything you think and feel. I want to share it all.* "Look," he said,

"I've known Phil less time than you have. But I have to tell you, I was glad you broke it off with him."

"Why?" she asked pointedly.

He shifted his look away from her for a second. "Because I didn't believe you were really in love with him."

"Oh, and what makes you say that?" She raised her eyebrows.

A teenaged boy arrived with a tray. "Who had the burger and fries?"

"Food's here." He shifted gears quickly. "She gets a shake. Man, I'm starved." He dived into his meal and avoided eye contact with Crystal while she continued to scrutinize him. Finally, she reached for a napkin and opened her straw.

She took a few sips of her milkshake. "This is really good. They must use real ice cream not that imitation stuff."

"Yeah, I hate that artificial junk that comes out of a machine." He smiled and lifted his cup in a mock toast. "Here's to the real thing; let's never settle for less." His tone was glib but the expression in his eyes was solemn.

She lifted her shake in response. As the two cups touched she returned the look and said softly, "Yes, never settle for less."

They each took a ceremonious drink and laughed when Crystal's straw made a loud bottom-of-the-cup gurgle.

BY THE NEXT WEDNESDAY construction on the float had become the focus of Crystal's class. Victor's father arrived with the back of his pickup full of rolls of chicken wire. Christine's parents brought lumber for the displays on the top of the float and Jordan's mother came loaded with tissue and crepe paper of all kinds.

"First, we have to decide if all of you are going to ride on the float or walk alongside," Crystal said.

"Ride, Miss Crystal, ride, please!" they all yelled, and Angela jumped up and down clapping.

"Okay, but we'll have to figure out how to make it safe for everyone and I—"

A voice behind finished her sentence for her. "—have just the plan." She turned to see Daniel smiling at her

She smiled back involuntarily. "And what exactly is this plan?"

"Yeah, Mr. Daniel, what's the plan?" Joey moved up beside him.

AFTER TWO HOURS OF lively discussion and work, Crystal raised her hand in the air and called for everyone's attention. "We need to stop now. You have homework." The children groaned and the parents began herding them toward their cars.

"Don't forget, we don't have much time so we'll need to do this again Friday. Can everyone be here?" Most waved in agreement as they left.

"Sorry, Teach, I gotta' work." Duke walked toward her as she spoke. "But Phil can probably get Joey on Friday." She noticed, as if for the first time, his square shoulders that were broad but not bulky suggesting latent rather than obvious strength. His beard was trimmed close which accentuated the line of his jaw and chin. The gaunt look she had noted months earlier had by now given way to a healthy leanness.

Crystal caught herself staring and blinked to break away from his gaze. "Uh, yes, I'm sure he probably can." He stopped right in front of her. All the while his eyes, crinkled at the corners with his playful smile, never broke contact with hers. She shifted in place and, with effort, looked away. Then rather abruptly she blurted, "Daniel, can we get together sometime before Friday?"

He perked noticeably to the question. Sensing his interest, she hurried on. "I—I'd like to talk more about your plan for the float. For the children's safety." By now she could feel herself blushing under his unrelenting scrutiny.

"Yeah, the children's safety." His eyes narrowed a little as they searched her face.

Crystal took a step away from him toward her car. "Okay. Good." Then she stopped. "Tonight I have to drive to the Agape Center and pick up the money for the float materials."

"Perfect. Penmartin's been nagging me about coming over to check in. We'll ride together."

Cautiously she ventured, "That might work out well." Then she stammered, "Logistically and time-wise, I mean."

"I was just thinking the same thing."

"Good," she announced. Neither said anything for a few seconds but Crystal looked around the parking lot.

As if understanding her increasing discomfort, the disarming young man offered, "You can follow me to my place and I'll drop off my truck. That way neither of us'll have to come all the way back over here later."

"Yes, yes, that's a good idea." She reached for the door handle of her car but he stepped in and grabbed it first, opening the door for her. Her body brushed his as she slid into the car. Had she never been that close to him before? She noticed for the first time that he smelled wonderful.

He closed the door carefully after her.

CHAPTER 14

On the way to the Agape center Crystal focused on the highway, eyes straight ahead. Her Daniel sat with his back to the passenger door and kept the conversation going.

"So tell me, what do you do when you're not teaching and building floats?"

"Uhm," she hesitated thoughtfully, "well I used to do very little but now I'm taking this correspondence course in auto-mechanics. You know, to have a second career to fall back on." She snickered, enjoying her own humor.

"Really?" He studied her as though her remark had been altogether serious. "Let me know if you need any help. Rebuilding transmissions is kinda' tough the first time." They both laughed and Crystal began to relax. She leaned her elbow on the door and cocked her head toward him, eyeing his expression.

He looked perplexed. "What?"

"Well, I don't know anything about your life before we met at the center."

He fidgeted a little then shifted in his seat so he was looking straight ahead. When he finally spoke his voice had an edge to it. "I already told you. I grew up, my parents died, I traveled around some and I ended up here. What's to know?" He continued to stare at the road.

Crystal returned softly, "Look I'm not trying to pry. I just thought that if we were going to be friends I'd like to—"

He turned to look at her. The transparency of her eyes showed only interest and acceptance and he couldn't take offense. He leaned back in the seat. "Crystal, I'd like to be friends too, but—"

Just then a tire bounced through a pothole in the road jostling them both and the car suddenly went dead. No lights on the dash, no sound from the motor. With the power steering and brakes also gone Crystal had to wrestle the car over to the side of the road as it rolled to a stop.

"What this time?" she moaned.

He opened the door and jumped out. "Pop the hood and I'll look but my guess is the battery cable."

He reached into the engine cavity. Crystal leaned out the window as he looked up from his assessment of the problem.

"Yeah, here it is. The bump must've severed the cable. Got any tools or anything in there?"

"I don't own a screwdriver much less a car repair kit."

"What about some tape?" he called from under the hood. "Electrical tape would be best."

"Daniel, I teach children. I have chalk, paper, paper clips and number cards. I do not have tools and electrical tape. Oh!" Crystal nearly shouted. "Wait a minute! I have one of those big flashlights in my trunk in case of—well—emergency." She quickly got out of the car and went around to the back. She opened the trunk and moved boxes and bags around.

"What all do you carry in here?" He came around to look over her shoulder into the full trunk.

"I told you, a teacher has—" she paused, "—teacher stuff." After taking two of the boxes out and setting them aside she again rummaged to the bottom of the huge Cadillac trunk. "Yes, here it is." She turned the light on and it immediately began flashing.

"Good. Then we'll set it on top of the car and just wait." He closed the trunk. "Someone's bound to come along sooner or later."

She cut her glance over at him as they climbed back into the car.

They chatted and laughed for over an hour. When the sun had set, the air became cool and breezy so they rolled the windows up. Flashing on top of the car, the red lantern continually contrasted light and darkness on their faces as they talked. Finally, a car pulled in behind them and headlights glowed against the foggy rear window. Duke opened the door and stood up.

Recognizing the driver, he called, "Hey, man. Glad you came along. The car broke down and we've been waiting forever."

"We?" Casper Penmartin raised a knowing eyebrow as Crystal rolled down her window.

"Sorry I'm late, Mr. Penmartin. The car just went dead." She gestured toward the offending engine.

"Got a wire stripper and some electrical tape?" Duke asked innocently.

Smiling slyly, Penmartin replied, "No, I don't, but I'm sure we do at the center. I can give you two a ride."

"Thanks." He slid into Penmartin's small pickup truck.

While they waited for Crystal to retrieve her purse and lock the car Penmartin turned to chide. "Car broke down, huh? I haven't heard that one in years. Way to go."

"No, it was—" The young man began to protest but stopped short when Crystal squeezed into the small truck beside him.

"Was what?" she asked and pulled the door shut.

"Cold. It was cold waiting." He hurriedly volunteered.

AT THE CENTER, PENMARTIN gave Crystal the check and found tools and tape for repairing the broken cable. On the way back to the car Penmartin asked, "Crystal, why was it you wanted all that money now?"

She dropped her head a few seconds then raised it almost defiantly. "Because this float is an important project. It will show what these special education children can accomplish and do it in a way that will get public attention." She paused. "Hopefully." As she finished, she looked out the window sadly.

"What's it going to look like?" Penmartin queried.

Crystal brightened and enthusiastically went over every detail of the float. "—But the best part was Daniel's idea." Admiration was in her voice and gratitude on her face as she turned to her companion.

"He figured out how we could let the children sit on the float and do things instead of walking alongside it. It's great!"

He returned her look, his face very near hers in the close quarters of the small truck. "Yeah, well, I was inspired."

After they arrived at the car, it only took a few minutes to fix the cable. He closed the hood and walked over to Penmartin with the tools. "Thanks, man. No tellin' how long we mighta' been stuck here."

"Don't think I'd mind much if I were in your shoes." Penmartin raised his eyebrows and tilted his head in the direction of Crystal who was getting into the driver's seat of her car.

"True, but I don't know. She's just broken up with this guy. And I can't say how long I'll be around here."

"Well, you do what you gotta' do. Just remember everybody has some baggage or other from the past and no one owns the future. Sometimes it's best just to do what you feel is right one day at a time. Don't throw away happiness worrying about what might go wrong."

"Yeah, yeah." He looked at the ground and scuffed the dirt with the toe of his boot. "I never used to care much, but this is different."

"Daniel, your life's been given back to you. You're entitled to a little joy in it." Penmartin again looked in Crystal's direction. She waved to him as the car started easily. "She's a nice girl and she likes you."

"You think?"

"No one looks at me like she does at you, and if they did I'd be counting my blessings." Penmartin started his truck as the young man backed away from the window. "Take it slow and easy just like you did learning to walk again. It'll come to you." He put the truck in gear. "See ya' around. Don't be a stranger." He started to pull away.

"Penmartin—".

The truck stopped. "Yeah?"

"Thanks."

Returning to Crystal's car, he opened the door and got in. Crystal asked, "What did Mr. Penmartin say?"

"Oh, just to take it easy." They turned around to head home.

WHEN THEY PULLED INTO the driveway, he reached over and turned the radio off. "Crystal, could we go out sometime? Not car stuff or school, just out—you and me."

"Like a date?"

"Yeah, like that."

"Daniel, I—" Crystal hesitated. She looked at him, and in the space of a few microseconds, weighed a dozen pros and cons. But when he lowered his eyes at her hesitation, she hurried, "I would like that very much."

When it soaked in that she'd said yes he perked up, his eyes brightened and the smile returned. "Hot—" He caught himself. "I mean, great!" He opened the car door and got out. "I'll call ya' later."

"Good." She put the car into reverse then looked up. "And thanks for tonight. The car and all."

"No sweat. Good night," he called and waved as she turned to back out of the driveway.

"Good night," she returned.
"Sweet dreams."

WHEN THE PHONE RANG Crystal jumped to answer it. "Don't bother, Mama, it's for me." She picked up the receiver with a bright, "Hello."

"Crystal, it's Daniel. You busy?"

"No, not at the moment."

"I was calling to see if you wanted to, uh, go out Saturday night."

"Yes, I would. What did you want to do?"

"Doesn't matter to me as long as it's not dancing. I haven't got my two-steppin' back yet."

She laughed the giggly laugh of a teenager.

Her mother walked by at about that time. "Who is that, Crystal?"

"Someone who's helping with the float. Mama, would you hang up the phone when I go upstairs? I'll pick up the extension in my room." Then into the phone she said, "I'm going to get on the other phone. Can you hang on a minute?"

"Sure." The masculine reply came before Ann took the phone.

Crystal trotted up the stairs like a runner in training. She went to her room and closed the door. "I've got it, Mama. Thanks."

Ann hung on for a few seconds.

Crystal repeated, "I've got it."

CHAPTER 15

Saturday night getting ready to go out Duke had an audience. "Where's your head at, kid?" Grunt's tone mocked him.

"What?"

"Oh, I get it now. The motor's runnin' but not all the plugs are firin'." Grunt shook his head. "Look, Duke, I've hauled your carcass out of more snake pits than I can count and I know what trouble smells like. You're goin' down in flames on this one. They're only gonna' be able to identify you with dental records. Get me?"

"Yeah, yeah. So she's different."

"Noooo. The woman with forty tattoos on her face is different. This one's more like hittin' the wall at 180 miles an hour."

"You here for a reason or have you just not stuck that ugly face into anybody's life this week?" Irritation was coming through his voice.

"So what're you going to do with this lady friend of yours?" Grunt continued to needle his friend who darted shirtless around the small apartment.

"I don't know. We're going to decide when I pick her up." He went to the chest of drawers, jerked one open and rifled through several shirts throwing them one by one onto the floor. "I got nothing to wear. This is great. I can just see me out with her in an old T-shirt."

"Would you chill, man? This ain't the prom… Daniel." Grunt dragged out the name in a formal, mocking tone.

Duke wheeled around and got right in his face. "Why don't you just get out?"

Grunt raised an eyebrow in momentary surprise then roughly pushed the smaller man aside as he rose slowly from the chair. "Yeah, this whole Barbie and Ken thing is makin' me sick."

After Grunt left, Duke stopped to look in the cracked dresser mirror. The scar down the front of his abdomen was still red but smaller than it had been. He reached up and touched the part of his closely cropped beard that covered the scar on his face. *Who'm I kidding? I don't even know what I'm doing in this town, much less with this girl.* He threw a rumpled black T-shirt angrily on the bed. "Forget it!"

As he did, the phone rang. "Yeah?" he answered sharply.

"Daniel?"

"Oh, hello." His voice instantly became more pleasant.

"I wasn't sure I had the right number. This is Crystal. Listen, I really don't feel like getting dressed up tonight. Would you mind if we just maybe went out for a burger or something and then you could show me that place where you work? What's it called?"

"Reggie's."

"Yes. Would you mind?"

He took a deep breath then smiled and tugged on the T-shirt. "No, sounds good to me."

"Thanks for understanding. See you in a little while?"

"Sure." He was still grinning when he hung up the phone.

CRYSTAL WATCHED AT THE window, not in an obvious way, but she watched just the same.

Ann came in from the living room. "Crystal, I don't know what you're trying to prove here but you'd better consider your reputation. This is a small town and everyone will know. I hope you're prepared to deal with that, you and this Daniel boy, whoever he is."

Crystal sighed deeply and headed out the door to the old porch swing. The antiquated truck painted primer gray pulled into the driveway. "I'm gone. Be back later." Crystal called as she left the porch not waiting for an answer.

She walked gaily toward the truck as her Daniel climbed out. "Hi."

"Madam, may I invite you to experience the nostalgia and sheer—raggedyness" He paused then gestured grandly toward the open door. "—of a true piece of automotive history?" He clicked his heels and stood at attention. Crystal giggled, enjoying the joke.

After they both got in, he began, "Sorry for the—"

"Shh. I'm savoring the nostalgia," she said. "You'll ruin the moment." They both chuckled as he started the motor.

Pulling out of the driveway, he asked, "Where do you want to go to eat?"

"I don't care, surprise me."

"Well, how about we go to our place."

"Our place?"

"Yeah, you know, that burger what-cha-ma-call-it."

"Burger Island?"

"Yeah. Where we had our first fight."

She gave a soft, natural laugh. Suddenly, though, her face turned serious. "Daniel, I—"

"What?" he asked nervously.

"This is all kind of sudden, and Phil and I just broke up, and it's Saturday night, and—"

"Got'cha. They have a drive-through. We can maintain our secrecy and steal away undiscovered into the night."

"You've thought of everything, I see." Her tone had an edge of suspicion to it.

"Well, I figured it might be too weird for you, out with the new guy nobody knows."

"No, that's not it," she hurried to explain.

"Look. It's okay. Relax. We're just hangin' out together. And it's nobody's business unless we want to make it their business. It's our choice."

She took a deep breath of relief. *I still don't know how he makes me feel like we're old friends, yet I barely know him.* "Yes, you're right."

"And if it's really warpin' your frame I've got a full-face helmet behind the seat. You wear it and I'll handle the drive-through guy."

She raised her eyebrows. "Are you serious?"

"Sure, reach behind the seat," he continued in his covert mode.

She pulled the seat forward and brought out a white motorcycle helmet with a tinted face shield. "This?"

"Yeah, try it."

While they drove, Crystal turned the helmet around in her hands then slipped it on. After she fastened the strap under her chin she looked at herself in the rearview mirror.

"Here, take my jacket and put it on. It'll complete the disguise."

She took the jacket, stuck her arms into a sleeve and pulled it around her. She looked in the mirror again.

"Here we are. Be cool."

When the truck pulled up to the drive-through he said, "We'd like two island burgers and two milkshakes, vanilla."

The teenaged boy keying in the order peered over at the other seat. Crystal sat still, facing straight ahead. "Would you like French fries with that?"

He turned to Crystal. "Fries?"

The helmet rotated left to right.

"No fries."

When the boy continued to stare, Duke leaned out the window of the truck and whispered, "Look, he's one of those actors who like to come to small towns and hide out from all their fans. You understand."

"Who is it?" the teen whispered back.

"You know, the one that goes to small towns to hide out."

He nodded knowingly. "Oh yeah, that one."

"Well, don't tell anyone you saw us. He likes his privacy and if anyone finds out he's here, well, you know."

Duke's seriousness evoked a solemn promise. "Oh no, I won't tell anyone."

"Thanks."

"Here's your burgers and shakes."

"Thank you."

"Oh, thank you too, Mr—"

Putting his fingers to his lips, he shushed the youth loudly.

"Oh, yeah, right. So long. And I really enjoyed your last movie."

As they pulled away, Crystal took off the helmet, tussled her hair with her fingers and howled with laughter. Duke steered into the driveway of a business a few blocks from the burger restaurant also snickering.

"Oh man! I thought I was going to lose it right there in front of the guy. Did you see him?"

Crystal wiped tears from her eyes and held her stomach. "Stop! I can't stand it. He'll probably go tell his friends as soon as he can get to a phone. By tomorrow I wouldn't be surprised to hear Tom Cruise was in town!" She doubled over in the extremes of her amusement.

When she finally straightened up her eyes were moist and she was still chuckling slightly. Duke suddenly leaned over and kissed her. She responded momentarily, leaning toward him and bringing her hand to his shoulder. Then they broke apart from the brief introductory kiss.

"What was that for?" she asked, a bit breathlessly.

"People are always nervous on first dates wondering when the kiss is coming. Best to just get it out of the way early so you can relax and enjoy the evening."

She peered thoughtfully at him then she chuckled again. "I never saw it quite like that."

"Well here, eat your burger while you think about it." He handed her the paper-wrapped meal.

Then just as she was beginning to wonder if he intended to kiss her again, he blurted, "Oh, that's right. You said you wanted to see where I work. C'mon. We got a machine in today that's a real museum piece. You have to check it out." Excitedly, he threw the truck into gear.

CHAPTER 16

They pulled up at the motorcycle shop. "Wait here. My key's to the back door. I'll turn on the lights then let you in."

She watched him go around the back of the building. Finally he opened the door and motioned her in.

"Come look at this. Can you believe it?" He led her past big muscular-looking motorcycles heavily appointed with chrome and laden with studded leather saddlebags, each in its own way massive and imposing. But the one he pointed to was more trim, less bulky. The condition was pristine like a new model. Light reflected off the chrome as with the other motorcycles but the heavy saddlebags were noticeably missing. Though it looked somewhat lighter weight than the others it in no way appeared fragile or delicate.

"See? It's a 1972 Sportster! I mean, the old ones were legitimate super-bikes in the 50s, but this is the first year they added the 1000cc overhead valve engine. It's a monster! Even by today's standards this is an awesome bike!" His eyes shone and his words raced in his enthusiasm.

"Daniel. I haven't seen anyone this excited since Joey got a remote control fire truck for Christmas. Men and their toys!" she chuckled, teasingly.

He looked down at the floor and took a deep breath. "Yeah, I guess I do get carried away. It's just that some of these bikes I've only ever seen in shows and working on them is—well—it's just cool. Sorry if I got a little carried away."

"It's okay." She walked over to one of the bikes. "Could I sit on one?"

"Sure. The Sportster is a little tall for a woman, though. Try this one. You might find it more comfortable."

"Well, I don't think comfortable is possible but one I could get my leg over would probably make more sense." Crystal let him direct her to a bike parked in front of the display window.

"What is this? The front wheel is sticking out two feet ahead of this thing."

He laughed. "It's called a Chopper and it sits a little lower than some of the others. Go ahead, climb on." He steadied the handlebars while she gingerly stepped over the bike and eased down into the deep leather seat. Warily she placed her hands on the tall handlebars.

"Vroooooom!" he said suddenly. Crystal jumped, startled, and stood up, awkwardly straddling the seat. He grabbed her elbow with his right hand while he continued to hold the bike up with the other. "Whoa! Don't let it get away from you there." She dismounted.

"I think I'll stick with four wheels." She laughed nervously.

"Aw, sitting on a bike that's parked isn't the way to experience one."

"Do you ride?"

He patted his side with his free hand. "No, not with this robotic hip. I just tinker on them. And I listen to the guys talk." *I have to watch myself here. Can't let her think— Not now, anyway.* Releasing the bike, he straightened and gestured around the small shop. "Well, here's my work. This is about all there is."

"I'm impressed." Crystal dropped her eyes, then looked up at his. "Thank you for bringing me here." She smiled sweetly. "Another piece of the Daniel Davis puzzle."

He met her glance, and while he held it, reached for her hand pulling it slowly up in front of him and placing his other hand on top of hers. "Crystal, I know I've been a pain but there's a lot in my life, past and present, I'm still sortin' out."

"Why don't you come to church with me tomorrow? Talking to God has always helped me make sense of things. I guess that's a pretty big part of who I am; just like all this is part of who you are." She looked at his hands that held hers then up at his face. He continued to hold her hand but avoided her gaze.

"Yeah, well, God and me aren't exactly on speaking terms." He cleared his throat then tugged her hand and started for the door. "C'mon. We should go."

Crystal let the subject drop. They left the shop and drove the sixteen miles to the ice cream bar in the next town. For an hour they sat in the parking lot and talked, he about motorcycles he was working on, she about the challenges of the children she taught. Finally he drove her home.

As he shut off the motor, Crystal turned to him.

"Are you sure you won't consider coming to church with me tomorrow?" She looked hopefully at the man who was becoming so dear to her, but his face was unresponsive.

"Is that a requirement for you to go out with me again?" His look was neither belligerent nor expectant, more controlled.

"No, I just wish you would consider it, that's all," she replied softly.

"Then I won't lie to you. It's not gonna' happen."

They were both awkwardly silent for a moment. Finally, Crystal spoke up brightly, "I had a nice time tonight and I learned a lot, too. It seems every time I'm around you I learn something new. And I'm supposed to be the teacher." She opened the door and started to climb out of the truck.

"Me, too," he uttered almost in a whisper. As she walked around the truck he got out of his side and walked with her to the door. The porch light was on. The open living room curtains revealed the TV playing.

"Mama's still up." She looked up briefly at the light. "And I believe she's put a hundred watt bulb in this time." Crystal snickered and Daniel smiled. He reached over and kissed her lightly on the cheek, squeezed her hand for a second, then turned back toward his truck.

"Good night," he called from the walk.

"Good night. And tell that mysterious actor good night too." She waved to him while he closed the door and started the motor. After he drove off she went into the house.

"Crystal, is that you, honey?" Ann greeted her as she walked in. "How was your evening?"

"Well, Mama, we talked a lot and I invited him to go to church with me tomorrow."

"Oh Crystal, how could you? So soon—and right in Phil's—"

"Don't worry," Crystal interrupted. "He's not coming. He said he and God aren't exactly on speaking terms." She looked thoughtful for a second. "Yes, I believe that's the words he used."

"You mean he's one of those atheists? Crystal!"

"No, Mama. I don't think that's it. There's a sorrow in him that he won't talk about. That might be the wall between him and God."

"Well, it sounds like—"

"Mama, please stop. He's a nice young man and I had a very pleasant evening. Can we just leave it at that?" Crystal moved toward the stairs. "I'm going to bed. Good night."

"Good night," Ann called just before Crystal's door closed softly.

THREE DAYS LATER AS Duke opened the door of his apartment a voice spoke from out of the darkness inside. "How 'bout some real food, kid?"

He turned on the light and snapped, "You know, if anybody but you called me that—"

"Yeah, yeah, I know. You may think you're a tough guy but you're still just a punk." Grunt laughed and lunged forward with his hand extended to rough Duke's hair as an adult would a child's. Duke threw up a fist to block him. Grunt grabbed the fist with the other hand and twisted Duke's arm around behind his back, overpowering the much smaller man. While Duke winced in pain and laughter Grunt rubbed his fist in his victim's hair. Just as Duke mustered all his strength to resist and swung his fist, Grunt released him and jumped out of the way.

"You—"

"Watch it now, Daniel." Again the sarcastic tone saying the name. "Don't say nothin' that cutie of yours wouldn't approve of." Grunt grinned in obvious delight.

Duke growled, "Did you say something about food or did you just come by to harass me?"

"Oh, right. There's an all-night place about five miles down the road from here. C'mon. You're still lookin' kinda' puny." Grunt's smile disarmed Duke, and he shook off his irritation.

"Okay, but we're goin' in my truck. I'm not ridin' on the back of that hog of yours. You're not my type." Duke grabbed his keys and strolled out the door. Grunt followed, shaking his head.

THE WAITRESS, AN AMPLE, curvy, early middle-aged woman with permed brown hair and a starched gray and white uniform worked busily at the coffee machine. Without turning around she called, "You boys just find you a seat. It's all first class here; we don't show no favorites."

Grunt and Duke looked at each other. "How do they do that?" They shared a laugh and took a booth around the corner from the cash register. Shortly the waitress came around to their table. She smiled at Grunt while she took his order. "And how would you like your potato, sweetie, baked or fried?" For Duke's order, she wrote down the number he gave her from the menu. "Thank you." With a wink at Grunt, she took the menus and walked away.

"How's the job goin'?" Grunt asked.

"Well, I like the work. Reggie gets in a lot of different bikes, mostly Harleys but they each have some custom work or other on them. Keeps it interestin'." He paused a second. "Grunt, I've never asked you but how is it you always have money and you don't work? I've never seen you do any of that illegal stuff either."

"No, that kind of life eats you up eventually. If the cops don't get you your habit will. I've seen enough of that to know I don't want no part of it."

"So, how do you live?"

"I get disability from the V.A."

"Disability? You can't be serious. For what?"

"My right eye. Can't see out of it."

"When? Were you in a war? Not Korea, surely. You're not old enough."

"Nah, one of them police action things when they started actin' up in the Middle East years after the war."

"Grunt, I've known you all this time and I never—"

"Yeah, well, don't lose no sleep over it."

Duke studied his friend. *What else don't I know about you?*

"Who had the steak and eggs? Like I had to ask." The waitress's sarcasm wasn't as grating as it was coy. She laid the plate in front of Grunt. "Here ya' go, hon. Ya' know, that's quite a beard you got there. A girl could get lost in that thing." She continued to smile at Grunt while she offhandedly put Duke's plate in front of him. "And here's yours, Babe." As she walked away she turned back and smiled one last time.

"You dog you!" Duke jumped in to tease.

"What?"

"That waitress. She was flirting with you."

Grunt chortled. "Get serious."

Though the big man had protested Duke's observation, during dinner he glanced more than once in the direction of the cash register where the waitress stood. At the end of the meal, Grunt got up and walked past the counter to the men's room. The waitress was drying glasses with a towel.

"Everythin' okay, honey? If you need anything you just call me. Name's Eugenia but everybody calls me Mama."

Grunt didn't say anything but his face reddened a bit under the long beard as he stepped aside to go around her.

While Grunt was gone a small man wearing jeans, a baseball cap and a denim jacket came in. In the reflection in the window Duke could see him fidgeting at the counter near the cash register. He wouldn't have paid attention except the man kept moving his right hand in and out of his pocket while looking intently around the diner. Duke's seat was out of the direct line of vision from the counter so the man apparently couldn't see anyone sitting there.

"Coffee, honey?" Eugenia turned the cup over at the man's place while she held the pot in her hand. He had been looking away and her sharp voice must have startled him.

He jerked toward her and thrust his right hand deep into his pocket.

"Uh, yeah, coffee," he stammered then looked nervously around again.

She poured the coffee, plopped two creamer containers next to the cup and turned away.

The man took one more quick look around the diner which appeared to be empty. He suddenly jumped up from his seat, yanking a gun out of his pocket. He shoved it into the waitress's ribs and grabbed her arm.

The woman screamed and dropped the coffee pot with a loud crash.

"The register! Open the register!" The man barked at her in an intense whisper.

Duke instantly sized up the situation and called casually from his seat. "Hey, did you drop my coffee? Do I have to come get it myself?" He stood up and strolled around the corner, momentarily distracting the man.

Startled, the man jerked the revolver toward Duke and cocked the trigger. The woman pulled free, immediately dropped behind the counter and crawled frantically around the corner out of the line of fire.

Obviously unsettled now, the would-be robber trained the gun on Duke. "I ought to just shoot you right here," he growled.

Suddenly a large, tattooed hand came from behind him and grasped the weapon. "I don't think that's a good idea."

Trying to regain control of the gun the man pulled the trigger, firing wildly in Duke's direction. Duke hit the floor while Grunt wrestled with the attacker who fought violently. In the scuffle, the gun went off again; Duke saw Grunt wince but he continued to struggle until he wrenched the gun away, tossing it out of reach. Then he threw one last punch that knocked the robber to the floor.

"You okay, kid?" he called.

Stunned at the near miss and Grunt's overpowering action, Duke stammered, "Yeah, I—I guess." He could see a dark streak oozing down the front of Grunt's shirt.

CHAPTER 17

Grunt reached down with his big hand and touched the red spot on his black shirt.

Duke grabbed his arm and ordered, "Lie down, you're bleeding!"

Grunt gave him a withering look. "What you all excited about? It was just a little .22." He did ease into a chair, though.

"Call 911! Now!" Duke yelled to the waitress who was already dialing.

When she got off the phone she threw Duke a towel. "Here, put pressure on the wound. You gotta' slow that bleeding. The paramedics are twenty minutes away and a man can bleed to death in fifteen."

Duke leaned over his friend who spoke, now sounding fatigued. "You sure you're okay?"

"Yeah, man. We all are. You just keep quiet, hero." The woman came over, bent down on one knee and looked at Grunt. She used her fingertips to smooth the hair back from the big man's face.

She glanced down at the towel almost completely soaked in blood then smiled through moist eyes.

"My, my, good looks and bravery, too. Didn't think there was any of that kind left."

"Where are those paramedics!?" Duke growled, impatiently striding toward the window. As he did, he bumped the gunman lying on the floor. The man came to and sat up. Duke exploded at him. "You! You did this!" He snatched him up by his shirt. The gunman's eyes widened and he brought his hands up to shield his face. Duke held him there for a few seconds then out of the corner of his eye noticed the pistol lying on the floor. Shoving the man against the counter, he scooped up the gun.

The terrified man, seeing his own weapon drawn down on him, went white. Duke breathed deeply in rage but his hand was steady and his jaw set. He held the gun ready.

"Please. I didn't want to hurt no one. I just brought the gun to—"

"To shoot someone, right? Well, maybe we ought to shoot some more. There's probably a couple bullets left in this thing. You think?" The man stood, paralyzed. Duke cocked the gun. He raised it then lowered it to set his aim.

"Don't—do—it—kid." Grunt spoke in a husky whisper. "Shootin' don't do nobody—no good."

Duke's eyes burned and indecision wracked him.

At that moment the door burst open and two county police deputies forced their way in. They both stopped when they sized up the scene. One stood directly behind Duke while the other moved to his side but within his field of vision. Both held their revolvers trained on Duke.

"Drop the weapon! Now!"

Duke stood immobile.

One officer cocked his pistol. "I said drop the weapon!"

The waitress stood up and cried, "Stan! Wait! He's not the one. This other guy came in to rob the place and then shot this man when he tried to stop him."

The officer glanced down at Grunt then at Eugenia's earnest face. He looked back at Duke and talked more calmly, "Okay, son. We'll take care of this now. Let's put the gun down and look after your friend."

Duke didn't respond.

The officer moved slowly toward him and extended his free hand carefully. "Let me have that now. Your friend needs help. You don't want to do this." Duke made eye contact with the officer then after a long moment lowered the gun. The deputy immediately snatched it from his hand. As he did, the other officer stepped in from behind, grabbed Duke's arms and handcuffed him.

While this all took place, the shooter made a lunge for the door. The deputy spun around and brought his gun to firing position. "I wouldn't try that if I was you."

The man froze. The deputy moved in, quickly cuffing him, too.

"Son, why don't you sit and settle down a little while we get this piece of garbage out of here." The officer eased Duke into a nearby booth but left the cuffs on him. "We'll need a statement from you."

The young man looked on helplessly as paramedics arrived and tended to the wound in Grunt's abdomen. "We need to get this one to the hospital, now!" a uniformed attendant said, hurriedly setting up an IV while another checked the prostrate man's pulse. It took both of them to get Grunt onto the stretcher. They wheeled him out at a run.

Duke stood up and shouted, "Wait, I'm going with him. Uncuff me, man! I've got to go with him."

"You just stay here, son, and cool down. There's nothin' you can do for him now." The deputy steered the now submissive man outside and put him in the back seat of a squad car. He closed the door and left Duke alone. Craning around, he could see the gunman sitting in the other police car. Through clenched teeth he vowed, "You'll pay for this!"

The deputy opened the car door. "Son, we'll need a statement from you. We talked with the waitress but she said she was hiding and didn't see the actual shooting."

"I need to go in that ambulance," Duke blurted insistently watching them load Grunt.

"Now don't worry, they're trained to handle this kind of stuff. You'd only be in the way. Tell you what. We can take you to the hospital and get your statement on the way."

His throat tightened as the ambulance door closed. The driver jumped into the cab and turned on the siren.

"All right," Duke glowered at the officers and said, "but take off these cuffs unless I'm under arrest."

The officers exchanged glances with the deputy near the other car then reached behind Duke and released the handcuffs. He rubbed his wrists. "Let's get going," he half-stated, half-commanded.

BEFORE THE POLICE CAR stopped completely Duke jumped out and dashed into the emergency area. "A guy came in here in an ambulance." He leaned over the counter close to the nurse's face and blurted. "Gunshot wound. Where is he?"

"Name?"

"Uh, I don't know. He's a big guy, beard, tattoos, like that."

"Oh yes, belly shot. He's being prepped for surgery. Are you family?"

Duke thought a second, "Not blood relative, but I'm as close as he's got around here."

The nurse studied him then pointed down the hall. "The waiting area for the O.R. is upstairs, second floor. Elevator's at the end of the hall."

"Thanks," he called over his shoulder as he hustled toward the elevator.

Several hours later a doctor in green surgical scrubs came out. "Are you waiting for Albert Hesterton?"

Duke jumped up. "Who?"

"Albert Hesterton. The gunshot wound?"

"Sorry, I never heard his real name before. He's gonna' be okay, isn't he? I mean, it was just a .22."

The doctor sighed and hooked his thumbs in the waistband of his scrubs. "Let me explain. Since the gun was a small caliber, the bullet went in and ricocheted around, nicking several organs. We removed the bullet and I think we found all the damaged places, but we'll just have to watch and see."

Duke's brow furrowed. "What do you mean?"

"If his vital signs stay good for twelve hours, that means we likely fixed all the tears and there's no internal bleeding."

"And if they don't?"

"We may have to go in again and look for what we missed. If we don't find it, it could be very serious."

"What do you mean, serious?"

"Let's not worry about that now. We'll just wait and see."

Real worry crept into his face as he looked at the clock. 2 a.m. He tried to shake off the dread creeping over him.

"SIR." DUKE WAS STARTLED when a nurse touched his arm. "Sir, wake up," she said. "We'll be monitoring your friend very closely. Why don't you go home? We've got your number on the call list if there's any change."

"No. Thanks, really, but I'd rather be here."

The nurse patted his shoulder and gave him a warm smile. "He's in good hands. And he may need you later. Go on home and get some rest."

"Well—" Her kind smile penetrated his concern. "Okay, but you'll call me if anything—" He stopped for a second. "—anything good or bad happens?"

"Yes, I promise. Now go on."

Duke looked at his watch as he walked toward the door. 4:30. Too early to call anyone. Nine and a half hours to go. He strode out into the darkness.

LATER THAT DAY DUKE was at work, somewhat distracted, but working. "Duke, it's for you; it's the hospital." Reggie handed him the phone.

"Mr. Davis, you might want to come down. Mr. Hesterton's being taken back into surgery."

"No! How bad is it?"

"It's too early to tell yet. But we generally ask family member to give blood in these situations. Would you like to do that?"

"Yes, okay. I'll come right now." Duke hung up the phone slowly.

"What is it? How's Grunt?" Reggie put her hand on his shoulder.

"They're taking him back into surgery." Duke moved toward the door. "I have to go," he announced.

"I will, too."

"What about the shop?"

Reggie looked down and said softly, "Grunt and I go way back. Back in the days when—back before I found the Lord. I have to go."

Duke raised his eyebrows. "Sure." *Reggie and Grunt? When?*

Reggie stopped long enough to lock up and put the CLOSED sign on the door.

AT THE HOSPITAL REGGIE and Duke both went in to give blood. Reggie's was a match; Duke's wasn't. "It doesn't matter," the lab technician explained to them. "We need all types to keep the supply up. Because someone else gave we have enough for him. Most people don't realize that."

Duke looked down as he slowly unrolled his sleeve. *What's going to happen?* He absently buttoned his cuff. He looked up, his eyes beginning to sting a bit and his thoughts seared. *Haven't you taken enough from me? He's all I have left. You're a greedy, thieving God.*

Duke slid down off the bed and stood. "Well, you're not getting this one." He muttered defiantly.

LATER, DUKE FOUND REGGIE in the waiting room. She stood by the window looking out. Her face was somber, her eyes fixed on some unseen spot outside.

"Reggie?" He touched her on the arm. She blinked and turned her face to him. "You okay?"

"Yeah."

"What were you thinking about just then?"

"I was remembering Grunt from earlier years. He's had so much trouble in his life. And now—"

"He's not going to die!" Duke's jaw flexed and he clenched his fist at his side.

"I wasn't going to say that." Reggie gently took his tightened fist in both her hands, coaxed it open and led him to the sofa. "I know you're worried. But the doctors say they believe they've stopped the bleeding. Now we just have to wait."

"But there's nothing we can do. I can't stand this." Duke leaned forward and put his head in his hands.

"We can pray."

He cocked his head in her direction. "Look, I know you're into all that God stuff, but he's never done me any favors. Do what you gotta' do." Duke stood up abruptly and strode across the room. "I'm gonna' take a walk. Watch for the doctor."

CHAPTER 18

As soon as Duke walked through the doorway a wave of weariness swept over him. He suddenly felt too drained to take another step. He leaned against the wall outside the waiting room. Why had God let this happen? Why? It seemed like God had always snatched away everyone that meant anything to him.

He braced his hands on his knees and let his back slide down the wall until he came to rest in a squat. Then from inside the room behind him he heard a soft, pleading voice.

"Lord, you're going to have to help me get through this one. But, in the meantime, could you help the guy in there? And while you're at it, Duke could use some of your comfort, too."

DUKE'S HANDS WERE SHOVED into his pockets and his head was down as he hustled toward the exit. He strode through the automatic doors and passed Crystal without even seeing her.

It suddenly registered that he had gone by and she turned around quickly. "Daniel!"

Already outside the door he continued across the parking lot oblivious to her call. She ran to catch up to him. "Daniel." She grabbed his arm. "What's happened? Are you hurt?" She stepped back and frantically scrutinized him up and down.

"Crystal." He smiled slightly at her insistent concern. "I'm okay."

"Well, what happened?"

"Let's go back inside. They've got a coffee shop. I could use some."

As they sat across from each other, he related the incident. "This guy took a bullet to protect me and now—" He couldn't go on.

His anguish brought a lump to her throat as well. She took both his hands in hers across the table. For a moment they sat unaware of their surroundings.

"He's in surgery now. He's bleeding internally. If they can't find where— He may not make it." He said the last part gravely.

She raised her eyebrows and drew back from him. "Die?" Crystal sat quietly for several seconds. Then she placed her hand on his arm, "Oh, Daniel—"

He put his forehead down on his hands. She moved to the chair beside him. Extending her arm over him, she laid her head on the back of his shoulder and held him that way for some minutes.

A HALF-HOUR LATER CRYSTAL left the hospital. She drove up the drive of the two-story Victorian style home past the huge pines that shaded the yard from thirty feet up. When she got out of the car she was shivering. She knocked on the door.

"Yoo-hoo, come in," she heard from inside the house.

As soon as she entered the house, Dr. Reasons welcomed her. "Please, sit down. We're glad you're here for this prayer group. We were just getting started. I have the list of Sunday's prayer requests and we've been going around the group for any more. Join us. Are there any other requests before we begin?"

"Well, yes, I have one," she said then took a deep breath. "There's a man in the hospital right now suffering from a gunshot wound. He's in intensive care after two surgeries to try to stop the internal bleeding. I would like to ask this group to pray for him."

Dr. Reasons began with a general prayer of thanks and strength for those who suffer. As he continued, Crystal made her own plea silently. *Dear Father, please help the man who is struggling for his life in the hospital. Also, comfort Daniel so he doesn't feel so alone in this. Only you can touch the part of him that's in pain now. Speak to his injured spirit and let him know your love as I do. Give him strength and hope.*

AT THE HOSPITAL DUKE stared out the window.

"Duke!"

He jerked his head around. "Reggie. What is it?"

"They're taking him back into intensive care now. We can see him tonight for a few minutes."

"What did the doctor say?"

"Hope."

Later that night in the intensive care unit Grunt lay still amid the tubes, monitors and soft lighting that was on 24 hours a day. Duke shuddered, remembering his own hospital stay. As he looked at the man lying there, he saw a face pink-cheeked from the replacement blood he had received. Duke stood motionless, regarding the man.

"He may come around in a little while." The nurse smiled pleasantly as she moved around the bed, checking monitors and tubes. She whispered, "If you talk to him, don't talk about what you see around here. Make conversation. Okay?"

Duke nodded. He sat next to Grunt's bed and watched silently for a while. Then he said, "Albert," softly, as if trying to get used to the name.

"Hey, buddy," the man on the bed mumbled through the twilight of sedation.

"It's me," Duke answered, unsure how to respond.

"You're okay? Good." Grunt spoke thickly and stirred. He opened his eyes wide, as if trying to bring his visitor into focus then sank back into stillness as his words trailed off.

"Just lay there, man. You need to rest now. We'll talk tomorrow. Just wanted you to know I was here."

The man on the bed smiled just slightly. Duke stood to leave but lingered a moment more. At first hesitantly, then with more surety, he touched the massive hand and held it in his own. After a few seconds he released it and left the curtained room.

REGGIE BOMBARDED HIM WITH anxious questions. "Did you see him? How did he look? Is he going to be okay?" They talked for a time then both sat quietly.

Finally, Duke stood abruptly. "I'm going for a walk."

As he strode through the halls, his mind raced. Twelve hours. Twelve hours they said. Then what? He shook his head not wanting to think about all the possibilities.

Eventually his meanderings brought him to the chapel. He didn't enter but a small brass plaque attached to the back of a wooden bench just inside the door caught his eye. "Vocatus atque non vocatus deus aderit. Bidden or not bidden God is present."

He frowned for a few seconds then cautiously took one step inside the door. He traced the letters with his finger. After a moment, he continued his walk through the hospital halls.

When he returned to the waiting room, Reggie stood and hugged him. Duke gave her a puzzled look. "I'm just glad you're here," she said.

As she released him he offered, "Look, I'm getting hungry. You wanna' go get something to eat?"

"No, you take off. They said they'd call us if he woke up and I want to be here. Just bring me something. Okay?"

"All right. Be back in a little while."

SHORTLY AFTER DUKE PULLED out of the parking lot rain began to fall. Lightning and thunder soon followed and he patrolled the road looking for some place to pull over that might be open. His headlights suddenly flashed onto a motorcycle off to the side of the road with two tent-like figures in rain ponchos hunched over it. Duke eased to the shoulder, climbed out of the truck and sloshed over to them, quickly soaked to the bone.

"What's the problem?"

They both looked up and rivulets of water from their rain-soaked hair ran down their faces. The taller of the two was a middle-aged man with a graying moustache and faded blue eyes. The smaller was a young girl whose eyes were also blue but a deeper shade.

"This thing sputtered a few times then just quit altogether. The man had to shout above the rain hammering loudly on the hood of the truck.

Duke yelled back, "Look, I've got a board in the back. Let's load your bike into my truck and I'll take you someplace drier. Then we'll see what's goin' on."

"Much obliged," the man called to him as he opened the tailgate. The two men wheeled the dead motorcycle to the truck and up the makeshift ramp. While they lashed the bike securely in the back, Duke motioned for the young girl to get into the cab. She smiled gratefully through the rain pouring off the hood of her poncho then got in.

When the men finished they both jumped into the truck. The two bikers shed their ponchos and stuffed them behind the seat. Duke turned on the heater. "One thing about this old truck; it's got a great heater. You two should warm up right away." He looked over at his shivering passengers. "You got anywhere to stay? It's late and it'll take awhile to figure out what's going on with your bike."

The man looked at the girl. "Actually, no. We thought we'd meet our friends by tonight. They got a motor home."

"You can stay at my place. I'm sitting with a friend at the hospital so I won't be there. I can't guarantee how clean it is. It's just me livin' there, so—"

"Thank you. I'm sure it'll be fine." The man smiled. "See, Amy? God's lookin' after us. Everything's gonna' be okay." He hugged her as Duke turned a quizzical glance toward them.

"Here we are. I'll back in so we can unload inside." As soon as they backed the bike off the truck, Duke turned to the travelers. "Door's unlocked upstairs. Why don't you go on up? You must be beat."

"Thank you." The man answered and the girl ducked her head shyly. Finally Duke parked the bike in the garage and climbed the wet steps to the apartment. As he came in the door he noticed the girl already asleep on the worn and lumpy couch with her father's jacket thrown over her.

"That old couch has ten years of gross stuff on it. Put her in my bed. It's cleaner. There's an extra blanket in the closet." The exhausted man gently scooped up the child and carried her to the bed. When he came back Duke was making coffee. "Want some? I'm not the greatest at making coffee but it'll be warm."

"'Preciate it." The man eased stiffly onto a rusting steel and vinyl kitchen chair.

"Where you headed again?" Duke asked.

"Christian biker's rally just south of Atlanta. Our fellowship group was goin' down for the week."

"Christian bikers?" Duke raised an eyebrow.

"Yeah, one of the clubs lets us use their clubhouse on Sunday mornings. Our preacher's been a biker for years. Heard the call ridin' down the road on his way to Myrtle Beach. You know, God spoke to him, said to go home and help lead people to faith. Glad he did. I don't know what me and my girl woulda' done without the fellowship this last year."

Duke filled a cup and set it on the table in front of his guest. "What happened?"

The man hung his head for a moment. When he lifted it again his eyes were tearing but his voice was steady. "Amy's mama got cancer and Amy and me took care of her. It was hard times for both of us. We couldn't a' made it without the group's help."

"I'm sorry." Duke joined the man at the table.

"Well, she ain't in no pain now; she's with Jesus. And Amy and me's got each other but she was always closer to her mama. The preacher said this trip might be good for us to kinda' get reacquainted. Our prayer group pitched in and paid for us to come down." The man leaned back in his chair, closed his eyes briefly and breathed deeply.

"Look, man, why don't you crash on the couch there? I'm headin' out. You're welcome to whatever's here." Duke stood to leave.

"I thank God for sendin' you along when he did," the man said. "I don't know what we'd 'a done."

"No sweat." Duke opened the door. "See ya' later."

"Hope your friend gets better. We'll pray for him."

Duke started to speak, then paused for a second. As he walked out the door, he responded. "Thanks."

A fifteen-minute drive brought him to an all-night gas station and store. He bought two slices of pizza and two soft drinks. On the way back to the hospital he sorted through a hundred racing thoughts.

Bidden or unbidden God is—

You don't have to believe for miracles to happen.

"No, I'm not fallin' for it," he shouted aloud. "If you got something to say to me then say it! I dare you!"

"I NEED YOU." The words popped into his brain like a loudspeaker.

"What? What was that?" He shook his head to clear it.

"I NEED YOU."

"Need who? You gotta' lot of nerve. You already got my parents and now maybe Grunt. Don't talk to me! Go get into Reggie's head or one of those other believers." He yelled the word sarcastically.

"THEY NEED YOU."

"Shut up!" He closed his eyes for a few seconds. As he did he saw the man and his daughter in the rain. He saw Grunt lying in the hospital bed. When he opened his eyes the truck was heading toward the ditch. He reacted instantly and stomped the brakes causing the truck to skid across the pavement and stop with the front wheel on the shoulder. Thrown against the steering wheel at the abrupt stop, he was momentarily stunned. Finally Duke straightened up and looked around. He saw that the pizza and drinks had fallen to the floor.

An image flashed into his mind's eye. *I remember now. The rain. The deer. Going too fast to stop then—*

As if in a daze, he opened the door and got out of the truck. Oblivious to the water soaking his hair and clothes he stared into the rain-walled blackness. *Broken hip, ribs and internal injuries. If that guy hadn't found me—* Penmartin's words came back. "With injuries like yours, you should be asking, why did you live?"

THE REST OF THE way to the hospital he paid close attention to the road.

CHAPTER 19

When he walked into the waiting area, he saw Reggie leaned against the end of the sofa her arm curled under her head and her eyes closed. Though he sat down quietly on a chair opposite her she stirred then opened her eyes.

"Duke?" She looked around sleepily. "Where've you been? You left over—" She squinted at her watch. "—two hours ago." She studied him for a few seconds. His face was tense and drawn, and he fidgeted with his hands. Sitting up and shaking off the sleepiness, she spoke with concern. "What's going on? What's happened? Is it Grunt?"

He put out his hand to stop her. "No, I just got here."

"The nurse came out earlier and said his blood pressure was a little erratic. They've got him hooked up to all those monitor things and they're watching him closely." She stared intently at him. "What's with you? And where's the food?"

"I got a little hung up," he said then explained about the man and his daughter he'd picked up earlier.

"That was a very Christian thing you did, taking them in like that. They needed you and you helped them."

"Reggie, do you know anything about biker churches?" he asked suddenly.

"Yes, I've been to a few. Why?"

"What's it like?"

Studying him, Reggie hesitated then answered. "Well, a group of riders gets together for fellowship and to get closer to God. Sometimes a church sponsors the group, helps them find a place to meet and offers some spiritual leadership. Just depends on the church and the group. Why do you ask?"

"Oh, that guy I picked up, he was telling me—"

"Mr. Davis," the nurse interrupted, "Mr. Hesterton's blood pressure has stabilized and his vital signs look good. You'll need to talk to the doctor when he comes in a few hours but it seems he's holding his own so far. Thought you'd want to know."

"That's great! Can we see him?" Reggie asked eagerly.

"He's resting now and you two look like you need a break. Go home and come back after seven when the doctor's been in. He'll be able to tell you more then." Her manner was kind and reassuring.

"Thanks." They both stood up and looked at each other. "Maybe we will go for a while." Duke turned to Reggie. "I'll drive you home."

He drove silently while Reggie leaned against the door and closed her eyes. When they stopped at her house she climbed out only half-awake. He walked her to the door. She hugged him and said, "He's going to be okay. I feel God's hand in this now."

"Reggie, when I was driving back here, I—" Duke began then changed his mind. "Forget it. It's late. So long." He left her and went back to the truck. When he climbed in he sat for a moment with his keys in his hand. Taking a deep breath, he slowly and deliberately put them in the ignition and started the truck. Like a man going to a funeral or a reluctant groom to the altar, he drove home.

When he arrived he opened the door and tiptoed in, careful not to disturb the sleeping man on the couch. He navigated in the dark to the chair on the opposite side of the room and sank into it. Within minutes, he was asleep.

WHEN DUKE FINALLY WOKE up the clock said 10:00. He shifted his sore, aching body in the old chair not intended as a bed.

"Morning. I borrowed your shower. Hope it's okay. Here, I fixed you something to eat." The man from the night before looked different. Except for the moustache he was clean-shaven and his hair was pulled back in a ponytail. He wore the same clothes but they were dry. Soon the girl came out of the bedroom wearing jeans and a fresh T-shirt, toweling her blonde hair.

"Oh, I didn't know you were up. We tried to be real quiet." She spoke softly as she had the night before, but the sleep had brightened her face.

"Your friend doin' okay?" The man's kind face turned toward Duke.

"Yeah, seems to be over the worst part."

"Good. We prayed for him last night. What happened?"

"He took a bullet from a guy who was going to shoot me."

"God was sure lookin' out for you—and your friend. Look, we've been here taking up your place and time long enough. Can you help me find someone who can work on my bike so we can get on down the road?"

"That'd be me around here. Let me call Reggie and tell her I'll be late, then we'll check it out."

BY NOON DUKE HAD finished the repairs on the travelers' bike. The problem was fairly simple and he was able to use parts Reggie had in stock.

"You've been a real blessing to us. Amy and me are going to make it to the rally because of you. What do we owe you?" The man pulled out his worn leather wallet attached to his belt loop by a silver chain.

"Just twelve dollars for the part." Duke smiled graciously.

"Are—are you sure? You did so much, letting us stay and all. Won't you let me pay you for your work at least?"

"No. Looks like my friend's going to be okay. Seems things worked out for everybody. Glad to help."

The man raised his eyebrows for a few seconds, then smiled broadly as he reached out to shake Duke's hand. "God bless you. And thanks." He called to his daughter, who came down the stairs with a small satchel. The man kicked the starter on the old Honda. It started immediately and went to an even idle.

Amy put her helmet on and tucked her hair up under it. Before she climbed on the bike she gave

Duke a quick bashful hug and a soft "thank you." The unexpected act caught him off guard, and he felt an unfamiliar smile come over his face, one that stayed while he waved the two on their way.

As he watched them go, he heard the loudspeaker in his head again. "THEY NEED YOU."

He stared thoughtfully down the road and was rewarded with a turn and wave from Amy just before they reached the curve that would take them out of sight.

"GLAD YOU'RE ALL RIGHT, Daniel," Casper Penmartin said that afternoon at the hospital. Duke was surprised to see him there. Had Penmartin come just to check on him? "Somebody from the church said you'd been shot. Something about a robbery?"

"Friend of mine got hit, not me," Duke responded soberly.

"Dodged the bullet again, did you? Excuse the pun. Somebody up there must really like you," Penmartin joked, somewhat inappropriately.

About that time Reggie returned from seeing Grunt. After updating Duke, she left to get something to eat.

"See ya'." Duke nodded to her then he turned to Penmartin. "Let's take a walk."

They exchanged small talk about Grunt and about Duke's work. When they reached the chapel Duke motioned for Penmartin to sit down. He pointed to the plaque on the bench. "Do you believe that?"

"What do you mean?"

"That God comes around and does his thing whether you ask for help or not?"

Penmartin was silent as if Duke's question had caught him off guard.

"Look," Duke continued, "God took my parents away from me." He paused and stared at his hands. "I've hated him for it ever since. So I wasn't about to ask for any favors." He paused again. "But then Grunt got okay. A few times there it coulda' gone either way for him." Duke looked up expectantly.

Penmartin shifted in his seat, put his elbow up on the back of the bench, and returned Duke's earnest gaze. "First off, I don't believe God takes people, I believe he receives them. It's a perilous world we live in. Things happen." He stopped as if expecting a protest. Receiving none, he continued. "Secondly, I believe God works through people. He intends for us to help each other. "

"You believe God talks to people?" Duke's intensity surprised even himself. He felt foolish after he had said it but Penmartin seemed to take the question seriously.

"I believe he makes things known to us. What do you mean exactly?"

Duke related the incident with the man and his daughter. "—And this thought blared into my head."

"What was it?"

"Well, first it said, 'I need you.'"

"First?"

"Yeah. It happened again and that time it said, 'They need you.'" Duke crossed his arms. "What do you make of that?"

"What do you think it was?" Penmartin peered at Duke, who answered almost immediately.

"I think—I think it was God talking. But I don't know why he would—"

Penmartin finished for him. "—talk to you when you despise him so?"

"Well, yeah. I mean, why not Reggie or Crystal or you? Or for that matter, the guy headin' to that Christian rally?"

"I don't have the answer to that. From the Bible we know that Paul wasn't always a fan yet God stopped him in his tracks and made him listen. I'll tell you this. If God spoke to me that clearly, I'd sure listen." Penmartin looked at his watch. Duke stood up with him. "Look, I've got an appointment. Wish I had more insight for you. I suggest you pray on it. Somethin' will come to you." Penmartin shook Duke's hand. "Keep me posted."

"Thanks." Duke responded vacantly. He watched Penmartin walk away then he shoved his hands into his pockets and headed slowly toward the waiting room.

PHIL AND JOEY APPEARED at church for the first time in several weeks. Dr. Reasons smiled broadly at them and shook Phil's hand before the sanctuary filled. Joey turned and waved at Crystal sitting a few rows behind them but Phil just looked straight ahead.

After church Crystal greeted them both warmly. "Good morning, Joey. Hello, Phil."

"Hi, Miss Crystal." Joey flashed his ever-present smile.

"Morning." Phil's manner was cordial and polite, nothing more or less.

"Phil, could I talk with you about something? We haven't had a chance much to have a conversation with the float and—everything."

"That's true." Phil's reticence didn't escape Crystal but she persisted.

"Joey, would you like to go to the fellowship hall? I believe Mrs. Henry brought ice cream for all the children."

Joey took off without answering. They both chuckled.

"That boy. He's got two speeds—stop and flat out." Phil smiled and appeared to relax a little bit.

"Yes, he's a powerhouse." Crystal gestured toward the path that led to the garden and she and Phil began to walk. She took a few deep breaths then started in. "Phil, I want to tell you—"

"—'Bout you and Daniel?" he volunteered.

"What? Where did you—?"

"It's a small town, Crystal. Somebody saw y'all at the Burger Island and well, things get around."

"Oh, Phil. We're not really dating. I wanted to talk to you, though, before—"

"It's okay. I just need to know. Were you seein' him before?" Phil's unguarded hurt burned her.

"I met him at the Agape Center. Penmartin introduced us. It was nothing really, just conversation over coffee. But—"

"—You like him." Phil's demeanor seemed to soften a little.

Crystal's eyes met his. "Yes, I do. And I wanted you to know it from me before, well, I guess it's too late for that."

"It's okay. He's a nice guy. Joey's crazy about him. You know what they say about someone who's loved by kids and—what's the other—dogs?" They laughed, and the tension eased further.

"Thanks for being okay with this. It's been difficult. I didn't want to—"

"No problem."

"Are you sure?"

"Yeah. Just don't bring him into the diner for a while." Phil smiled then added, "I still need to get used to the idea."

"You're great, Phil." Crystal kissed him on the cheek.

CHAPTER 20

When Duke went the next day to see Grunt he had been moved out of intensive care and was sitting up in the bed.

"Well, hello, Albert," he laughed. "You look like you're back from the dark side."

"Hey, kid. You remember Mama?"

Duke turned to see the waitress from the diner sitting in the corner. She smiled at him. "Hi, I just came by to see how our hero's doin'." She joined him at the side of the bed and squeezed Grunt's hand. "And to thank him." She dropped her eyes then cut them over at Grunt who blushed just slightly under his beard.

Duke watched them in amusement. "I don't want to intrude on your little party here, Grunt, so I'll come back."

"Watch'it, punk." Grunt grinned and playfully punched at Duke's arm, but winced instantly in pain. "Oooooo. I tell ya' for a puny little .22 bullet, they sure carved me up."

"Yeah, well, they figured they'd never seen anything quite like you so they thought they'd poke around inside to figure out what makes you tick. Kinda' like those alien autopsy things." Duke chuckled. Grunt growled.

"Boys! You two are worse than young'uns," Mama scolded.

Both men sobered instantly in response to the feisty woman. After a few seconds pause Grunt spoke again in a conversational tone.

"Mama here's offered to let me stay at her place when the doctor finally lets me out."

"That's the least I can do. Besides it's just me alone in that ole house. I'd enjoy the company. Haven't had a man to look after in some years now." The woman looked at Grunt tenderly.

Duke grinned. "I can't compete with that, man." He started for the door. "Look, I got something I need to talk to you about but I'll catch you later when you're not so—busy."

Mama jumped and dropped Grunt's hand. "No, you boys can talk all you want. I got groceries to buy and sheets to wash." She kissed Grunt on the cheek. "See you later, Sweetie."

Grunt was still smiling when Duke pulled the chair up close to the bed. "Sweetie? Well anyway, Grunt, you believe in God?"

The big man leaned back on the pile of pillows behind him and the smile left his face. "Do you know something I don't?"

"No, no, nothing like that. We never talked about this stuff, and well, I was just wondering."

"Why you bringing this up now?" Grunt looked at him skeptically.

"A lot went on while you were out and it's eatin' at me."

"I can't leave you alone for—"

"This is serious." The tension in Duke's whole body signaled for silence. Grunt listened quietly to the events of the past few days. "—And you see what a weird trip this all is? What do you think?"

Duke's intensity was unmistakable. Grunt paused thoughtfully before he spoke. "Well, I can see where some people might think you'd lost it."

"I don't care what some people think. What do you think?"

Grunt shifted in the bed before he spoke. "I never was one much on that God stuff as a young fella'. Maybe if I had been—" He stopped as if unwilling to reveal some secret thought.

Duke regarded his friend sympathetically. "Maybe now isn't a good time to talk about this."

Grunt raised his head and looked Duke in the eye. "I'm no expert but I don't think God talks that way to just everybody. So if he's talkin' to you, you better listen."

The words surprised Duke. "Funny, that's what Penmartin said. Now if I could just figure out why me. I'm no saint." He shook his head in confusion. "Why doesn't he pick on somebody else?"

"Just lucky, I guess," Grunt said, reassuming his tough-guy demeanor.

"Feels kinda' like a building falling on me."

"Well, what're you gonna' do about it?"

"I don't know. Maybe first figure out who 'they' are and what I have that anybody could possibly need." Duke put his hands on his knees and stood up.

Grunt reached for Duke's hand and shook it firmly. "Whatever you come up with, kid, I'm there. You know that."

"Yeah, I know. You've always watched my back," Duke responded, grateful for the firm grasp of the huge hand. "I owe you big-time."

"Well, I'm gonna' collect one of these days," Grunt laughed.

TWO HOURS LATER DUKE pulled into the church parking lot dressed in a plaid shirt and fresh jeans. Taking a deep breath he got out of the truck and headed for the church office.

"Hello, Daniel." Dr. Reasons came from behind his desk and shook his hand.

"I'm glad to see you. You look great. How's everything going?"

"I'm fine. Listen, there's a buncha' stuff going on in my head I need to talk to somebody about."

"Sit down and tell me."

They both settled into chairs in front of the desk. Dr. Reasons leaned back with a relaxed manner yet Duke felt the clergyman's eyes focused intently on his.

"I've been around church people all my life but the last few years I've been kinda'—well—away. The reason's not important now but what's happened lately is…." He rubbed his hands on his pants before blurting, "…well, I think God's talking to me and

I don't know what it means. I mean, I don't know why it's me or what I'm supposed to do, or—" He didn't continue.

"I see." Dr. Reasons asked, thoughtfully, "Can you give me a few more details?"

An hour later, the office door opened and the two men walked through the empty church. Dr. Reasons offered one hand to Duke and placed the other on his shoulder. "I think you're headed in the right direction, Daniel. I've heard of the Christian Motorcyclists of America. God apparently has something for you to do and that might be a good place for you to start."

"Yeah, and thanks. It does seem clearer now. I'll talk to a few people and see what I can come up with." Duke turned to leave, smiling.

CRYSTAL DIDN'T SEE HER Daniel or hear from him for several days. She checked with Phil and Joey but they hadn't seen him either. Not knowing who else to ask, she checked with Rev. Reasons.

"Don't worry about our young friend," Rev. Reasons told her. "He didn't say where he was or what he was doing but I know he had some things to sort out. Maybe his boss knows something more. Have you checked with her?"

But Reggie wasn't able to provide any information either.

Finally, Duke appeared one evening at Crystal's house.

"Where have you been? Why didn't you call me? I've been worried—"

He placed his fingertips over her lips. "I'm sorry I didn't call," he said, "but the last few days have been intense. I had some things to work out."

Gazing into his eyes, she quieted. "Well, can I get you some coffee?"

"I think that would be good," he said.

They sat at the table, and she leaned back in her chair, waiting. He also relaxed and took a sip of the coffee in front of him.

"Now, the long version would take all night."

She remained silent.

"The bottom line is I believe God has called me to a motorcycle ministry and I'm going to start one here." He paused to let what he had said soak in.

"A motorcycle ministry?" Crystal's surprised look made him smile.

"Yeah, see the idea is to offer people—bikers mostly—a way back to God and a place for believers, who are also motorcycle people, to get together with others like them. Groups like this are all over the country. I had no idea the numbers who were into this."

"Wait a minute, Daniel."Crystal interrupted. I thought you and God weren't 'exactly on speaking terms.'"

"Right. We weren't. But then he— Are you ready for this? He spoke to me."

"What?" She chuckled her surprise. "What makes you think that?

"I know it. I heard Him inside my head. I didn't even want to have anything to do with Him. I didn't even really believe in Him. But He spoke to me. He said, 'I need you.' Then later, He said, 'They need you.' See, I had picked up some cyclists broke down in the rain and helped them."

Crystal felt her mouth hanging open but it didn't matter to her. She had prayed, yes. And she had asked God to speak to him but this was beyond her expectations. "What do you think He meant?"

"I think He was tellin' me it's time to quit feelin' sorry for myself and get on with my life. See, I didn't know what He meant either. I asked some people what they thought but I just couldn't figure it out. So I had to get away for a while."

Crystal sipped her coffee and waited. Duke appeared to struggle with how to explain what he wanted to say.

"Me and God, we used to be pretty tight. Then I got messed up about some things. I started running, trying to find some peace. But I was really running away from it. So I had to stop and settle things with God. I had to confess my bitterness and give it up."

"I see." Crystal's heart ached for him. She didn't know where he had come from, what pain he carried, but she thanked God silently for helping this man she held so dear come to terms with it.

"Before, I never thought about anybody but me. It was all about my pain. My problems. Then God told me He needed me. And these Christian bikers needed me."

"So what's your involvement?"

He chuckled. "I'm still not a hundred percent sure but this was God's idea so I figure He'll—I don't know—do something. I can't believe He'd do what it took to sell me on this and then hang me out."

Crystal studied him before she spoke. "I—I didn't expect this. You seemed so—"

"Yeah. I spent a lot of years blaming God for my parents being gone. I know now that's not the way it all works. Maybe it's time I started looking at contributing more and complaining less." He laughed.

She raised her eyebrows.

"I know this may seem like a quick decision, but it wasn't. A lot of circumstances and people guided me in this direction. Now it just feels good to chuck that old stuff and look forward to going somewhere besides just down the road. I kinda' like it."

Crystal sat quietly for a few seconds, appraising him. "Well, you do seem less—less—"

"Freaked out?"

"No, less angry, troubled."

"Well, I am." He beamed.

"But why motorcycle people?"

He thought for a moment as if carefully deciding exactly what he wanted to say. "These people seem to have the most need and are the least likely to go to a traditional church for a spiritual connection. They just stay on the outside feeling like there's no place for them. I've been there and maybe I can help."

Crystal leaned forward laying her hands on the table. "I'm just amazed," she said. "You look calmer and happier than I've ever seen you."

"I'm not completely sure," he said taking both her hands in his, "how it's all going to play out but I'm gonna' give it a shot. Rev. Reasons said he'd help. He's been great about all this."

"I'll certainly support you. I think it's wonderful you've found such a calling."

"Thanks." His eyes held hers tenderly. "I'm counting on you."

THANKSGIVING WAS COMING. FOR the next two weeks Crystal's time was consumed with building the float for the parade. Duke worked long hours at the shop then spent evenings and weekends meeting with people who wanted to become involved with his group. Only elaborate telephone planning allowed the couple to spend any time together.

Finally, he phoned Crystal to set up an outing. "Listen, I've found out there's a swap meet about two hours from here," Duke said. "There are some people I've been trying to catch up with who'll be there and the drive down could give us some time together. Wha'dya say?"

"What's a swap meet?"

"It's kind of like a flea market for motorcycle people; parts, clothes, custom bikes, stuff like that. It's pretty interesting. I think you'd enjoy it."

"Okay, what time?"

"We'll need to leave early Saturday morning, by seven anyway."

Crystal groaned. "My one morning to sleep late and you want to drag me out at seven o'clock? Well, it looks like that's the only way to get your undivided attention."

"Good. Then I'll see you Saturday."

CHAPTER 21

At 7:15 a.m. Saturday Crystal looked out the window at the sun just beginning to rise into view. Her mother stumbled into the kitchen where she was sitting. "Honey, where is it you're off to so early?"

"I told you, Mama; Daniel's taking me out of town to a motorcycle flea market kind of thing."

"I'm not sure you should go to something like that."

"Mama, this is Daniel's work and I need to understand it." Just then lights pulled into the driveway. "He's here." Crystal bounded to the door. "Bye, Mama."

Crystal hurried cheerfully past Ann's disapproving look to the parked truck. As the driver's side door opened a haggard-looking Duke climbed out.

"Here, would you drive?"

"Daniel? What is it?" She peered into his face. "You look like you haven't slept at all."

"Actually, I haven't. The ex-husband of one of the women in my group showed up at her house and I had to go over to try to keep the lid on things.

I'm really too tired to drive that distance safely. This is automatic, not hard to drive. You'll do fine."

Not sure she wanted to do fine or otherwise driving the old truck, Crystal stoically stepped up into the driver's seat. She pushed papers and burger wrappers out of the way while Duke cleared empty Styrofoam coffee cups from the dash. "How do we go? Do you know the route?"

"Yeah, I think so but I have a map in here somewhere just in case." Crystal settled in behind the wheel adjusting the seat and mirrors. He leaned over and kissed her on the cheek.

"And what was that for first thing this morning?" she asked coyly.

"For being a good sport. Not many women would come out like this and ride in an old, raggedy truck."

"Well, you just keep that in mind when I call on you to help with the float," she returned cheerfully. "The parade's in a week and a half and we're going to need lots of bodies and hands to get it ready." She put the truck into gear. Within fifteen minutes Duke was asleep.

An hour and a half later she stopped at a Waffle House. "Hey, wake up. We're here." Crystal pushed him gently on the shoulder.

He stirred then blinked awake. "Sorry, I must have dozed off."

"Yeah, for the last hour," Crystal responded flatly. "I thought this was going to be time together."

"C'mon." He cocked his head at her in his boyish way and took her hand. "I'll get some coffee and we'll hang out here awhile. Okay?"

She was completely disarmed. "How is it you can make me smile just like that even when you don't deserve it?"

He gave her a peck on the cheek as he leaned across her to open her door. "I have that effect on women." She opened her mouth to protest, but he was already pushing her out of the truck. "C'mon, let's go."

"All right!" she laughed. "Has anyone ever told you, you were pushy?"

With coffee still in hand they drove the last two miles to the swap meet. The parking lot was filled with motorcycles of all kinds as well as numerous cars, trucks and vans. He took her hand and started for the booths that were stretched out in long rows. Almost immediately he pointed excitedly to a motorcycle that was parked in a line of colorful chrome-outfitted bikes. "Look, see that one? The blue Harley with the eagle painted on the gas tank? I worked on the motor." They walked closer as he admired the bike.

"I don't get it. What are all these doing here and why do people fix them up so fancy? I mean, look at this one. It's bright pink all over and the reflection off the chrome hurts my eyes. Doesn't it cost a fortune to do all this?" Crystal pointed at a bike further down the row. "And this—a horse saddle that looks like it's bolted on over the seat. What's that all about?"

Duke laughed. "It's hard to explain but these bikes are part of their owners' lives. Serious bikers never go a day without riding—rain, shine, snow—whatever. Oh, some buy a bike and keep it covered in the garage and take it out only on Sunday afternoons. Some fix theirs up for show primarily. But they all love the power and the feeling of freedom you can't get anywhere else."

Crystal studied him intently as he talked. The fervor in his voice suggested an intimate understanding of the subject. For just a moment there was something familiar about him squatting next to a row of motorcycles. *No, that's silly.* She shook her head. *That man was clean shaven and he rode, what did Joey call it? An Indian?*

As they strolled among the tables and booths Crystal said nothing, overwhelmed by it all. Duke stopped occasionally and poked through boxes of salvaged motorcycle parts. They strolled past displays of various hats, T-shirts and jackets with Harley-Davidson written on them; leather clothes, heavy black jackets adorned with studs, zippers, chains or fringe. Leather chaps, boots and even vests and tops for women.

"Why all the leather? Isn't it hot in the summertime?"

He smiled. "Leather is by far the best protection from cuts and abrasions in a crash. Asphalt will rip other clothes and skin right off if you ever lay one of these down. Leather will get scraped but rarely tears, and it won't burn either." He picked up a woman's vest and cocked his head to admire the effect as he held it up to her. "Doesn't look too bad on either."

Crystal blushed and dropped her eyes. They moved on down the rows. Suddenly, Duke looked up. "Oh, I see one of the people I came here to meet. Can you entertain yourself for a few minutes?" He asked hurriedly as he dropped her hand.

Before she could answer, he was off. He walked rapidly toward a group of men who were standing next to a table of motorcycle parts. Crystal watched him approach the group. Two of them had denim vests that said, "Ride in the Word." They both smiled and shook hands enthusiastically with Duke. After chatting for a few minutes he followed them to a booth further down the row and took a large cardboard box they handed him. He nodded and smiled a thank you while one of the men slapped him on the back. They exchanged a few more words and parted company.

"Look, I got fifteen brand new Bibles," he beamed. "They had some extras that were donated so they told me I could have them for my group. Let's go to the truck so I can set these down. God's word is heavy."

As they walked, she asked. "Who are those people with all the tattoos and chains and stuff?"

"Well, the short guy with the black cap has done some time but had a rebirth of faith in prison. It's an amazing story. Now he goes around to prisons hoping to bring back others who've lost their way. He's a pretty tough character which, I guess, is what makes him believable to cons." He shifted the box to get a better grip. "The taller, heavier guy with long hair and beard is a nomad."

"A nomad?"

"Yeah, he was a member of a seriously rough club years ago so he's still technically a member for life, but he's allowed to travel around on his mission work. He goes to rallies, talks to people on the roads, speaks to Christian biker groups all over the country and actually to anyone who'll listen. He'll talk your ear off but he's serious about Jesus' role in his life and about showing others the way of God. You might say he rides for his faith."

He stopped and set down the box. Crystal turned to face him. "What is it? Too heavy?"

"No, it just came to me."

"What?"

"The name for my group: Riders for Faith. What do ya' think?"

"I think it fits—from what you tell me about these people."

He picked up the box again. "Good."

"I'm looking for a few specific parts for Reggie. You mind if we stay a little longer?"

"No, I'm actually enjoying myself. It's a whole different world."

"Yeah, it's a society of its own. Actually, more like a family. A biker will stop to help another biker who's broken down on the road or in trouble. Many of them organize rides for charities and donate to all sorts of causes."

At that moment a tall woman with long light brown hair turned suddenly from where she was standing looking at T-shirts and bumped into Duke, nearly causing him to drop the box. Her face was strikingly beautiful and seemed not to fit with the worn jeans, denim vest and dusty black boots she wore. She looked him in the face for a moment then shook her head and mumbled, "Sorry, thought

I heard a voice I knew." Duke stood for a few seconds and stared as she walked away.

"You know, really we could go," he blurted. "I found one of the parts I needed and got some names and numbers for guys who might have the others. I bet you're tired with all this walking around." He hurried Crystal in the opposite direction from where the woman had gone.

Crystal, a little surprised at his sudden concern for her comfort, answered, "Well, okay. I am getting tired. I didn't get to sleep most of the way like somebody else I know."

"Okay, okay." He laughed. "Guilty. Look I'll drive back and you can sleep all the way if you want. Let's go find that barbecue place they told me about."

They returned to the truck. Crystal noticed that he glanced nervously over his shoulder only once.

ONE O'CLOCK ARRIVED ON Thanksgiving Day.

"Crystal, where is this young man of yours?" Ann asked impatiently. "I can't keep the turkey warm much longer."

Crystal pulled back the drapes for the twentieth time and fidgeted with the pendant on her necklace. "I don't know, Mama. Maybe we should start. Something must have happened."

"Well, he could at least have had the courtesy to call. It's so rude to—"

"Here he is, Mama." Crystal dropped the curtain and dashed to the kitchen. "Let's go ahead and put the food on the table. Daddy, would you get the door?" The two women scrambled to place all the separate dishes on the table at once.

"Sorry I was late, Mrs. Harper. One of our regular customers was trying to get to his mom's house for Thanksgiving and he had clutch trouble." He surveyed the table as they sat down. "This all looks great! I haven't seen a meal like this since—well—in a long time."

Ann softened a little. "We're glad you could come and share Thanksgiving with us. Crystal's never brought anyone but Phil over to eat." Crystal shot her mother a stern look. "And since we know you so little we were delighted when she invited you."

Crystal jumped into the conversation. "Dad, I haven't introduced Daniel yet. This is Daniel Davis." Her father smiled pleasantly and reached across the table to shake hands. "Daniel, this is my dad."

"Good to have you, Daniel."

"Crystal," Ann said brightly, "would you ask our guest to say the blessing?"

Crystal looked apologetically at the young man. "Mama, I don't think—"

"No, it's okay." He smiled graciously. "I've got a lot to be thankful for this year."

All bowed their heads. "Dear Heavenly Father, this day we remember all the gifts we have received—old burdens laid down, wisdom gained from experiences, new worlds opened up to us by your grace. We thank you also for friends, old and new, and for the opportunity to serve you in ever-increasing ways." He sneaked a wink at Crystal who caught it with her own sideways glance at him. "We are grateful for this food and for those who have provided it. Bless this house and all who live here. In Jesus' name, Amen."

Crystal whispered, "That was nice," as her father began passing plates of food around.

"Well, Daniel, how long are you planning to be in this area?" Ann began the inquisition as she handed him a bowl of gooey sweet potatoes.

Crystal rolled her eyes but he responded cheerfully, "That's not certain. I've started a small lay ministry here and there seems to be a great need but I would have to eventually go to ministerial school to become official. And that would be out of town."

Crystal's father showed some interest. "I hear you work on bikes. I had an old Triumph when I was in the Army. Do you remember that, Ann?"

"Yes, I do," she answered curtly as if to dismiss the subject. "Now, Daniel where is it you're from?"

"Mama! He didn't come here to be interrogated," Crystal said, knowing his sensitivity to talking about his past.

He answered affably, however. "All over really, the last few years."

"Oh, and what have you been doing—?

An electronic version of a bird chirping suddenly interrupted Ann's question. Glancing down at the cell phone he pulled from the holder on his belt, he apologized. "I'm sorry," he blurted, jumping up. "I need to go. I have to take this call. One of our group lost his wife and daughter in a car wreck this time last year and it's kind of rough on him."

Crystal rose and followed him from the room. After he finished talking she said, "Do you want me to come with you?"

"No, I'm not sure what I'm going to find when I get there and it might be better if I went alone."

He turned to her and kissed her on the forehead. "Thanks for offering, though."

"If you get a chance," Ann called from the dining room, "stop by for dessert later. We're having pecan pie that Crystal made. We'd love to chat more."

"And pry more into your life," Crystal whispered conspiratorially into Duke's ear. "I'm sorry. She's just that way."

"I don't mind," he whispered into her hair. "I think it's great she cares about who you go out with." He grinned playfully. "I know I do."

She socked him in the arm.

Giving her a quick peck on the lips he put on his coat and went out the door.

"WELL, WHAT ABOUT THAT?" Ann said when Crystal returned to the dining room. "What kind of person comes late and leaves early?"

Crystal bristled at her mother's tone. "Someone with a dedication to God's work."

"I should think he would show you a little more consideration, dear. Say, have you talked to Phil? Do you think he and Joey would like to come over for some pie?"

"Mama, don't start," Crystal said wearily.

"Start what? I was just concerned about them being all alone on a holiday."

Crystal rolled her eyes, sighed and left the room, retreating to the porch swing. She gazed off down the road while the swing creaked back and forth. She was glad her dear one had found something he believed in but she wished it didn't take up so much of his time.

CHAPTER 22

Friday morning the alarm went off at five. Crystal groaned, lay there a minute with a pillow over her head, then finally pulled herself upright. Dressing and brushing her teeth quietly, she left the house without waking anyone.

She drove into the staging area for the parade at 5:45 with hot chocolate and two boxes of doughnuts. Sleepy parents were arriving with their children, who were anything but sedate.

"Miss Harper, I want to thank you so much for doing this with the children," one parent told her. Jordan climbed onto the float and sat in his seat at the front. He had his violin in his hand. "He has never wanted to play in front of anybody before, but he's really excited about doing this."

"Jordan, honey, the parade's not for three more hours," Crystal called to him, laughing at his enthusiasm. "We'll let you know when we're ready for you." She turned her attention to the adults finishing the last details of preparation. The old hay trailer had been transformed into a bright yellow, blue and white stage for the students.

As the setup continued, Phil and Joey appeared with sausage biscuits and juice for everyone. The enthusiastic last-minute work made everyone ravenously hungry and the hot chocolate made the cold air less chilling. The tractor that was to pull the float came and hooked up.

When all the children were dressed and the details were complete they were towed to their position in the parade line.

"Okay, one last 'abandon ship' drill. Everybody in your place," Crystal tried to shout above the roar as the children climbed onto the float. "Volunteers set? When I blow the whistle, all of you rip off your seatbelts and move quickly to the sides of the trailer. A parent will be there to get you. Don't worry if it's not your parent." With everyone positioned, Crystal blew the whistle loudly. The sound of Velcro ripping and the scrambling of the children into the arms of the volunteers played out a well-choreographed and rehearsed safety dance.

At last the bullhorn blared, "All drivers, please take your places in line. We will leave in five minutes."

Phil came over to Crystal and put his arm around her briefly. "It looks great. You did a terrific job." He squeezed her briefly.

"Yeah, I'd say it's all going according to plan." A man's voice from behind her caused Crystal to break free and wheel around. Though there was no edge to his tone, his eyes questioned for a split second.

"Oh, hi, Daniel! Isn't this great? Look, it's worked out just as you suggested."

Phil, cordial but reserved, also greeted him. "Hello Daniel. Joey'll be happy to see you." He moved away from Crystal.

The bands played to the people lining the streets. Rarely did anyone in the small town miss the annual Christmas parade and it had become a countywide celebration. As the transformed hay trailer inched along with the other floats Jordan played his violin. Christine, with large flourishes of the brush, painted shapes on the easel. Joey and Victor took turns showing each other large flash cards of addition problems. Angela, dressed in a sequined costume trimmed in white fur, twirled a baton. Tim sat very still and held a book, the pages of which he turned and smoothed slowly.

"How did you get him to do that?" Duke asked in amazement. "Isn't he the one that hates noise?"

"Look closely," Crystal giggled. "Ear plugs, just like the ones they use around the big jets at the airport." Duke laughed with her as he waved to the passing float. Joey stopped his flash cards for a second and waved back to him.

"You two are really something," Crystal beamed. "I wouldn't have thought—"

Duke continued to wave to Joey as he passed. "Yeah, I never did either but now—" He cupped his hands around his mouth and yelled, "Hey, Joey, show 'em that wheelie!"

While Joey took advantage of the anchored wheels of the chair and tilted his seat back, Duke cheered and gave a thumbs-up. Joey beamed.

Crystal stared, amazed.

DUKE SQUATTED BESIDE THE skeleton of the wrecked Indian motorcycle. The rear wheel and fender were missing as well as the saddlebags. The red gas tank and leather seat with fringe sat atop a bare frame that was propped on milk crates. Duke lifted a new chrome wheel and fitted it into the frame behind the seat. He was so engrossed in his work that he didn't even look at a lone motorcycle passing on the road.

Suddenly, the cyclist snapped a look and throttled down quickly. Turning carefully around, the tall, leather-clad, helmeted biker returned and pulled into the yard. The soft murmuring sound of the engine stopped after the bike parked several yards away. Duke straightened up as the rider swung a leg over the seat to dismount and at the same time pulled the helmet off to reveal a woman's face, beautiful in its structure but drawn and hollow-eyed. Tendrils of light brown hair escaped a ponytail at the nape of her neck and flew after the helmet.

Duke smiled in recognition but approached slowly. "Hello, Camira. How's it going?" Her black-brown eyes stared at him, a confused expression on her face. She looked toward the wrecked Indian then back at the man. "Yeah, I grew a beard and it's really this color," he explained.

She stared a few more seconds then looked down sadly, unmoving as he approached. "Duke, Jerry's dead," she announced flatly.

He studied her and gently took her hand. Her shoulders sagged and her face contorted into anguished tears. As she sobbed he pulled her to him and held her. "I'm sorry. I'm so sorry for you, Camira." They stood that way for some time occasionally rocking gently left to right and back again. When she quieted he pulled back slightly to look into her face. Even though her demeanor was calmer the tears still flowed freely from her reddened eyes. Tenderly, he lifted her chin. "Let's go inside. You look like you could use a cup of coffee."

They climbed the steps to the apartment, his arm around her waist. He glanced over his shoulder. "Still riding a BMW, huh? Do you ever use those tools I bought you?"

Camira smiled back faintly and wiped her eyes. "Nope, never. That's why I ride a new bike, remember? No skills."

Duke laughed as they entered the apartment.

WHILE DUKE MADE COFFEE Camira excused herself. "I'm gonna' go clean up a little." She smiled now in familiar company. "Then you can tell me what made you trash a one-of-a-kind motorcycle. To see if you could put it back together maybe? Sounds about like you."

Coffee turned into dinner and the conversation never stopped. "—So I still don't remember exactly what happened when I wrecked. And I guess I lost about a month in there somewhere."

"Are you okay now?" she asked earnestly.

"More or less. The therapy's been a real drag and I'm not able to kick start a bike yet but the good news is I can predict when rain's coming." He laughed, and she joined him. He studied her familiar visage, remembering.

Though every bit as beautiful as she had been in those earlier years, she now carried a weariness that hadn't been there before. He shook off the reverie. "Camira, what happened to Jerry?"

The shadow of grief returned but allowed her enough composure to tell her story. "We were riding through Atlanta on the way to the Myrtle Beach rally. Somehow we ended up on the wrong street at the wrong time and they shot him. I never saw anybody. No challenge, no warning, nothing. And then, just like that, he was gone." She stopped and looked at Duke. "You know how it was with us. He never treated me like just his 'old lady.' We were together, really together. I know that's not the way it is for some but it was for us." Camira looked down and was quiet.

"I remember when you left me for him," Duke interjected, hoping to lighten the conversation.

One corner of her mouth turned up a little then dropped again. "We were both just passin' through in those days, you know that. But we did have a good thing for a while, didn't we?" Camira rose and stepped toward him. Before he could react, she kissed him.

For a moment he responded to the familiar feel of this woman from his past. And then he remembered, *this is my past, but it's not my life anymore.* He pulled back from her and blushed. "Camira, I—there's someone—things are different."

"Oh, yeah, well, that was nothin'. Just for old time's sake." She stepped back but managed to sound casual. "What's a little kiss among friends, right?"

"Sure, among friends."

Camira sat back down at the table. "Can I have another cup of coffee? And while you're at it, how 'bout bringin' me up to date?"

Duke welcomed the break from the awkwardness and quickly turned the stove on for the coffee. "I haven't weirded out or anything; it's just my life is going a new direction."

"Oh? You didn't go and—"

"I'm a lay minister now. I work with bikers who want to get connected with God." He paused.

"Well now." Camira leaned back in the metal chair and propped her feet on the counter. "I'll bet there's some kinda' story in this. Why don't you tell me all about it?" She smiled smugly. "Then you can tell me about this 'someone'."

Duke eyed her with a sideways glance then found himself relating to his old friend everything that had led up to where he was. As the hours passed he told Camira about the months in therapy relearning to walk, about his new job, about the shooting and also about his Riders for Faith group.

"What made you get into this church stuff? I don't remember you ever being religious. In fact, you were—"

"Yes, I was." He stopped her from finishing. "But my parents devoted their whole lives to God's work. I guess I've just come back to that—in my own way."

"So what do you do with these people? I mean, what's it like? I just can't see a bunch of bikers and their old ladies sittin' around listening to somebody preachin' at 'em."

"No, it's not like that. Yes, we do sing hymns and read scripture but we talk about what we're reading. Everyone says what they feel or think. But also, we support each other."

"What? Money?"

"Sometimes, but more often with a phone call or a prayer, or maybe even a cup of coffee at 2 a.m. for someone who's at the end of their rope. Things don't look so bad when you know you're not in it alone." Duke smiled. "You might try it." Camira squirmed in her chair.

"Yeah, well," she quickly changed the subject, "what about this girl? How did you meet her?"

"Well, I met her once. Then we met again later but she didn't know it was me." He related the story of his chance encounters with Crystal before and after the accident.

"What? You mean you fell for this gal but she wouldn't have anything to do with you because she thought you were some bad guy? Then she met you in this disguise you have." She unfolded her arms and waved up and down, appraising him. "And now everything's sunlight and roses. Does she know anything about before?"

"Some," he responded evasively.

"Well, what is she like? Oh wait!" Camera snickered. "I know. That was you at the swap meet and you were with that chick. Kinda' a goody-two-shoes type, isn't she?"

"She's great. Teaches handicapped kids." Duke ignored the dig and went on enthusiastically describing Crystal.

Finally, as she got up to grab a roll from the counter, Camira looked out the window. "Hey, Duke, sun's coming up. We've been at it all night."

"You're kidding. I've got to get ready for work! Quick, you fix whatever you want for breakfast. I'm going to take a shower."

Half an hour later a car honked outside. "Oh no! I forgot. Crystal's picking me up today. This is just great." Duke hurried toward the door, grabbing a jacket on the way. "Camira, just make yourself at home." Then he added, "And keep out of sight."

"Sure thing," she called. Then she grinned to herself. "I just can't resist this."

CHAPTER 23

"Daniel, what's that motorcycle over there?" Crystal asked when he got into the car. "Bringing your work home with you?"

"Oh, that? Uh, no. It's just an old friend who was having some problems stopped by and stayed late, that's all."

At that instant Camira stuck her head out of the window and called, "Hey, where do you keep the stuff for the dishes?"

"Old friend?" Crystal glared.

Duke shrugged sheepishly. "Crystal, it's not—I mean, nothing—we just—"

"Just what?"

Though Duke couldn't see her eyes he could tell they were blazing.

"I guess you're going to tell me you sat up all night drinking coffee and holding her hand like you do all those others." Her face reddened. "Wait!" She blurted. "That's that woman, the one at the swap meet who said she recognized your voice." Her own voice grew louder and more shrill. "What's going on here?"

He winced at her unusual vehemence. "Crystal, you have to hear me in this," he began in a controlled tone.

"No, you have to hear me. I've been patient with you standing me up or running off in the middle of a date or even Thanksgiving dinner. And you know what? I finally figured it out. Daniel, they get more of your time and attention than I do. All I get is a minute here, a phone call there. And now—!" She stopped the tirade as tears began to slip down her face.

"Crystal, stop the car. We have to talk, right now, and it's not safe to drive like this." He spoke as gently as he could. She pulled off the road but continued to look straight ahead.

Suddenly, her voice switched to a level tone that was in marked contrast to the emotional volcano only seconds before. "Look, I don't know what went on with that woman or what she is to you, but…."

"Crystal, she's not—"

"No." She turned to him and laid her hand on his arm. "No, let me finish, please." Her controlled but intense demeanor mesmerized him and he was quiet. "As I said, I don't know what happened and I'd like to think that you are a man of principle. But, Daniel, that's the problem. It's not just this time. I can't be second in someone's life." She paused and looked out the car window avoiding his penetrating look, the deep, troubled look that she had seen in him when they first met. "At least with Phil I was always—"

His calm changed to a storm. "Oh, is that it? Phil again? Look, I explained and that's that. But hey, we got no commitment here. My work is important and I thought you understood that. But if he's what you want, lady, then don't let me keep you!"

He pushed open the car door, jumped out and slammed it shut with such force the old car shook. Hunching his shoulders he shoved his hands into his pockets and crossed to the other side of the road where he began walking in the opposite direction, quickly adding physical distance to the emotional chasm that had just blasted open between them.

Crystal dropped her hands into her lap and sat for a moment, stunned. *What just happened? Where did all that come from?* Then still in confusion she slowly and mechanically moved to start the car and drive away. Putting it into gear she shot a timorous, expectant glance at the rearview mirror. With his back to her he had his thumb out, hitchhiking. *Please turn around and look*, she cried inwardly. She watched for several seconds, shook her head then slowly and deliberately pulled out onto the road.

A WEEK PASSED. NEITHER Crystal nor Duke called the other. Thursday evening Crystal drove out to visit a student who had missed school.

"—And we'll look forward to seeing Victor back on Tuesday. I'm glad his surgery went so well." Crystal rose to leave the warm country home. "I know he's looking forward to walking without those braces. Here is his schoolwork that I've graded and the new assignments. The children will be happy to have him back."

She leaned over to the smiling ten-year-old. "See you soon, Victor." Crystal pushed the screen door open. The boy's round-cheeked, soft-eyed mother hurried to the light switch.

"It's awfully dark out, Miss Crystal. Do you want my Andrew to follow you to the main road?"

"Oh no, Mrs. Richardson. Daniel just—" She caught herself. "Uh, my car is running fine. Besides, there's a moon rising and it's going to be a beautiful night for a drive. With my hectic schedule I'll actually welcome the quiet time alone. Thanks anyway but I'll be fine," Crystal reassured her then walked to the car.

Waving goodbye, Crystal turned on her headlights and pulled out onto the road. She drove slowly to savor the night. The blowup she had had with Daniel replayed in her mind. She hadn't realized that his work bothered her so much. And why had she said that about Phil? She knew why. That woman! She had seemed awfully comfortable in Daniel's place. It was obvious she wanted Crystal to see her. But who was she? And more importantly, what was she to him? She shifted in her seat and set her jaw. "Well, who cares!" she said aloud. First she gripped the steering wheel defiantly with both hands. Then she sighed, "I do."

The lump in her throat led to a burning sorrow as it had so many times since the argument. She pulled to the side of the road and turned off the car. The moonlight paled her face. "Dear God, what does all this mean? I believe in dedication to your work but don't I count? Don't we count as a couple? Must we give up everything to serve?" She paused. "You have to help me on this. I want to understand but I just can't seem to."

After an expectant half-hour she took a deep breath and turned the key. Instead of a prompt turn-over of the engine or even a grinding attempt to start, the car emitted a flat klunk. She tried twice more with the same result.

Oh, why didn't I get a cell phone like Phil told me to? Well, I'll just sit here a few minutes until the engine is ready to start. Then I'll be on my way. She patted the door of the car and leaned against it, looking out at the clearing sky. She noted the moon coming out from behind the clouds. *See Crystal? God's looking out for you after all.*

After a time she walked around to check the engine. *What was it Daniel had said, "Look at the battery cable contacts?"* She shook her head and smiled. "Daniel, you're always looking after me." Lifting the hood she leaned in and checked the connections to the battery. There was just enough light from the moon to see. She moved the cables slightly back and forth then backed out from under the hood. As she stepped back toward the car door, a pair of headlights appeared in the distance. She slid into the seat and tried to start the car, noting in the rearview mirror that the lights were coming closer. The ancient Cadillac klunked a few more times but would not turn over.

While she tried again and again, the vehicle approached—an old pickup truck with bright lights on. The sound of loud laughter reached her before the truck did. It pulled in behind her. Crystal began to feel nervous. *Billy Nyson's truck. He's probably drunk again.* She watched a man push open the door and stumble out. He laughed loudly and swore, recovering his balance, then walked to the driver's door where Crystal had rolled the window up nearly all the way.

"Why, look here," he called to the truck. "It's Miss Crystal."

"Well, I heard a lot about her," an answer came back. "I need to meet this fine piece o' handiwork."

"Billy Nyson, are you drunk again?" she asked, trying to sound amused.

"Why, yes, Miss Crystal, I guess I am." He staggered against the car door. "And it looks like your old piece of junk has quit on you again. What about that?" Then to the truck, "Hey, her car is broken down. Maybe we can help her out."

"Oh, yeah, I'd really like to help that young lady out." The other man in the truck reached out the window and opened the truck door, pushing it hard with his shoulder. It gave and he tumbled abruptly out of the truck with a grunt. "Did you see that? I fell out of the truck!" He guffawed loudly from the ground. Crystal felt chills. Billy Nyson was an irritating but harmless drunkard. But this other man—she didn't know.

The man approached the rider's side door. "Now I'll just come in there and see what I can do." He tried the locked door, hit it with his fist then yanked it sharply, causing it to pop open. First, he leaned in and leered at the now thoroughly frightened woman. Then he slid into the car placing his arm around her. The reek of the cheap alcohol he was drinking nauseated her as he leaned over to kiss her. Billy spoke up.

"Hey, now, I seen her first. Let me in there!"

Sizing up the situation quickly, Crystal volunteered, "No, Billy, I'll get out."

"See? She likes me best." Billy taunted.

"Well, we can't have that now." The other man, older than Billy and now beginning to appear less jovial, quickly jumped out of his side of the car and stomped around to where Billy and Crystal stood.

Genuine terror was taking Crystal as the men began to argue. Each grabbed one of her wrists. Billy laughed at the amusing game. The older man became gruff and roughly pushed Billy away. He hooked his arm around Crystal's waist.

Crystal, frantic, said nothing. Her breathing was shallow and quick and her stomach churned. The arguing became more violent. Crystal prayed desperately, *Please, God, no!*

PHIL WAS ROUSED BY a pounding on the door. "Phil! Wake up! Phil!"

He awakened slowly and raised the window. "Who is it?" he called to the dark shadow on his porch. "What do you want at this hour?"

"It's me, Daniel. Get up and open the door. I need you to help me."

"Do you have any idea what time it is?" he grumbled. "And why should I help you?"

"It's 12:30 and Crystal's not home. Her mother called me. We've been—well—apart lately. So I thought maybe she had uh, that she might be—"

"No, I haven't seen her." Phil was fully awake now and clarity was bringing worry into his face. He spoke to the young man who was nearly breathless. "She had to go over somewhere near Cloverton to see a student or something. Said she'd be back in time for dinner with Joey and me. When she didn't come, I thought maybe she had—" He looked at the young man again and stopped.

"Phil, you have to help me find her." The shaky edge to Duke's voice further alarmed Phil.

"Okay, I'll call the sheriff and tell him what's going on."

"Great. I'm going to look for her."

"No," Phil said sharply and grabbed Duke's arm. Duke looked down and bristled in sudden offense. "No," Phil repeated more softly. "I know these roads better'n you. It won't take but a minute to call the sheriff's office." He took his hand away. "We'll go together."

"Yeah, yeah, you're right." Duke calmed slightly.

"Alright." Phil quickly made the call to the sheriff and threw on his jacket. He rushed down the hall and scooped Joey from his bed. "I'll take him over to Crystal's mom," then added soberly, "We could be awhile."

CHAPTER 24

A waitress approached. All kinds came into the roadside grill that stayed open until 2:30 in the morning so she didn't seem surprised to see the long-haired bearded hulk of a man who had come in on the Harley motorcycle sharing the booth with the fair- skinned, neatly dressed young woman.

"What is it you called him? Duke, is it?" Sitting near the window she looked intently at the leather-clad, tattooed man across from her.

"Yeah, that's what he told me his name was. I didn't know no different until the hospital."

"You were the one I saw leaving the rehabilitation center."

"Yeah, probably. He didn't have nobody and we hung together, so—"

She studied the face of this person who had caused her such fear on their first meeting just an hour before. She now saw a softness around his eyes when he talked that belied the image projected by the long, heavy beard, biker clothes and intimidating size. In addition, she noticed the small cross he wore around his neck.

"So, how long have you known Dan—uh, Duke?" She was immensely curious about this other life of the man she was so involved with but now seemed to know so little about.

"Well, it's been about two years, I guess. We was in New Mexico at the Labor Day rally."

"What was he like—you know—then?"

Grunt answered quickly with a laugh. "Mad. At everybody and everything, until—" He stopped and regarded her, smiling at the intense look on her face.

"Until what?" she blurted like a child who couldn't wait for the next line of the story.

"Until he saw you." Grunt sat back with a satisfied look on his face.

"At the Agape center?"

"No, before that."

"Before? We never met before." Crystal puzzled while Grunt smiled, enjoying the game.

"Yes, you did."

"No." She thought carefully. "I don't think so."

"You remember the day your car broke down and you went to that diner? You were using the phone, and a guy came up to you—"

"—And he said something about my hat," she broke in, remembering the incident. "But that guy had black hair and no beard."

"No, his hair was real short, covered up with that black leather du-rag he always wore. He thought it made him look dark and tough. Guess it worked, huh?"

Crystal sat back for a few seconds, stunned. "I remember his teeth. Isn't that funny?" She recalled her impressions at the moment. "I was afraid of him but then he was so nice, I wasn't." Pausing for a moment then beginning again, "And at the gas station? When Billy nearly ran over me?"

"Oh, yeah. He wanted to kill that guy. I had to drag him out of town."

Hesitating for a bit, she ventured timidly, "Why—why did he just disappear?"

"Do the math, honey. How long was he at that rehab place? He was in a coma for three weeks before that."

"Oh." She stared out the dark window that reflected the two of them in the booth. "What happened?"

"We was partyin' pretty good. It was the kid's birthday. All of a sudden he left. Tore out of the parking lot. Left ol' Dolores just standing there."

"Who?"

"Nobody." He waved his hand as if dismissing the subject. "Anyway, he didn't come back."

"How did you find him?"

"Well, the party got rowdy and the cops came. One of 'em said something about one of 'our kind' smashin' up an Indian that night."

"An Indian? Did he hit someone?"

Grunt chuckled. "No, an Indian is a kind of bike. They don't make 'em anymore. He was always doin' somethin' to it, fixin' or polishin'." He stopped for a few seconds then continued, "Anyway, the local yokels tried to haul us in but, well, let's just say we talked 'em out of it."

"So where was he?"

"I figured if he wasn't with the bike he was wrecked up pretty bad. Since we didn't hang with a club the other dudes took off. I went to the hospital and found him. He didn't have no family anybody knew of, so they let me sit with him. He was out a while."

Crystal regarded the man with a new respect. Here was a loyalty she didn't know existed among men she had stereotyped as being without values. They were both quiet for a bit. Suddenly, a spark of memory lit up her face.

"And the shooting? The man who saved his life. Was that—?"

"Aw, he made a big deal out of nothin'. I was just showin' off to impress Mama."

Then, Crystal reached across the table and touched Grunt's hand. "He's lucky to have a friend like you. And I am, too."

Grunt squirmed a little and pulled his hand away. Crystal dropped her head and lowered her voice. "Grunt, I have to ask you. About that woman—"

"Oh yeah, Camira. He told me."

"Is he—did he?"

"Nah, they was tight for a little while a couple years back but then she split with some guy runnin' from the law. Liked livin' on the edge I guess."

"Did he love her?"

"Well, I don't know about all that but he never got ignorant over her like he did you."

"Ignorant?" Crystal snorted in offense.

"Yeah, talkin' all that stuff about you bein' 'right'," Grunt teased but stopped as he sized up the look on Crystal's face. "In case you're interested, she's gone.

Duke sent her off as soon as he got home. Never seen a man that fired up to get a woman outa' his sight before. It was right humorous."

Crystal smiled in understanding. "Thank—" she started, but was stopped in mid-sentence by a commotion as Phil and Duke burst in.

"Where is he?" he barked harshly at the lone waitress.

She calmly met his assault. "Who you lookin' for, honey?"

"A big guy—beard—the guy that came in on the—"

"Over here, kid." Grunt stood up. "Quit makin' such a commotion."

"Grunt, have you seen anything tonight? Crystal's—"

"—Right here." Grunt stepped aside and gestured across the table.

Duke darted around the big man and grabbed Crystal, jerking her up from her seat. A startled but amused look came over her face as he hugged her tightly. "Oh, God. Thank you. She's safe." He held her close and for several seconds buried his face in her hair. "You're safe," he whispered to her.

She pulled back and took his face in her hands. Seeing the fear mixed with joy, she spoke softly, "Yes, I'm fine." She stroked his cheek. "I'm okay."

Phil watched the two of them with a look that reflected both relief and sadness. As he dropped his head to look away Crystal called, "Phil, come sit down. Let me tell you what happened!"

There was an awkward moment as they shuffled to determine seating. Finally Phil grabbed a chair and placed it at the end of the table. Duke blushed and Crystal pulled him in beside her. Their shoulders touched and he held her hand under the table. Grunt, chuckling, returned to his side of the booth.

"You two should have seen what happened!" Crystal, now completely removed from the danger of the situation, bubbled excitedly, turning first to Duke and then to Phil and back again while she talked. Her voice echoed in the empty café and the others listened, quiet as she related her frightening ordeal.

"—And I was paralyzed! I had no idea what might happen but you can imagine I feared the worst." She paused and looked at Duke and Phil, then at Grunt. "Finally the two of them began tugging at me and threatening each other. I just closed my eyes. Suddenly, they stopped. I heard this loud, roaring engine, opened my eyes and saw a huge motorcycle pull up with a giant, terrifying man riding it."

Grunt smiled proudly. "That'd be me."

Crystal continued with animated gestures, "I thought I was really done for. Two drunks and now some outlaw!" She stopped to take a breath and let the full effect soak in.

Duke looked over at Grunt. "Outlaw, eh?"

"Let the lady tell the story."

"So this huge bear of a guy gets off the bike and walks over. I couldn't believe what happened next. He goes right up to Billy and says, 'Excuse me, but the lady's with me.' Billy just stared up at him and said, 'Yes sir.' He backed off but the other guy swung his fist. Grunt caught the punch in his hand and pushed. The guy fell over. Grunt walked toward him and the guy scrambled away. "

Crystal smiled over at Grunt. "He took my arm and in a very gentlemanly way said, 'Can I give you a ride somewhere?' I was so stunned. I followed him a few steps. When I stopped and pulled away he said, 'You don't have to be afraid. I'm in Davis' "Riders for Faith" group.' I hesitated, still not sure, then he added, 'Jesus says that I'm okay. You want to ask him? I'll just stand over here and wait while you do that.' Then he left me, walked over to his bike and stood there with his arms folded. He was so genuine and disarming I climbed on that great big motorcycle behind him and here I am!" She grinned excitedly and clasped her hands, setting them down on the table to mark the end of the story.

Duke smiled and reached across to punch Grunt. "You snake you. I've been trying to get her onto a bike all these months and you just ride up and off she goes."

"It's my charisma, kid. Charisma." Grunt spread his hands in a grand gesture and beamed. Everyone laughed out loud.

Duke and Phil replayed their search. Finally, Phil jumped up. "Oh no, I'd better call the sheriff. He's probably got half the county out looking for you. I'll be right back. And I'll call your mom, Crystal."

"Thanks, Phil," she called after him.

"Well, Grunt. Looks like I owe you again, man." Duke's sincere gratitude made the big man lower his eyes.

"Well, guess I've had about all the fun I can stand for one night." Grunt rose to leave. "I believe the lady's in good hands."

Crystal pushed Duke out of the seat and went over to Grunt. She hugged him and said, "Thank you—for everything."

Grunt smiled at her after a quick sideways look at Duke. "Sure, anytime. Glad to help out."

After he had gone Duke turned to Crystal. "Everything? Is there something I should know?"

"What, I can't have a cup of coffee late at night with someone without arousing suspicion?" Crystal grinned slyly.

"Ouch," he winced. "That shoe on the other foot kinda' pinches." Both chuckled and they exchanged a look that said the storm was over.

Phil returned and offered, "If you can stand to step down from being a biker woman and ride in an ordinary truck, we can go."

Crystal laughed and took both men by the arm as they left the diner. On the way home Crystal chatted gaily at first then the fatigue of her ordeal took her over. She laid her head on Duke's shoulder and he put his arm around her. Phil kept his eyes on the road.

When Phil's light shined in Crystal's drive her mother hurried out. "Are you all right?" She hovered solicitously as Crystal roused from her sleepy ride.

"Yes, I'm fine. The angels were with me tonight but I have to tell you, they don't look like you'd expect." Crystal yawned loudly.

Walking to the porch Phil glanced at Crystal and Duke then said to Mrs. Harper, "Ann, how 'bout if we go in and check on Joey. I'll probably leave him here and pick him up in the morning if that's okay." The two went inside leaving Crystal and Duke on the front porch.

There was an awkward moment as the circumstances of their separation of the past week nagged. Duke spoke first. "Crystal—I— Tonight when your mother called, my heart stopped." He paused and took a deep breath. "Just the thought of anything happening to you— Well, about the other day, with Camira and all—"

"It's okay, Duke." Crystal stopped him.

He looked at her questioningly. "What? What did you call me?"

"Grunt told me everything. I understand now. I didn't at first. I admit I had resented the time you spend away from me. But if Grunt hadn't come along when he did, well— What you do is more important than—"

"Crystal, nothing is more important to me than you. It took tonight to make me see that. I love you and I believe I have since the first time I saw you. But now, it's different. Before I just loved the vision of you. Now if I think of being without you my stomach sinks and I get the shakes." His words came in a passionate rush. "If it means giving up my mission or changing it in some way, I will. I'll do whatever."

She put a finger to his lips. "Stop. We can sort all this out in the morning. But know that I love you and believe in what you do. We all have to serve God in the way that works for us. Let's talk tomorrow."

He touched her cheek then put both arms around her, holding her against him as if protecting her from an unseen evil. Finally, he pulled back enough to look her in the face. They both smiled and he kissed her. The two sank into each other, yielding to the powerful force that was pulling them together.

CHAPTER 25

Christmas brought a few days of unseasonably warm weather as sometimes happens in the South. Crystal's father grumbled while he set up the nativity scene in the yard. "This feels like Florida or California. How can anyone get Christmas spirit with it 75 degrees out?"

"Well, considering where Jesus was born it might have been this warm for the first Christmas," Crystal offered.

"Yeah, yeah, but Christmas morning without a fire in the fireplace just doesn't seem right somehow."

Crystal held up the two panels for the stable. As the sound of a motorcycle reached her ears she turned suddenly dropping the panels and leaving her father grasping at air.

"Crystal!" he yelled.

She turned back around and picked up the fallen panels. "Sorry, Daddy." Duke pulled into the driveway and shut off the bike. "Now what kind of 'head' is this?" Crystal called.

Duke laughed out loud. "A little knowledge is a dangerous thing, isn't it?"

"Well, you're always talking about a panhead or a flathead or whatever."

"No, actually, this is a blockhead, one of the newer ones. It belongs to the guy I'm doing that evening job for. He's out of town so he let me use it."

"How's your bike coming along? Have you been able to find the parts?"

"Yeah, most of 'em. That guy in Atlanta, T.C.—got his name at the swap meet—he's really helped a lot. I found a motor too but I still can't afford it." He frowned for a second then brightened. "So, you tied up here or can we take a ride? This weather's perfect."

"Daddy, do you need me?"

"No, I guess not. But get your mother out here so I have another set of hands."

"Okay." The screen door slapped shut behind Crystal then in a few moments she returned with her mother.

"Hello, Daniel," Ann said politely.

"Hello, Mrs. Harper," he returned with equal formality.

"We're going now. See y'all later." Crystal called from the back of the motorcycle. Then to Duke, "Let's go." She laughed with carefree delight. The rumbling motor revved and they spun out of the driveway.

After they had ridden for several minutes Crystal leaned forward and shouted above the engine roar, "Where are we going?"

"There's some people I want you to meet; they've invited us over."

Crystal nodded and held on.

After a half-hour's ride into the country where only an occasional house or mobile home interrupted the landscape they slowed and pulled onto a somewhat overgrown dirt road. Bringing the motor to a slow idle, Duke navigated carefully, avoiding branches that might scratch his borrowed ride.

"Hello, Duke! Great to see ya'." A small, wiry, balding man wearing a carpenter's belt with tools hanging from it came out of an old tin-roofed shed to greet them.

"Crystal, this is Watt. Watt, my friend, Crystal."

"Pleased to meet you. Walt, did you say?"

The man grinned as if at his own joke. "No, it's Watt, like in electricity."

"See, Watt was struck by lightning a few years ago so now he glows in the dark," Duke explained. Both men laughed.

Watt walked over and shook Crystal's hand. "So you're the one our fearless leader's been talkin' about." Then he turned to Duke. "I see now. A good-lookin' woman like that's enough to make a man get religion."

"Who's good-lookin'?" A woman had walked out of the shed also. She was no taller than the man but was solidly built, muscular and heavy. "Oh, I see Duke's finally brought his honey around. I was beginning to think he made her up." The woman came toward Crystal who had by now climbed off the motorcycle and removed her helmet. The woman hugged her warmly, which took Crystal by surprise.

"May's our official greeter," Duke commented. "When she welcomes people they know they've been welcomed." They all laughed again.

"Duke, show her what we're doin'," Watt directed then turned to Crystal. "Since our man here helps us get closer to God we thought the church we built him ought not to get in the way."

Duke led Crystal down a narrow but worn footpath. They walked through the trees. Suddenly the forest gave way to a grassy area around a small pond. At one end a creek ran into the pond contained on the other end by an earthen dam. A small half-moon platform—not much more expansive than a large living room in a house—stood next to the pond. Large upright poles encircled the platform and bare rafters were bolted into them. The whole thing looked much like an umbrella cut in half. A single new wooden bench sat in the middle with lawn chairs also scattered about on the platform.

"He leadeth me beside the still waters—" Crystal said softly as she took in the scene.

Duke's eyes widened. "Yes, that's it exactly."

"This is also the place where 'he restoreth my soul,' right?" she added. "So this is where you run off to every Sunday morning right after early church."

"Actually, we met in the home of one of the group members for a long time but Watt and May offered us this place right after Thanksgiving. People help out when they can with materials and labor. Our group is truly building its own church." The pride in Duke's eyes was unmistakable. "We've got a work party planned for New Years. A couple wants to get married here on Valentine's Day."

"Married?" Crystal looked at him in surprise.

"Yeah, believe it or not they want a traditional wedding ceremony. Reasons is gonna' handle it."

"I bet he's wondering what he's gotten himself into," Crystal said.

"Yeah, he's a little freaked but he said he'd support this so he can't really refuse."

"And you did all this?" Crystal's admiration came through in her voice.

"No, God did it. All I did was talk to a few people and tell them what I was trying to start here. Then it just took off, kinda' on its own. I had no idea how many bikers are out there looking for the Holy Spirit in some way, shape or form. Either because of things in their past or the way they look they don't feel like they fit anywhere. And they're right. Most bikers don't look like typical churchgoers."

Crystal dropped her chin and said softly, almost apologetically, "I know. I was one of those. The first time I saw you I—"

"I know," he interrupted her, "you fell madly in love with me in spite of yourself." Grabbing her around the waist he pulled her to him and kissed her. In the middle of the kiss she pulled away and ran, laughing, to the water's edge, scaring the ducks that were swimming there.

"I think you're a little too sure of yourself there mister. What makes you think you're so irresistible?" He tackled her onto the grass, still laughing. They both sat up and he picked the dried grass out of her hair. Then his demeanor became sober.

"You. I don't believe you give your heart lightly and I'm grateful that you give it to me."

She reached up and stroked his face tenderly. "I love you." Then she kissed him.

"I love you."

"Yeah, and anybody who's seen you two together knows it so we figured we'd better come down here and chaperone." Watt and May walked out into the clearing carrying a newly-made bench seat.

"Here, we'll help you with that," Duke said. He and Crystal stood and helped lift the eight-foot bench onto the platform.

"Well, it's not exactly like a church pew, no velvet cushions or nothin', but it'll let five or six more have a place to sit." May sized up their work.

"You two are great," Duke said.

"Well, we've had good fortune in our lives—found each other and found Jesus. That's sure worth a few benches." Watt walked over to May and kissed her. She put both arms around him and kissed him back deeply.

After standing there for an entire minute waiting for them to separate Duke cleared his throat. "Uh, hum," he teased. "Who did you say needed the chaperone?"

"Hey, that's what's so great about being married. You don't have to hold anything back."

"I think these two need to be alone," Duke snickered as he took Crystal's hand.

Walking up the path Crystal looked back for a second then commented, "Who would've ever put those two together?"

"Yeah, isn't it a trip? They've been married for twelve years. They lost a daughter to leukemia about four years ago. Something like that either breaks people up or makes their relationship stronger. They survived it. Now, they're just like teenagers together."

"What do they do for a living?"

"He works for the phone company and she's an emergency room nurse."

"I'm glad you brought me to meet them. I didn't have any idea what kind of people you worked with in this group. I mean, the only one I've met is Grunt and well, he isn't exactly like other people."

"You got that right. But he's had trouble in his life, too." They walked a little further. "You just can't tell about a person to look at 'em."

Crystal squeezed his hand and smiled. "No, you can't."

CHRISTMAS EVE DUKE WENT with Crystal's family to the candlelight service. Rev. Reasons delivered the message then handed a miniature hand-carved tree ornament to each of the children—a manger with hay and a tiny doll baby glued inside.

"Watt and May made those," Duke whispered to Crystal.

Walking out at the end of the service they noticed several bikers from Duke's Riders for Faith group sitting near the back and shook their hands. Several of the church members stared at the visitors. Some even frowned in disapproval. But a few greeted them and wished them Merry Christmas.

Crystal's mother tugged on her husband's arm slowing their progress until the bikers were outside.

At Crystal's home the family tradition of opening presents on Christmas Eve included Duke this year. Crystal handed him a large box wrapped in green foil with an oversized red bow. He gave her a smaller long box that was noticeably heavy.

"You first," Duke grinned boyishly. "I want to see if I guessed right."

Crystal tore off the paper. The box inside was marked, "Deluxe Tool Set—37 pieces for any auto maintenance or repair job."

Ann rolled her eyes and looked at Crystal's father who was smiling as he watched Crystal opening the box, gleefully taking out the tools and naming them.

"Look, here's a spark plug socket wrench! Oh, and a timing light! What's this?"

"You use that when you change the belts."

She hugged him squealing, "No one but you would give me car tools." She kissed him enthusiastically while Ann looked away. "Now open yours."

He tore off the paper and lifted the lid on the plain, white box. Opening the paper, he looked in surprise at the black leather motorcycle chaps. He lifted them out. "Crystal," he said in awe. "These—these are great. I've never had any this nice before."

She hugged him. "I remember you said that leather helped protect you from injury better than anything else."

Duke blinked back tears that welled in his eyes and cleared his throat before he spoke again. "Thank you, Crystal." Then he turned to her father and mother. "And thank you for including me in your family celebration. It's been a long time and, well—"

Ann looked in surprise at the young man. "You're welcome," she replied softly. She paused as if carefully selecting her words, and for the first time in speaking to the young man, sincere warmth crept into her voice. "And thank you for the care with which you treat our daughter."

Mr. Harper stood and shook Duke's hand. "You're welcome anytime."

Crystal's own throat tightened and her eyes gleamed with tears. "I love Christmas."

With his back turned to her parents Duke mouthed silently to Crystal, "I love you."

CHAPTER 26

Throughout the winter and into spring both Duke and Crystal jealously protected their regular Tuesday evening dinner and their Saturday afternoon out. Occasionally, they were even able to attend early church together if Duke hadn't been up all night with members of his group.

Then, one day in late May Crystal's principal came into her room after class.

"Crystal, I wanted to tell you I submitted my recommendation for next year's funding of your program." He smiled confidently. "The parade and some of the stories the paper has printed on the children have really gotten attention. The members of the school board would be fools not to approve it."

"Thank you. Many of the children have made great progress this year. Victor has gotten rid of his braces and his speech is also improving. Joey is reading two grade levels above average. Christine will be able to go into regular classes."

"Whoa! You don't have to sell me. Hardly a month goes by that one of your parents doesn't call me to say what a great job you're doing. I'm convinced, and I think this report will convince the folks that hold the purse strings, too. I wouldn't worry about anything."

"I appreciate your support."

"No problem."

AT THE END OF the school year Crystal and Duke, along with some of the parents, took all of Crystal's students to the beach for a long weekend.

"Don't they make a darling couple?" Jordan's mother commented to Phil as she watched the two playing in the waves. "You know, I heard he's planning on becoming a minister. They just seem so right for each other."

Phil smiled graciously as Duke and Crystal coaxed Victor into the water. "Yes, I have to admit they're both fine people."

THEY HAD ONLY BEEN back two days when Crystal's father called her from the den. "Crystal, you'd better come hear this."

"The school board this morning announced several cuts designed to reduce the growing deficit in the county budget," the female news anchor reported. "But one that is causing concern among some parents is the elimination of the resource support for special education at East Gold elementary. Several parents of the children affected by this cut have been waiting outside the school board meeting.

"Mrs. Berg's son is autistic and is in the class that will be discontinued. Mrs. Berg, what do you think of this decision by the school board?"

"It's an outrage! There is no other place my son can go. Miss Harper has done so much with him. Now he might just as well sit home all day."

"Other parents had similar comments."

"My Jordan had just made the transition from homeschooling to a class with other children. Miss Harper was wonderful with him. His reading and speech were improving."

"We asked the school board to comment. Here's how they responded—"

CRYSTAL STARED AT THE television but didn't hear any more of the broadcast. Stunned, she sat back in her chair. They did it. She couldn't believe it. Her job. The children.

The phone rang. "Crystal, it's for you." She didn't respond.

"Crystal, come get the phone," her mother called insistently. "It's rude to keep people waiting."

Crystal stood and walked past her mother toward the porch door.

"Uhm, she can't come to the phone just now. Can I take a message?"

Her mother wrote down the number then followed Crystal outside to the porch. "What is wrong with you, Crystal? That was—"

"I don't have a job anymore," she responded flatly.

"You what?"

"My job. The school board cut the funding for my program. That means I won't have a job anymore."

"Oh, that's silly. There aren't any more special education teachers in the area. What will they do with the children?"

"Very little."

"I'm sorry, dear. I know you love working with them. What are you going to do?"

"I don't know, Mama. I just found out five minutes ago."

"Oh, don't worry. I'm sure you'll find something else. I mean, you have a degree. Or maybe you could take a little time off. Sort of relax and enjoy yourself for a while. You've been under such pressure. You know you don't have to work right away."

Crystal responded only with an exasperated sigh.

ALL AFTERNOON CRYSTAL MOPED around the house. Much of the time she spent in her room. *My career—my life's work—shot! I have no prospects of any other job. God, is this some cruel joke you're playing? If it is, I don't find it very funny. Haven't I given my life to your work?*

Finally, her mother knocked on her door. "Crystal, come on out of there.

The women in this family don't mope. We hold our heads up and bear with whatever comes and find a way to make the best of things."

Crystal opened the door. "Is that what you've done, Mama? What could possibly have come in your perfect life that compares to this?"

Ann looked as if her daughter had slapped her face. "That was uncalled for. You don't have any idea what my life has been like. I was just trying to help."

Seeing she had hurt her mother's feelings with her misdirected rage, Crystal began to cry, "Yes, yes it was. I'm sorry. I'm just so lost."

"I know. But things will work out for the best. You'll see. Now go on, get out of the house. Maybe a drive would help you think."

THAT NIGHT DUKE CALLED. "Crystal, guess what? I finally got enough money to buy the motor for my bike and the guy can send it to me by the weekend. Isn't that great?"

"Yes," she answered without enthusiasm.

"Hey, don't overwhelm me with your excitement," he joked.

"Look, I don't really feel like talking now."

"What is it? What's wrong? Are you okay?" The tone of his voice shifted instantly as he expressed his concern.

"The school board cut the funding for my class."

"What does that mean exactly? What will you be doing instead?"

"It means I don't have a job in the fall." The finality in her words didn't escape his notice.

"Crystal, honey, I know how much your work means to you and to the children."

"Well, apparently the school board doesn't care."

"Look, I'm coming over right now. We'll talk. Okay?"

"I won't be much company."

"Crystal, everything you go through I go through. We'll look at this together. I'll be there in half an hour."

"HI, SWEETIE." DUKE KISSED her on the cheek and smiled.

She kissed him back half-heartedly. "C'mon, let's go."

"Where're we going?"

"Someplace private so we can talk."

Duke didn't offer any more conversation for some time. They drove for twenty minutes; then he turned off the road down a gravel driveway. At the end appeared what looked like a giant golf ball. Though generally round at first glance, its angles and facets became clear as they drove closer. About two thirds of the structure was closed in, leaving a piece of the top open.

"What is this? Where are we?" Crystal stared in amazement.

"A geodesic dome, a structure that combines tetrahedrons and hexagons to make a building system that gets stronger the larger it gets." He stopped and laughed at her incredulous stare. "I memorized that because I thought it sounded so cool."

"What?" She laughed, opening the door and joining Duke behind the truck.

"A kind of house made by engineers." Duke laughed. "One of Reggie's customers is building this, and I've been helping with the construction." He looked over at her sitting on the tailgate of the truck. "It's good to see you laugh. Look, I understand today's been rough on you but it got me to thinking. I talked to Reggie and she said she knows several people in Atlanta that own bike shops and she could get me on at one of them."

"You're leaving?" Panic pushed through all the other emotions she was feeling.

He moved to sit beside her and took her hand. "I've been thinking about this since we talked earlier. You could come with me. Atlanta has lots of schools and I'm sure they would be happy to have a teacher like you."

"What are you saying?"

"Well, since—uhm, maybe we could—you know I love you and—"

Her eyes widened as realization hit. "You want me to marry you and move to Atlanta?"

"Yeah, that is, I mean, we've both thought about it, haven't we?"

"Duke, I— Well I'd have to admit I'd hoped maybe someday, but—" She paused. "Why now all of a sudden?"

"With your job and all, and I can make more money there, enough to support you, us, whatever." He looked at her eagerly.

"Wait a minute. You mean you're only bringing this up now to rescue me?" She stood up, clenched her fists by her side and blurted, "You of all people! I thought we understood each other, that we were partners." She glared at him. "And now I see you don't get it either!" She jumped off the tailgate and stomped toward the cab. "Take me home! Now!"

Duke's confusion turned to hurt. He climbed into the truck. "Why are you so upset? Crystal I never meant—"

"It doesn't matter what you meant. It's how you think of me." They drove silently for some time. Finally, Crystal spoke. "Duke, stop and pull over. Please."

He eased the truck to the shoulder of the road. When he turned off the ignition, he looked at her.

She took a deep breath and exhaled slowly. "I'm sorry I got out of control back there." She put her hand on his arm. "This job thing has really hit me hard. But it's also made me see a lot of things clearly for the first time. My whole life has been careful and nice and planned. I went to school where my parents told me to go. I chose special ed because a professor recommended it. I almost married Phil because he made me believe it was right."

Duke looked down and didn't respond to her touch. She reached up and gently lifted his face toward hers as she continued. "I never loved anyone this deeply until you came along, and then suddenly my life was different." She smiled and he smiled back thinly. "But when I marry it's going to be my choice—to build something—not because my other prospects don't look too good."

"Then you're saying no." His abrupt response surprised her.

"I'm saying I still don't know what yes would mean to me. I have to know that, now more than ever. I want my life to be a gift I give freely not a responsibility you lovingly agree to take on. Can you understand that?"

He didn't say anything for a long while. Then finally, "Yes, I think I do. But Crystal, I've come to that point and I'm ready to give my life to you as I've given it also to God."

"Then where does that leave us?"

"I guess we wait, but—" He took her hand and stared at it, tenderly stroking his fingers across hers. "Crystal, I have to register for classes the end of August."

"That soon? Why didn't you tell me this before?"

"I never thought I could get in. Reasons talked to some friends at Columbia and they took me on his recommendation. I just found out this week. I wanted to tell you but I was waiting for the right time. Guess this wasn't it."

She leaned in front of him to look up into his face. "You know I love you, don't you?"

"Yes but that doesn't seem to matter much here."

"It always matters."

"Look, for the next two weeks I've got to work after hours on that dome, so I'll be pretty much tied up. Why don't you think about what you have to do and I'll do the same. We'll talk after that."

"Not see each other for two weeks?" Her voice quavered.

"That's about it," he answered with quiet resolve.

"Okay, then, two weeks."

He started the truck. They drove the rest of the way to her house without speaking. When they arrived he stayed in the driver's seat. She leaned over and kissed him on the cheek. "Good night."

"Good night," Duke answered quietly after she got out of the truck. Then after a few seconds he leaned out the window and called, "Sweet dreams." *And please, God, let them be of me.*

Crystal watched him go, smiled tentatively and waved. "Tell me what to do, God," she prayed out loud. "Show me the path I should follow and how this man I love can walk it with me."

CHAPTER 27

Sunday brought the morning late to a sleeping Crystal. Her mother came into her room and threw open the curtains. "Time to get up, sweetie. I know you want to go to church today. The mission group from Guatemala is speaking and they always have wonderful stories to tell."

Crystal groaned and pulled the covers over her head. "Go away, Mama."

"Breakfast is ready. C'mon down soon or your father will eat too many Danish. You know how he is; if there are some on the plate into his stomach they go."

Crystal rolled over. "I have to get up so Daddy won't eat too much? I don't see the connection." But it was apparent Ann was going to hover until her daughter emerged from her bedsheet-hideout and rejoined the world for the day.

Finally, an hour and a half later the whole family arrived at church. Just after they took their seats Reverend Reasons appeared at the front of the sanctuary. "Today we will not have our regular service because we have special guests who will give us a message that is far more compelling than any I could bring you. I would now like to introduce the mission group that has just returned from a month in Guatemala. Please give them your attention."

Reasons' entreaty was unnecessary as the group immediately captivated the audience. They told of the first shoes brought to children in one of the villages, of the school where the retarded boy sat on the steps outside because he was not allowed in with the others, and finally of the intense faith and hopefulness of people who had so little to be hopeful about.

Crystal sat enthralled by the compelling stories of the dedicated people. After the service she hurried to the reception in the fellowship hall. As she entered, Rev. Reasons called to her.

"Crystal, oh I'm glad you came. I want you to meet Rachel. Rachel, this is Crystal. You two have many things in common." Then the minister moved on to speak to others.

"Reverend Reasons tells me you're going to have a little time on your hands over the next few months and that I should recruit you for a mission trip," Rachel offered. "I don't know what he wants me to say but I'll tell you that working with people so different from us but yet so rich in faith is a life-altering experience."

"I could never do what you and your group have done," Crystal objected. "I mean, I don't know what I would have to offer." She paused, feeling the pressure of Rachel's insistent gaze. "And truly, I've never been anywhere outside the U.S. ever."

"All the more reason. Look, I grew up in small town Florida a long way from even Disney World. I went to the community college, got married, found a job in my same town. Then one day I woke up and realized I didn't know anything about life outside my very small world."

"But isn't going for something like this a little extreme?" Crystal asked.

"No, it's exactly what I needed. I got a better picture of the whole of God's world and of my place in it."

Crystal studied the mission volunteer who looked to be about her own age. Though the woman continued to talk, Crystal's mind raced. *"The whole of God's world and my place in it." Is that what I need to find my own place, time away from my life to see real life?*

Her head was still awhirl when she left the church. Two days later she made an appointment to see Reverend Reasons.

THE DOOR TO REV. Reasons' office opened and he and Crystal walked out. "Crystal, I admire what you're doing. I did the same thing when I was young. For me it was to seek adventure I think. I believe you'll have a lot more to gain."

"I hope so. Later I may not be so free to go. Now is definitely the time." Crystal's resolve was strong, the result of 48 hours of gathering information and praying for guidance.

"Someone from the group that's scheduled for July will call you in the next few days. Better update your shots, be sure you have a passport, visa, that sort of thing."

"Yes, I've already made appointments and filled out paperwork for most of that."

"I envy you in some ways but I have to warn you to be careful. There's always uncertainty in a foreign country, though things have been pretty quiet there for a couple years now."

Crystal turned. "Rev. Reasons, this was a very personal decision that I had to make on my own. Please don't say anything to anyone until I've had a chance to tell….well, please don't say anything yet."

"Oh of course, if you wish, but if you're as serious about this young man as we all think you are, you should talk this over with him right away."

Crystal felt her cheeks burn.

LATER THAT AFTERNOON THE doorbell rang at the Harper home. When Crystal opened the door, Duke burst in. "Just when exactly were you going to tell me?" His face was flushed.

"What? How did you hear? I made Rev. Reasons promise."

"Never mind. Then it's true. I didn't believe it when I heard." He was yelling. "What happened to us talking?"

Ann came out of the den. "What's going on?" she asked in alarm.

Crystal herded Duke through the door. "Mom, we're going out for a little bit," she said. Then as soon as they were alone, she spoke to Duke. "Stop yelling. You said we wouldn't meet for two weeks. I was going to talk to you today."

"I don't care about today or tomorrow. You're not going!"

"What did you say?"

"You heard me. You are definitely not going." His commanding tone caused Crystal to bristle.

"I know this is sudden," she said soothingly, "but it's something I've been thinking about for awhile and—"

"Well, stop thinking. It's crazy; it's suicide. If you want to do something risky why don't you just walk out in front of a truck?" His face was red and he was pacing on the porch.

"Please calm down," Crystal said, a bit agitated herself. "I understand you're surprised but it'll be all right. It's in many ways a cruel country and they need a strong faith to sustain them."

"How could anyone in their right mind walk into a situation like that?" Duke shouted. "And what about me? I thought we were talking about—" He stopped in mid-sentence. "I guess I can see what you've decided. Well, if you're determined to become some kind of martyr, then so be it. But don't count on me to wait around for you. I'll be gone when you get back! If you get back!" Duke wheeled around and stormed to his truck that he'd left running, jumped in, slammed the door and peeled out of the drive.

Crystal stared after him open-mouthed, not understanding what had just happened. She stood in place for some time, tears rolling down her face. Finally she set her jaw and with a determined look, went into the house to get her keys. The old motor in her car started right up as if it didn't dare cross her today. She tore out of the driveway and roared down the road. By the time she pulled into the yard in front of Duke's apartment so intent was she on her speech that she didn't notice the huge black and chrome Harley motorcycle parked beside his truck. She jammed on the brakes. The tires screeched. She threw the gearshift into park, got out and slammed the door. Creaking from both age and the force with which Crystal was stomping, the steps to the apartment sounded as if they might break.

The door was open. "Daniel Davis, you—"

"He ain't here," Grunt answered from across the room.

"But his truck's out front."

"He got the motor put into his bike. I just got here and passed him going out at about light speed."

"Oh, I was going to talk—"

"Well how 'bout talkin' to me? Reggie ran me down and told me the kid was freakin' out over somethin' and I needed to get down here." He sat forward with his elbows on his knees. "Now what's goin' on?"

"I don't know."

"Try again." Grunt motioned toward the only other chair in the room. "Sit down."

Crystal shifted back and forth on her feet, uncomfortable under his scrutiny. "Since I lost my job, he suggested we get married and move to Atlanta. He's going to ministerial school and he didn't even tell me. Did you know?"

"I knew he was wanting to." He sat back in the chair. "I didn't know about the marrying part."

"Oh, then he hadn't said anything to you and he was just offering because he felt sorry for me?" Her indignation rose to the surface.

Grunt looked hard at her. "Reggie said the guy was losin' it big time. What's goin' on?"

"I don't know. He found out that I volunteered for a mission trip to Guatemala for a month and he just—"

"What did you say?"

"I said he just—"

"No, the volunteering thing."

"That I'm going to Guatemala for a month?"

"So, that's it."

"What? I don't understand."

"Let's just say he's got reasons he don't want you to go."

"I have to do this. I'm sorry he doesn't approve but I'm committed." Her face was beginning to tense in indignation. She turned to leave. In the doorway she paused then added more softly, "I don't expect you to understand." For a few seconds she looked away down the road then riveted her eyes back on Grunt. "But if you care for him, as I expect you do, you'll find him so I can explain it all when I get back." With that she strode out the door.

He rose quickly and lumbered down the steps behind her. "Explainin' ain't what's got him shook."

THE NIGHT BEFORE SHE was to leave on her mission trip Crystal was in her room packing. The weight of sadness seemed to cover her. There still had been no word from Duke. Nor had Reggie heard anything from Grunt. Ann walked into the room and sat on her daughter's bed by the duffel bag she slowly stuffed with clothing.

"Tomorrow the adventure begins," her mother said brightly.

"Mama, look, I don't need your Suzy cheerleader attitude tonight. I just don't think I could take it." Crystal never looked up from her packing.

"I'm not the one you're upset with," Ann responded gently, "so don't take it out on me."

"Tomorrow I get on a plane to a place I've never seen and a culture I don't begin to understand to do God only knows what and the man I love has disappeared so I couldn't even say goodbye." Crystal broke down in tears and her mother stood to hug her. "Why would he do that Mama? I just don't understand. If he loved me he would want to be with me this last night."

"Sit down, honey," Ann began, "and I'll tell you a story about when your dad and I were stationed at Dobbins Air Force Base."

"Oh please, Mama, not one of your stories." Crystal moaned. "I'm miserable enough."

"You need to listen to this. Once your father was on what we were told was a training mission. Later we heard his plane had gone down in an unfriendly country. For six days I had no idea if I'd ever see him again. The terrible waiting, the awful, excruciating anguish of not knowing." A slow tear slipped down her face as she finished. She quickly wiped it away and composed herself.

Crystal was in shock, mouth open and eyes fixed on this woman she felt she had never truly known before this moment.

"So you see, this man of yours may have his own fears of you going. I can understand that. If I could have run during that awful time I would have." She smiled warmly then put her hand on Crystal's.

"Don't worry. If you two truly love each other you'll find your way back together. And this will be just one of the bumps in the road of your relationship."

Crystal leaned over and hugged her mother tightly. "Thanks, Mama," she whispered.

AT 5:30 THE NEXT morning Crystal and eight other mission volunteers met in the Charlotte airport. Sleepy but excited, they huddled together around the complimentary coffee machine at the gate. When the flight was finally called her mother hugged her and her father handed her a small leather-bound journal.

"These next few weeks will change your life forever, Crystal. You need to record every minute of it you can." With tears in his eyes her father hugged her hard and whispered, "God be with you."

"And also with you," she whispered back.

Entering the loading ramp, Crystal took one last look around. Though disappointed, she still smiled and waved to her parents. They smiled back and waved enthusiastically.

AS THE PLANE TOOK off, the just-rising sun glinted off its wings and cast a shadow on a single man on a motorcycle parked roadside just out of sight of the runway.

CHAPTER 28

In Guatemala, Crystal had been warned, any break in the jungle that included a quarter mile flat spot could qualify as a landing zone for the bush-equipped planes flying supplies in and out. Still her eyes widened and she clutched the strap around the crate nearest her at the abrupt drop in altitude when the pilot approached for landing.

Birds scattered as the small cargo plane touched down on the tiny dirt runway, its wheels screeching. It taxied to within fifty feet of a lone wooden building that looked more like a produce stand than a terminal. The pilot and co-pilot dressed in army fatigues and T-shirts climbed out of the cockpit and opened the side door, releasing the six passengers who had been sandwiched between boxes and sacks.

"I don't want to know what's in those crates," a small, blonde-haired woman with a soft Irish accent commented, stiffly maneuvering around the cargo to the door. The others clambered out, jumping to the ground behind their duffel bags and landing with the same dead thud as their bags.

Crystal put on her hat and surveyed the mountains. "Are there any active volcanoes in the area where we'll be working?"

"Actually no, not in the immediate area," a deep voice replied, "but the mosquitoes are big enough to be classified as UFO's."

A short, stout, pleasant-faced man, late-middle aged with graying black hair and broad shoulders, deftly grabbed two bags in each hand as he spoke.

"Hello, I'm Crystal Harper." She smiled and he nodded.

"I'm George, George Mack, or Jorges as the locals say." He had already turned his back to her and led the way to a small, four-wheel-drive pickup truck. "I have room for one in the cab but I'm sorry, the rest of you will have to ride in the back."

"I think I'd just as well run alongside," the blonde woman remarked dryly. She bent her body left, then right, grimacing with each movement. "Every joint aches already from that 'economy' flight."

"Ah, Kelsey. Welcome back." George smiled and shook her hand.

"You've been here before?" Crystal asked, surprised.

"Yeah, well, you get used to it after awhile," Kelsey growled good-naturedly. "Except for riding with the baggage, that is. I really hate riding with baggage."

"Here, why don't you ride in the cab with George?" Crystal offered. Then to George, "Are we all going to the same place?"

He pulled out a wrinkled piece of paper. "No, you and Kelsey are joining up with the Red Cross field hospital. That's near the river about two hours from here."

"Alan Redhawk's camp," Kelsey offered. Then she looked at Crystal and smiled smugly. "Wait till he sees what we've brought with us."

Crystal, still bewildered from the long ride and the strange surroundings, gave Kelsey a puzzled look, which she ignored, and walked around to the passenger side door.

For an hour the little truck bumped over rough roads before reaching a small village. Four of the group unloaded there. "This is a building project," George explained as they made their way to where he had directed them, "a structure to be used as a church and a school." Then to Crystal he said, "Why don't you squeeze in up front here with me and Kelsey? No point you sitting in the back all alone."

"Thank you, I think." Crystal responded looking skeptically into the tiny cab.

"Oh, come on, girlie, might as well get used to close quarters. Not a lot of facilities where we're going and what's there, the patients get." Crystal found herself liking this gruffly disarming woman. Kelsey had pushed over against George and Crystal pressed in, barely able to close the door.

The next hour's ride brought the setting sun and Crystal marveled at what she was seeing. *Okay, Crystal, you're here. You wanted to know what it was like away from home, well this is about as far away as you could get.* The lush jungle-forested areas thinned a little as pines and other trees spread large branches over a more open floor. After a long time George pointed to the left.

"There's the river. Not much longer now."

As the tents and pavilions of the hospital camp came into view, Crystal's excitement edged out her fatigue. Eyes wide and mouth open like a child at a carnival, she took in everything around her. A bell ringing atop a tall pole. The smells of food. Young college-aged men and women in khaki shorts and T-shirts. Dark-skinned women wrapped in long shawls in the cooling evening air.

"End of the line, ladies." George flashed a friendly smile and offered a handshake to Crystal. Kelsey gave him a warm hug, the kind reserved for old friends.

One of the Red Cross volunteers got up from a long table.

"Welcome. I'm Calvin." He offered a hand and Crystal shook it. "A couple more sets of hands will sure help. The soldiers have started coming in here. Treating them, too, it's getting kinda' hectic."

"Why's that?" Kelsey's eyes flashed. "Since when does the Red Cross treat people who torture and butcher their own countrymen?"

Calvin sighed, shrugged his shoulders, and dropped his head. "I'll show you where we sleep." He took them to a large canvas enclosure set up next to the main hospital tent. "Women are on this side. We're over there."

Kelsey stomped off, and Crystal hurriedly offered, "Thank you. She's just tired; we've had a long trip."

The young man looked at her seriously. "She's right but in this country civil wars of one kind or another have been a way of life for 35 years. We don't take sides or judge, and we're not here for the politics."

"Oh. Well," she offered brightly, "thank you for showing us to our place. I look forward to working with all of you."

"This is your first trip, isn't it?" he asked.

"Yes, yes it is."

The man smiled as he turned away. Crystal lugged her duffel bag to the tent where Kelsey was unpacking. She didn't speak. By the time they had both put their things into trunks under the cot-type beds, the fire had subsided in Kelsey's eyes.

She smiled smugly. "So, why are you here?" She studied Crystal momentarily. "Let's see. Are you the liberal idealist who wants to right the wrongs of the world? Or maybe you're one of those who are trying to find themselves someplace besides home."

Crystal blushed at the ridicule. "I—I'm an unemployed special education teacher from a small town. I just want to know what role I'm supposed to play in God's scheme of things. They say the real way to discover what you're made of is to face a challenge. So, here I am."

Kelsey sized up this newcomer. "Well, like they say, be careful what you wish for." She chuckled. "Let's go find something to eat. I'm starving."

THE SOUTH CAROLINA SUMMER had turned hot and dry with temperatures near a hundred degrees.

Duke, shirtless in the heat, was working on his bike. Grunt leaned against a shade tree surveying the situation.

"So you're really gonna' do this? This preacher stuff?" Grunt prodded.

"I know it sounds off the wall but if I'm going to do this biker ministry right I've got to be the real thing." He grinned boyishly. "Besides, a man's got to grow up and do something with his life."

"Well, I think you've busted a piston myself. And what about Miss Girlie?"

"That's none of your business," Duke snapped. "Drop it."

Grunt was quiet for a moment then asked, "So what's the story this Sunday?"

"Watt and May have finished our pavilion. We'll keep the service short and have a dedication. Reasons is coming out. It ought to be a trip. He means well but he always weirds out a little around our folks."

"Considering some of them, I can see why." The big man's affable laughter elicited the same in Duke.

"HONEY, WE'VE GOT A letter from Crystal!" Ann called to her husband as she came in the door.

"Already? I didn't think we'd hear from her for awhile yet."

Opening the letter, Ann read:

HI MOM AND DAD,

We finally arrived and started to work immediately. I've met some great people here. The most interesting is my tent-mate, Kelsey. She's in her forties and has been coming here for five years. She takes her four-week vacation and volunteers. Amazing!

Oh, did I tell you I'm working at a hospital compound? Most of what we do is routine medical care but sometimes people come in with injuries from the fighting. It's so sad what these people suffer through.

A physician's assistant runs the hospital. He's an American Indian with red hair. Can you believe it? I can't tell you how good he is in these conditions. I feel grateful to be able to work with all these people.

Gotta' run. It's lights out and the day starts before sun-up.
Love to you all.
Crystal
P.S. If you see anyone, tell them I said I miss them. Thanks.

"SOUNDS LIKE SHE'S HAVING quite an adventure," Crystal's father commented.

"Yes, it's good she's so busy. She's got a lot to work through," Ann observed thoughtfully.

Day six— I've gotten into the routine here. Not much time to think. Up early, work all day and go to bed late. Kelsey's a real gem, though. She jumped right in. I'm starting to work with the children more and more. Alan's amazing. I wonder if Grunt found Duke okay. What must be going through his head now? I wish I knew how to tell him I'm safe.

CRYSTAL SAT IN THE mess tent and wearily sipped coffee. The long day had been spent traveling up into the hills to inoculate children and to make calls in the area villages. Every place they went a long line awaited them. The only semblance of healthcare within fifty miles, the Red Cross truck brought people from remote areas.

A tall lean red-haired man slung his leg over the bench and slapped Crystal jovially on the back. She looked up and smiled through the fatigue of the day. "Alan, I've grown dearly fond of you and admire your work but I've seen more of you today than I want to see of anyone."

"What?" He set his own cup of coffee on the table. "You mean you don't find my company compelling?"

"Yeah, you're compelling alright—always compelling me to work. If I had to pick up another child or box of supplies I think I'd have to be carried away myself." She took a sip of coffee then held up the cup to him. "See? You're driving me to drink. I could never stand coffee before coming here but now I'm beginning to welcome it."

"Coffee is much better down here. It's fresh, not like in the stores at home." Alan's amiable relaxed manner always made Crystal feel at ease.

"Where is home? I've never heard you say. Do you live out west somewhere?"

Alan laughed out loud. "Actually, no. I live in Cleveland, and I even used to have an apartment. I left my teepee with my grandparents."

Crystal blushed. "I didn't mean—I just—"

"No sweat. It's a little hard to stereotype me."

Crystal reached over and touched a stray strand of his bright red hair. "And I guess there's a story here?"

"My mother's Irish." He grinned and quickly changed the subject. "So, what's your story? You said you teach. What else do you do there in grits country?"

"I'll ignore that cliché." Crystal elbowed him playfully. "Actually, I lost my teaching job—funding ran out. Politics, you know."

"What happened?" His sincere interest and intent look caused her to forget the fatigue and the late hour. Among other things, she confessed her sadness and confusion over the events of the last few months.

"—And I'm here trying to figure out what life, if any, I have left to go back to."

"So this guy says he's moving away and leaving you forever, and you've got no job," he stated matter-of-factly. "Hmm. I'd have to wonder why you'd be in any hurry to go back at all." He squeezed her hand then stood. "Get a good night's sleep. Tomorrow starts early."

Crystal looked down at her hand then watched Alan go. Finally, she shook her head slowly, stood up and walked to her tent. As she quietly pulled back the covers of her cot, Kelsey spoke from the darkness.

"So what do you think of our young doc?"

Though startled, Crystal answered quickly, "He's not like anybody I've ever met."

"Oh, that's original."

Crystal laughed softly. "No, but it's true."

"That's our boy," Kelsey whispered. Crystal heard the smile in Kelsey's voice.

CHAPTER 29

"And we dedicate this structure to God's work and to the congregation that seeks to know Him. Let this forever be a place of worship and peace for all who come here. Amen."

Cheering followed Rev. Reasons' dedication. Watt and May beamed from the back row as did Duke from his place beside the Reverend. Duke raised a hand for quiet. When the cheering had died down he announced, "There's food and drinks up at the work shed. We need some volunteers to bring it down and to set up tables." Two of the burly men and one woman nearly as stout started up the hill. Several others followed.

When everything was ready, Rev. Reasons rapped on the table a few times. "May I have your attention, please, for a quick announcement?" The crowd quieted. "Some of you may not know it yet but Duke here has been accepted at Columbia Seminary where he'll begin work in the ministerial program."

A burst of applause followed. Those near Duke slapped him on the back and there were a few shouts of "Way to go!" Then somebody called out, "Does this mean you're leaving us?"

Murmurs rippled through the mass of people. "Yes and no," Duke answered. "I'll be up here every other weekend for services and to keep up with you all. Rev. Reasons, Casper Penmartin from the Agape Center and guests from other biker churches will pinch hit in between. Watt and May and Grunt will wear cell phones and respond to emergencies. But remember, people in a church take care of each other. Anyway, I'll be around fulltime until the end of August."

Discussion picked up again and Duke surveyed the crowd with some anxiety.

When the gathering began to break up, Duke, Watt and May cleared the tables and bagged the trash.

In the midst of the cleanup, a late arrival rode in. "Am I too late for the food or the fun?" Camira looked directly at Duke with a coy smile.

He stopped what he was doing. "Uh, there's some chicken left over there and some salad, maybe some chips. Grab a plate." He seemed somewhat uncomfortable but added graciously, "Glad you could come, Camira."

"Well, you did invite me so I thought I'd check it out." She turned to Grunt, who was frowning. "I'm happy to see you too, Grunt."

Camira picked up a plate of food and chatted with several of the people still sitting around in chairs under the shade trees. Duke busied himself with putting away tables but kept an eye on her.

Even at a distance Duke thought he could see a new sadness about her.

Grunt followed her. "What brings you here, Camira? Didn't think this Jesus stuff was your thing."

"Things are different now since Jerry's gone. Just thought I'd hang around for awhile, maybe see what it's all about."

Grunt's skepticism showed on his face. "That all?"

"Yeah, why not?" she shrugged innocently.

Day 14—Somehow it doesn't seem like half a month has gone by. We've been so busy. Soldiers have come through once or twice for patching up. It gives me the creeps to see them with their guns here in the camp. They seem to like Alan, and I heard them talking in the mess tent long after we all went to bed tonight. I miss Joey and the children sometimes. I miss Duke terribly. I hate feeling so apart from him. But maybe Alan's right—he may not even be there when I get home.

THE SOUND OF A vehicle pulling up outside drew Crystal's attention away from her diary entry. It would be George with mail and supplies. But as she looked out she noticed that a soldier was with him. The uniformed man stood stiffly at attention as Alan approached. He handed Alan a large envelope.

Alan opened it and quickly scanned its contents. He looked up and called in all the volunteers and workers.

"Good news, everybody! It looks like peace is just about to break out here after nearly half a century." The announcement brought cheers from everyone.

Alan gestured for quiet. "The government wants to show their good will and invite us into the prison to tend to the 'care of the inmates' as they put it. No doubt CNN is in town, and they want to look their humanitarian best." Everyone laughed heartily. "Anyway, it's a long trip and there's a lot to do here so I only want to take a few people with me. Any volunteers?"

He looked right at Crystal. She nodded silently. Several others raised their hands. Kelsey also nodded then muttered, "Sittin' with the cargo again."

That night Crystal and Kelsey packed a small bag for the trip. "You asked me why I was here," Crystal said. "This isn't your first time. What brings you back over and over?"

"I believe in what Alan's doing," Kelsey answered as she continued her work. "I think he's great."

Crystal puzzled over the answer. "Are you and Alan—"

Kelsey looked over at her and laughed out loud. She pulled back her blonde hair to reveal auburn roots. "Does this give you a clue?"

"Oh—" Crystal felt her cheeks burn a little with chagrin. "He said his mother was Irish. I just didn't think— You seem so young to be— I just didn't get the connection."

"Yes, I was a child bride," Kelsey laughed, "and I'm older than I look, so they tell me." She winked at Crystal then continued, "So have you thought about staying on after your time is up here?"

Crystal paused, played with the idea in her head. "I hadn't considered this to be more than a temporary volunteer mission."

"Well, we each serve in our own way. There's a lot to do here still. And I can tell you from personal experience, your life will be richer for having invested some of it in this kind of work. It's a tough life but I highly recommend it, even for my own child." Kelsey snickered again and this time Crystal laughed with her.

Day 16—I've learned a great deal here so far, like how little sleep I can get and still function and how many different ways corn can be prepared. Everyone works hard but it's not about pay. It's about humanity. About a few people doing God's work in whatever way the spirit moves them. It's humbling and inspiring at the same time. Today I showed the mother of a deaf boy how to sign to him. She spoke no English nor I Spanish but the joy in her eyes went straight to my heart.

"YOU WERE RIGHT. THIS biker church stuff isn't as lame as I thought." Camira smiled at Duke as they walked up the hill from the pavilion.

"Everybody comes for a different reason I guess. That's what makes it such a good group. I'm going to miss being around as much."

"Bet you won't miss being on call 24-7." She laid her hand on his shoulder. He kept walking. Camira frowned just slightly then perked up. "Hey, this weather's great today. Why don't we just take off and go somewhere? Don't you get the urge to watch those white lines flash by?"

Duke looked thoughtful for a few seconds. "You're right. I've been so into—well, everything lately—I haven't taken any time off."

"Time to go then—that is, if you think that antique of yours can keep up." She raced to her bike, jumped on and started the motor.

"No helmet?" Duke asked. "You think that's a good idea?"

"No need. It's cool. Not much traffic, great weather. Nothin' to worry about."

"I don't want to risk this pretty face of mine," Duke said, fastening his own, full-face helmet. "I wouldn't think you would either."

She smiled flirtatiously at the compliment.

Duke started his bike and revved the motor to warm it up. Just then Grunt pulled up on his powerful 'hog' with Mama behind him.

"You guys goin' somewhere?" he asked innocently.

Camira flashed a "What're you doing here?" look at him but Duke answered congenially, "Hey, why don't you two come along? We got the urge to see how much asphalt we could cover in one afternoon."

Grunt turned to Mama who nodded and pecked him on the cheek. "Sure, we're up for it."

Camira forced a smile. "Great," she said flatly, then opened the throttle and roared out onto the road ahead of everyone. "Catch me if you can!" she hollered over her shoulder. Duke peeled out onto the road with Grunt and Mama right behind.

Though Camira's newer machine pulled ahead immediately, the Indian's powerful motor inched the speedometer gradually higher and higher. The desolate South Carolina back roads invited speed. Duke caught up with Camira after the first mile and pulled ahead. They were both laughing with the game.

Suddenly Duke throttled back while Camira zoomed on. Clamping down on the brakes, he slid the back tire sideways. When the bike had come to a full stop he planted both feet on the pavement and sat motionless. Camira, finally realizing he wasn't immediately behind her, turned around and came back to where he was.

"Hey, you quit just because I was beating you?" she goaded him playfully. He didn't respond. He just looked left, then right, surveying the area. Grunt and Mama approached and eased in beside him.

Duke spoke vacantly. "This is it." He turned to Grunt. "Isn't it?"

Grunt nodded.

Duke dismounted, took off his helmet and placed it on the seat. While Camira stared questioningly, he climbed down the bank off the shoulder of the road. He stepped deliberately through the tall grass and weeds, staring at the ground and dragging his hand across the tops of the stalks. Finally he stopped and pushed back the weeds. He squatted in a depression in the ground. Slowly he rolled his head up toward the road. Unmoving, he held that position for some time.

"Duke," Camira called to him, "what is it?"

"Shut up." Grunt barked.

"What?"

"Leave 'im alone. This is where he cracked up."

"Oh." She nodded her head knowingly then continued to observe.

For several minutes nothing moved except the grass gently swaying in the breeze. Finally Duke climbed arduously up the steep hill. Back up on the road, still silent, he surveyed the site again. Then he turned to Grunt. "I remember the bike coming off the road but then I felt like I was floating in the air watching it all from above. I saw the bike hit and roll over two, three times, but I didn't feel anything. Like being at a movie."

Grunt listened intently, as they all did.

Looking down the hill at the crash site again Duke asked, "Did you say a cop found me walking on the road?"

"Yeah, said you looked like an escaped autopsy but you was walkin'."

Duke stared thoughtfully a few more seconds then shook his head and turned back to his bike. Immediately, Camira was beside him. She put her hands on his shoulders and pulled him around to face her.

"Are you all right?" She stared at him, her demeanor the picture of concern.

"He's fine," Grunt called with an irritated tone. "Ain't cha, kid?"

"Yeah." Duke answered. He turned to Camira. "I'm okay, really." He gently removed her hands but held them for an extra second before releasing them. She lingered briefly then went back to her own motorcycle.

After he started his bike Duke took another long look at the site. *Thank you, Lord. I will try to serve as you would want.* Finally he rode off with the others following.

CHAPTER 30

As the little pickup jostled along the narrow roads its passengers chatted to pass the time, Kelsey and George in front, Crystal in back with Alan and Calvin.

"Can you believe that?" Alan commented. "The man can sleep anywhere, anytime." He poked Calvin lightly with his foot causing little more than a grunt in reaction. "That's why he's so perfect here. He can go on for 24 hours or more with fifteen-minute naps. It takes me an hour to get to sleep sometimes."

Crystal squirmed uncomfortably under Alan's intense gaze. "What?"

"You just amaze me."

"How? What are you talking about?"

"Well, I expected a small-town Southern girl to be sort of, I don't know, prissy. But you've been right in there through all the hard work and long hours. I mean, you even changed the spark plugs on the truck!" Alan picked up her hand and examined it. "Yet your hands have a quiet grace about them, competence without coarseness, I guess you'd say."

Crystal pulled her hand back blushing a little and turned away.

"What?" Alan responded at her change in demeanor.

Crystal dropped her chin slightly. "I was just reminded of someone else who called me competent." She looked off into the distance, daydreaming for an instant. Then she shaded her eyes. Far to the east was the outline of a small town. She touched Alan's arm. "Is that where we're going?"

"I think it is." He leaned forward to the driver's window and spoke to George. "Yeah, George says it's up here."

Crystal's stomach felt suddenly tight and she didn't think it was the jostling ride. "What do you suppose we'll find at the prison?"

"No telling. My guess is some malnutrition and the related stuff—scurvy and such. There are a lot of respiratory problems in poorly ventilated, dirty places. But they're not going to trot out anyone who's too bad off if they're trying to make an impression."

"Yeah, I guess you're right," Crystal commented uncomfortably.

Alan punched Calvin several times to wake him. When they arrived at the prison, guards saluted and swung open the large metal gate. Across the street two men, one with a large camera and both wearing armbands with the word "Press" on them, started toward the gate.

Alan touched Crystal's shoulder and pointed. "What'd I tell you?" They both smiled in amusement. "Only I think it's the BBC."

Inside a perfectly appointed officer greeted them. "Thank you for coming." He spoke in English and shook Alan's hand as he cast a quick glance in the direction of the now-rolling camera. "Please, tell us what you need and we will get it for you."

Alan responded without enthusiasm. "Mostly we'll need our supplies from the truck and a clean room that has hot running water." The officer barked commands to the guards who saluted crisply then dashed to the truck, returning with bags and boxes marked with the Red Cross insignia.

While they walked through the halls the news reporter was speaking into his recorder. Crystal shuddered as gates and doors were locked behind them.

Finally they reached a large room with a tile floor that shone and a spotlessly clean sink. A hospital-type bed was wheeled in while they set up their equipment. Alan questioned the officer. "Will we be seeing any of the prisoners in their cells?" Wide-eyed at his boldness, Crystal looked sharply at him.

The officer responded formally but congenially. "The facilities are better here. Isn't this what you asked for?" His teeth gleamed for the camera under his heavy black mustache.

Alan frowned but kept his composure. He asked if they had anything with a flat surface strong enough to be used as an examination table. The officer bowed slightly and sharply called out instructions, sending another guard briskly on his way.

For five hours straight Calvin, Crystal and Alan took vital signs, treated minor cuts, scrapes and rat bites and administered many vitamin shots. No one appeared to be in horrible condition, though many were thin. All were subdued and meek. They only spoke when one of the Red Cross workers asked them a specific question which the guards insisted upon translating.

Finally the officer reappeared and announced, "You must stop now and join us in a meal." He gestured grandly then beckoned them to follow him out of the room.

He led them to a large mess hall with clean metal tables and bench seats. Many of the prisoners they had seen that morning filed obediently through a cafeteria-style line then took seats away from the group. One of the tables was set with plates, napkins and silver flatware along with glasses and a bottle of Coke at each place. "No doubt to impress us with their worldliness," Alan whispered.

Crystal noticed that two guards stood at the door. As the visitors took their seats a young woman moved quickly toward their table. The officer spoke briefly to her then motioned her away. "We will be served shortly," he said.

"Who is that young woman?" Crystal inquired. "Does she work here?"

"No, no. She is a prisoner but we allow prisoners who behave themselves to work in other areas. We are very self-sufficient."

"General—" Kelsey began.

"It is Colonel, senora," the officer interrupted, "Colonel Vasquez."

"Colonel," Kelsey stressed the title, "what are these people in prison for? What are their crimes?"

The officer responded curtly, "Our country has been struggling a very long time. There are people who do not want peace. It is sad that politics can cause such hardship."

Kelsey smiled sardonically then dropped her head, whispering to Alan, "Yeah, and that these guys are so effective at delivering that hardship."

"Shhh," he hissed a warning. "We're not here to start anything."

The server brought a large platter with three roasted chickens on it. Two other kitchen workers brought other dishes and set them in front of the guests. As they ate, the conversation stayed light and congenial. Several times the young woman returned with more bread or water. Once she bumped Crystal's chair spilling water on her. The woman apologized profusely and began wiping Crystal's clothes and hands with a towel. The colonel screamed invectives at her.

As he was shouting, the woman whispered hurriedly in broken English, "American prisoners in cell under here." She continued wiping frantically and apologizing in Spanish. Finally the officer ordered her out.

"I am sorry for the mess. I am afraid we just cannot get good help here." He laughed heartily at his own wit while the others offered uncomfortable, subdued polite chuckles. Crystal sat pale and stunned.

After lunch was finished the colonel excused himself. "I have matters to attend to. Please feel free to rest here or return to your work. The guards will direct you so you don't become lost."

"—Or poke our noses where they don't want us to," Kelsey said softly. Then she noticed Crystal's face. "What's wrong, honey? You look like you just found out you ate octopus."

Crystal didn't answer. Instead, she spoke to the guard. "Excuse me. I need to go to the ladies room, the bano de mukeres. Can you show me—uh, us—where?" Crystal touched Kelsey on the arm and made a beseeching, urgent face.

"Okay. Uh, yes, I'd like to go also." Kelsey responded to Crystal's entreaty, though she looked puzzled.

One of the guards at the doorway bowed slightly and led the two ladies down a short hallway. When they arrived he stood at attention immediately across the hall.

Once inside, Crystal gasped as if she had been holding her breath. "Kelsey, that woman in there," she whispered urgently, "she told me—"

"Whoa." Kelsey touched her arm. "Slow down. What's going on?"

Still whispering, Crystal continued, her manner compelling Kelsey to listen. "When she spilled the water, she told me that Americans were being held here." Her eyes were wide and her face flushed in agitation. "What're we going to do?" She was taking rapid, deep breaths now.

"Take it easy." Kelsey chewed her thumbnail in thought for a few seconds. "We've got to tell Alan somehow." She puzzled a moment longer. "Wait, I've got an idea! Lie down on the floor and don't move. Close your eyes." Kelsey helped her down then called to the guard, "Por favor—can you help us, please?"

She pushed open the door showing Crystal lying on the floor. "Get the doctor. Senorita is ill. Infirmo." She gestured to illustrate the problem. "Don't just stand there, go get the doctor!" With that, she shooed him away. "Andele!"

Within a minute Alan knocked on the door. "Kelsey, Crystal, what's wrong?"

"Come in—now." Kelsey motioned him inside. As she did, she waved at the guard. "Gracias. Would you bring us some water? Agua?"

"Si." The guard scurried away.

"Crystal? What happened?" Alan knelt beside her. As he did, she opened one eye.

"Are we alone?" she whispered.

"Sure," Kelsey said. "Now tell him what you told me."

Crystal explained about the message. "What can we do?"

Alan shook his head slowly. "I don't know. They're not going to just walk us down to meet these folks for a big reunion. For now we might just have to play it cool and see what we can do from the outside." He smiled warmly as he offered her his hand. "C'mon, get up. You can stop acting now." He held her hand briefly as she remained seated on the floor. Then he glanced at Kelsey who was snickering. "What's with you?"

"Oh nothing, I just don't remember the last time I shared the ladies room with a man, that's all." All three of them laughed.

The guard returned with a pitcher of water. Alan thanked him then turned back to Crystal. "You do look a little pale. Maybe you should sit here a few minutes longer." He dipped a paper towel in the cool water and gently stroked it over Crystal's face. She smiled at first then looked up at Kelsey who was observing the scene with a raised eyebrow. She blushed.

"I think I'm all right now, thanks." Crystal stood up on her own and Alan backed off, still holding the towel.

"C'mon, you two. We've got work to do and plans to make." Kelsey matter-of-factly pushed past them both and out the door.

CASPER PENMARTIN, WITH HIS eyes closed, sat on a wooden box and leaned against the tree. Duke wiped his hands on a rag.

"So, you're riding again?" Penmartin asked.

"Yeah, I finally got to where I could kick-start this thing."

"How's your friend, the one that was shot?"

"He's over that but I'm afraid he's suffering from a heart problem now."

Duke couldn't contain his amusement as Penmartin looked at him with concern. "Yeah, he's gone ape over a woman and I believe it's terminal."

Penmartin grinned. "But you look like you're doing okay." He sat forward. "What about that young woman, Crystal, wasn't it?"

Duke looked away and remarked casually, "She took off to Guatemala."

Penmartin peered at Duke. "So, where does that leave things?"

"I told her I didn't want her to go and she went anyway. So I'm moving on without her."

"Well, then I think you'd better come back to the center with me."

"What're you talking about?"

"Anyone who'd let a woman like that get away has obviously got brain damage we overlooked somehow."

Instead of laughing at Penmartin's joke, Duke' anger flared. "She didn't have to go there." He stood up, nearly shouting. "People die in places like that!"

A knowing sadness dawned on Penmartin's face. "Dear Lord. Is that what happened to your parents?" He leaned forward and clasped his hands around his knees. "I'm sorry, man." He paused a second. "Look, maybe if you wrote to her, told her what you're feeling—"

Duke slowly returned to his work. "Even if I did it probably wouldn't get to her before she left to come back."

"Well, do this. Write to her now and tell her where your head's at. You can give her the letter when you see her. She'll read what's in your heart and understand." He rose and patted Duke on the back on his way to his vehicle. "Hope, son. That's what God teaches us. Hope and trust—hold onto that."

LATER THAT EVENING DUKE sat at the old kitchen table. For only a brief instant he paused with pencil in hand. Once he put it to paper he didn't stop until he had completed four pages. The task engrossed him completely and he didn't notice the sound of a motorcycle pulling into the yard. The knock at the door made him jump.

"It's open," he called without looking up from his task.

"Reggie said you got off early today." Camira glanced down at what he was writing.

My dear Crystal,

I love you. I have to say that first because with the way I've been acting lately you probably are having doubts about it. I don't know if there's a tool to fix what I've broken, or if it can even be fixed. But I know that—

DUKE STOOD AND HURRIEDLY turned the papers over. "Oh, yeah. I had to meet with Penmartin. He still thinks he has to check up on me I guess."

"Uh, hum—" she responded.

"What did you want?" he asked politely but with no invitation in his manner.

She pulled out a chair and sat. "There were some things I've been thinking about the group that I wanted to talk over with you."

"Well—" He looked down at the papers on the table then back at her. "I guess I can take a break. What is it?"

"I was hoping we could go somewhere. Aren't you hungry? I haven't eaten and I'm starved. C'mon," she urged playfully, "my treat."

He looked around, hesitating, then shrugged. "Sure, why not?"

"Where you want to go, that diner just outside town?"

"Yeah, I guess." He hustled her out. "We'll need to take my truck."

"Okay," Camira answered brightly.

CHAPTER 31

"George," Kelsey asked on the long ride back to the hospital compound, "could you get some information on the plan of that prison?"

"Sure, I'll check around. What have you got in mind?"

In the back of the truck an exhausted Alan, Crystal and Calvin chatted lightheartedly for a few miles but soon Calvin nodded off.

"There he goes," Alan laughed.

"Oh, I'm beat," Crystal yawned, "and no coffee to keep me going." She poked the boxes and duffels under her. "This seat isn't exactly first class."

Alan shifted back against the cab of the truck. "Here, lean on me and doze awhile if you can." Crystal hesitated only a second then laid her head on his shoulder and cuddled into a comfortable position.

"Thanks, Alan. I can barely keep my eyes open. Let me know when we get to camp and I'll help unload," she mumbled in near-sleep. Alan put his arm around her, steadying her as the truck hit a pothole. She only slightly stirred. He held her that way for several minutes. Just before she drifted into oblivion she thought she felt him softly kiss the top of her head.

When they arrived at camp they all muttered groggy goodnights and stumbled to their respective quarters except for Calvin who jaunted off to night duty in the ward area.

When Crystal finally dragged out of the bed the next morning she found that George had gone before the others rose and that Alan and Kelsey had gotten up early to tend the patients while she slept.

"I don't know what happened," she said apologetically. "I slept so hard. Kelsey, why didn't you wake me?"

Kelsey just laughed.

"Why don't you go get something to eat?" Alan asked with a twinkle in his eye. "Wouldn't want you fainting on us."

Crystal blushed but obeyed. When she returned she immediately became absorbed in the care of patients. At lunch the conversation turned to more serious things.

"I've been thinking about the situation at that prison," Kelsey said. "But I'm not sure what we can do. I mean, we're not exactly 'special forces' here."

"No, but I'd like to think someone else would want to help me if I were in that place," Crystal remarked soberly.

Alan held Crystal's gaze for a few seconds before averting his eyes to Kelsey. "Let's look at this from several angles—getting word to someone, making contact with the Americans in the prison, figuring out how to free them—all those things." The big bell rang, signaling visitors. Alan rose quickly. "We'll talk again tonight."

TWO DAYS LATER RAIN began to fall. Crystal sat in her tent writing in her journal.

Day 20—So much is happening I haven't had time to write anything down. I'll try to catch up. We discovered Americans being held in a prison about 60 miles from here. I feel so helpless. As I look over my life nothing I've learned has prepared me for this. Alan and Kelsey are going through their contacts to see what can be done. Right now I can only pray for God's help in this. Alan thinks I should consider staying on here. He's a fine person and I've grown fond of him. Maybe I can do more good here—

The wind suddenly whipped the tent violently and threatened to pull it loose in places.

"What's going on?" Crystal shouted to Kelsey over the noise of flapping nylon and canvas. "I know rain is common but is this wind?"

"No," Kelsey yelled back. "We're trying to find out on the radio what's happening and how long it's going to last."

George battled his way through the weather and drove in that night. "Have you heard? A hurricane's working its way toward here. This is just the edge of it. It's stalled off the coast. They say it's gathering strength but it's a big one already."

"What happens here if there's a hurricane?" Crystal asked nervously.

"We'll have to mobilize in case the river overflows." Alan had assembled the entire group together. He began assigning duties. Everyone scurried out into the rain to pack up critical supplies. In the midst of all the preparations, George burst into the hospital tent.

"I just got word on the radio. The hurricane's going to hit us in about six hours. We'd better be ready to move."

"Where's it coming ashore, George?" Kelsey asked.

"About twenty miles up the coast from the town we went to but heavy rains are predicted for this entire area."

"We definitely have to move," Alan said. "A flood or a mudslide could wipe out this whole place! Let's go!"

Crystal noticed Kelsey pulling George aside. "Did you find out anything about the layout of that prison?"

"What? Oh, the prison. Yeah, I found out there's a ground level, where we were, then there's two more levels below that. If there's a flood anybody down there won't be able to get out!"

Crystal gasped. "Oh, God, no!"

PHIL'S DINER WAS SLOW for a Thursday night. "Baseball game's running late, I guess," he speculated to two men sitting at the counter. "No one leaves till it's all over." They both grunted in agreement.

Just then the door swung open and the screen slapped shut behind two new diners.

"Well, hello, Daniel," Phil greeted him and nodded to Camira. "Joey, your buddy's here."

Joey wheeled out of the kitchen. Duke remained standing to greet Joey. He pulled him up out of the wheelchair and sat him in his lap as he slid into a booth. Camira sat opposite the two.

"Who is this, Mr. Daniel?" Joey asked.

Duke blushed for a second. "Uh, Joey, this is Ms. Camira. She's in my motorcycle church group."

"Hello," Joey said politely but his attention was on Duke. "When're you going to take me for a ride on your Indian? It's soooo cool!"

Duke laughed and wrestled with Joey a minute before answering. "We'll have to ask Phil but it's running better all the time. I think it's about ready to take out and be sure we'll get back without walking."

The whole time Duke and Joey were talking, Camira looked at the menu then out the window. Finally she interrupted. "Hey man, can we eat?"

"Sure." Duke sat Joey back in his chair. "Joey, what's good tonight?"

"I made the soup," Joey said proudly.

"Then soup it is. You want soup, Camira?"

A little impatient, Camira looked again at the menu then called to Phil behind the counter. "You got any chicken left this late that's not all dried out?"

He paused a second. "Yes, ma'am. And the potatoes are fresh-mashed."

"Well, ain't that just wonderful," she muttered under her breath. "Great," she called. "I'll have that."

"Phil, can I have some of Joey's soup? That is, if it's not POISONED!" Duke raised his voice and tickled Joey.

"Joey, c'mon," Phil said. "Leave 'em alone."

"Okay. Bye, Mr. Daniel. Bye, Miss—uh—Ca—"

"Camira," she finished for him curtly as Joey wheeled out to the kitchen.

"What's with you?" Duke asked.

"When did you get so into rug-rats?"

"I don't know. Joey's just a kick, that's all. You don't like kids?"

"No, and don't hope to, and I remember a time when you swore off 'em, too." She flashed her coy smile. "Remember those days?"

Duke responded matter-of-factly, "Yeah, I guess. Seems a lifetime ago now, though. So much has happened since then. So much is different." He looked her squarely in the face. "What about you? Don't you look back on those years and wonder how you lived through it?"

She laughed out loud. "Look back? All there is for me is forward. Times past are times past." She caught herself. "Except the time you and me were together."

He noted her look. It was hopeful yet questioning. "Camira, I—"

"Here's your chicken, ma'am. And your soup, Daniel. Joey made me use a big bowl. I told him it was too much but leave whatever you don't want I guess. Eat up."

After Phil walked off Camira snickered condescendingly. "Can you believe that guy? 'Here's your chicken ma'am, eat up.' Where did he come from, the hayfield?"

"He's just being polite. It's called courtesy. You know, where you treat people with respect whether they deserve it or not." His own voice had the slightest edge to it.

"Hey, don't get all tweaked. I was just making a joke." She frowned. "You know, Duke, you used to be fun."

"Yeah, well, none of us are what we used to be, are we?" He started on his soup.

Phil and Joey watched from behind the kitchen doors. "Who you think that woman is, Joey? She's got a pretty face but she looks irritated like she ate a dill pickle." Joey and Phil laughed then ducked away from the window in the door as Camira looked up.

THAT NIGHT LONG AFTER Camira had left in a huff the door to Duke's apartment opened suddenly and Grunt burst in.

"Well, come in, I guess," Duke said jokingly.

Grunt walked over to the old television set by the window and turned the channel. "You better see this."

The newscaster announced, "—The hurricane has gone slightly south but the heavy rains have already caused flooding and mudslides in parts of Guatemala. There is no report currently of loss of life but property damage is estimated in the millions."

Duke's face blanched and he sat back in the large chair, unable to speak. Grunt volunteered, "Look, one of the guys has a brother that's a ham radio operator. He says he can reach that far. Move it now and we can go over."

Seconds passed and Duke's expression turned hard. "I can't. I told her—"

"Are you through yet?"

"But—"

Grunt pulled him up from the chair. "Shut up and get in the truck."

CHAPTER 32

Gouging chunks out of the bank, the swollen river ripped trees down and towed them along with the other debris. The Red Cross crew had moved over half the camp's supplies with borrowed trucks and strong backs. Tents struck in a hurry were folded and thrown on the back of a collection of motorized vehicles that also groaned with loads of patients.

Crystal found Alan in the melee. Shouting, she stopped him. "I know there's still a lot to move, but Alan, the river goes right by that prison. We have to do something!"

He shook his head. "I'm sorry Crystal, but these patients are my first priority! We can go after we get everyone to safer ground but not now."

She put her hands on her hips and scowled as Alan jumped on the running board of a loaded farm truck as it rattled by. Making her way through the frenzied evacuation, Crystal searched the crowd until she found Kelsey.

"I'm going to that prison." Kelsey looked down at Crystal's hand on her sleeve.

"Somebody has to! Can you help?"

"Okay," Kelsey yelled and nodded through the torrent. "Find George. I'll finish here."

George had just returned to the site from an uphill run of supplies. Crystal jogged alongside his truck shouting, "George, we're going to the prison. Will you drive us?"

"Who?" he shouted back. "Who's going?"

"So far, you, me and Kelsey. I don't think Alan can spare anybody else."

"Does he say it's okay for you to go?"

"He says he'll be along later," Crystal hedged, hoping George wouldn't notice.

"All right, let me try to find a gas barrel that doesn't have water in it and fill up. You two meet me by the road. Bring some ropes, some tape, a flashlight of some sort if you can find it and empty gallon water jugs."

Crystal scurried around trying to round up the items George had asked for and returned to the meeting site with ropes thrown over her shoulders and two water jugs in each hand. "Couldn't find any tape," she told him.

"Okay. This old truck sometimes needs a little putting back together. Look under the seat. You should find a roll there."

In a moment Crystal held up the tape she had found. "Let's go get Kelsey."

They sloshed through camp, even the four-wheel drive slipping on the watery path. Kelsey flagged them down and, after Crystal threw open the door, squeezed into the tiny cab. George barely slowed.

"Made it," Kelsey declared as she slammed the door. "Let's get going!"

The intrepid little truck slid but continued to go forward. After they reached a roughly paved road and headed in the direction of the town George asked, "So, what's the plan?"

Kelsey and Crystal looked at each other, shrugging in embarrassed ignorance.

George looked over at the two of them. "So, we're going into a possibly flooded, possibly still guarded prison to look for people we don't actually know are there and certainly don't know where they are?"

Crystal and Kelsey both looked at him. "Well, yeah."

Throwing his head back he guffawed, barely maintaining control of the vehicle. "This is certainly going to be a night to remember." They all laughed for a few seconds before a thoughtful silence took over.

EVERYTHING THAT COULD BE moved from the compound was already on safer ground or loaded into the last of the trucks. The warning bell clamored intermittently as the wind rocked it back and forth. When Alan and the remaining workers arrived in the new camp, Alan began a headcount.

"Everybody here and okay?" He looked around the soaked group huddled together in the one tent they had been able to erect in the wind and rain. "Where are Crystal, Kelsey and George?"

"They left over two hours ago," Calvin answered. "I thought you sent them for something."

"Two hours? Where could they—" Alan stopped in mid-sentence. "Oh no! Calvin," he barked, "what have we got that's drivable right now?"

"Nothing that could go in this mud. George's truck is the only thing that's four-wheel drive."

Alan clenched his fist against the tent support as he looked out into the downpour. Desperation mixed with anger contorted his face.

"Why would anybody do anything so—" He closed his eyes and leaned his head wearily against the post. After a few seconds, he straightened, shook his head slowly and turned his attentions to the patients in the tent.

LIGHTNING FLASHED, KEEPING THE road more or less in view. The truck fishtailed and nearly spun out in the watery mud washing over the asphalt, eradicating the road.

"The rain's slacking up a little," Crystal offered hopefully.

Kelsey frowned. "Yeah, but run-off from the mountains can cause the worst flooding after the rains have subsided."

"Look, over there," Crystal shouted as she pointed to the right. "Isn't that the town? Wasn't the prison on the west side?"

"Yeah," George boomed.

Though the four-wheel-drive truck had considerable ground clearance, the water was threatening to drown the engine. About a hundred yards from the prison they climbed a slight rise. George stopped.

"I'm afraid if we go any further we might not be able to drive out. We can leave the truck here and wade. The water's not moving that fast yet."

Crystal swallowed hard. "Okay."

"Yes, ma'am." Kelsey got out of the truck. "Hey, this rope is probably a couple hundred yards or more. Let's anchor to the bumper and feed it out as we go."

"Got it!" Crystal fastened the jugs to the remaining bundles of rope, causing them to float in the water.

"Good thinking, girl," Kelsey shouted.

GRUNT AND DUKE LISTENED while the ham radio operator set up his signal-hopping network.

"What we do is find someone close to where we're targeting," he explained. "Then that person will raise another and so on, until we have a line of contacts to relay messages. Did you say your friend is with a Red Cross group?"

"Yes," Duke answered. "It's a hospital camp or something like that."

The operator nodded. A voice crackled from the speaker. "Affirmative. Say again." To the anxious pair, he said, "They've reached a Red Cross group with only portable radios in the trucks. The signal's not clear. We may have to wait until morning."

"Please keep trying," Duke said. "Tell them it's for Crystal Harper."

"Okay. What's the message?"

"Say—say Duke's waiting for her to come home."

"I'll do the best I can."

"Thanks man. I appreciate your help."
"No sweat. Glad to."

EVERYTHING WAS WET INCLUDING the radio Calvin was talking on but he found Alan. "Message came over the radio for Crystal. Some guy back in the states, David or Duke or something like that, I think, says to tell her he's waiting for her. That's it. When do you think she'll be back?"

Alan looked out into the wet void. "I don't know."

"Well, will you tell her? I've got the memory of a flea."

"Yeah, I'll give her the message."

"Great. Thanks."

"Sure. No problem." He took a tired, deep breath. "So, his name is Duke."

"What was that?" Calvin asked.

"Oh, nothing," Alan muttered then turned back to the patients huddled in the makeshift shelter.

GEORGE, KELSEY AND CRYSTAL waded through the deepening water with George feeding out the heavy rope as they went. The darkness was occasionally interrupted by lightning but no one except them appeared to be out. After a few slips and dunkings, the rescuers reached the end of the rope.

"Let's tie the rope off to that tree," Kelsey suggested. "It doesn't look that far now."

With the water dragging at their legs with every step they finally made it to the prison. The front door was open and unguarded. Water poured in. No lights were on.

"We've got this one flashlight but that's it," George offered.

"Okay." Crystal's adrenaline was pumping, and she pressed forward with a new drive. "The woman said the Americans were down below."

"That could be anywhere," Kelsey offered.

"Well, let's see where the water's flowing," Crystal said. "It'll go to the lowest point. There must be stairs."

"That college education kicking in?" Kelsey grinned.

"Girl scouts."

"Over here, you two." George motioned them down the hall. "I hear water rushing."

Crystal shuddered. "This place was eerie enough in the daylight with people in it. In the dark it's worse."

"Yeah, but no prisoners. Maybe they had enough warning. The Americans may not even be here."

"I have to know for sure." Crystal pressed forward. She pointed to water flowing steadily down some stone steps. "Look here."

"Watch out. Those could be slippery," George cautioned.

They began to descend carefully. The small flashlight shone a single beam just large enough to make shadows. With no railings, they stayed close to the wall. Kelsey slipped and was on her way down when George grabbed her arm. At the bottom of the stairs they came to a landing with water eddied against closed doors.

"No locks on this side," Crystal said and tried unsuccessfully to open one.

George labored through thigh-high water. "These old doors have swelled." As soon as he freed the door, it jerked out of his hands and the force of the water nearly took Crystal off her feet.

"Let's secure a rope here," Kelsey suggested. "It might be hard to get back up." "Good idea," George said.

One door opened onto a long hallway while the other led to another set of stairs. "What do ya' think?" George asked. "This hall or go down another level?"

"The lower level will fill first if it hasn't already," Crystal said. They exchanged glances.

"Okay," they said in unison.

CHAPTER 33

The swelling, sweeping river threatened to overwhelm everything in its path and was attacking the foundations of the prison. Pieces of stone and mortar began to shift in the face of the powerful onslaught of water and debris. The trio strained against fatigue and futility, calling to the walls, listening for some sign of the Americans.

Kelsey stopped to listen. "What's that banging in the pipes above us?"

"This water is too noisy," George answered. "I can't hear anything else."

"Move down this hall a little farther," Kelsey said, leading the way.

"Yes, I hear it too now," Crystal said. "But I can't tell how close it is." The three pushed through the waist-high water. Finally they came to a huge waterlogged wooden door. Muffled shouts came from behind it.

"Hello! Are you all right?" Crystal called.

From the other side a faint answer came in English. "Yes, get us out. Water rising. Hurry."

George studied the door in the minimal beam of the flashlight. "If we open this door the cell's going to flood." Kelsey and Crystal looked at each other, then at George.

"Well, we have to do something quickly," Kelsey said. "This water's really rising fast."

"Hello in there," Crystal shouted. "We're going to unlatch the door. On three, okay?"

"Yes, on three."

"Okay, ladies. If you've been savin' up strength for something now's the time. Ready?" George challenged. "One! Two! Three!"

The door groaned and jerked out of their hands. George, Kelsey and Crystal struggled to stay upright in the torrent. "Here, Kelsey, pass this rope in but hang onto that wall," George instructed.

"Here's a rope." Crystal shouted above the rush of the flood. "Tie it around you."

A scream came from inside the cell as the river crashed through the outer wall. Stones began to fall. The rope jerked hard while George, Kelsey and Crystal strained, dragging the weight of the prisoners against the current. They hauled in line, inch by inch.

"C'mon," Kelsey shouted. "This foundation won't hold much longer!" Stones splashed all around them. George threw himself behind the door and backed up to the wall to anchor Crystal and Kelsey.

"Get against the side and pull around the door," he shouted above the roar of the water.

The three pulled mightily and finally dragged the prisoners clear of the torrent.

"C'mon, we've got to hurry," Kelsey barked.

"We'll head up these steps. Hang onto the rope." Crystal assisted a woman who was disoriented and bleeding from the head. The weary band half climbed, half crawled up the eighteen steps to the doorway. But the heavy wooden door was jammed shut and wouldn't budge. They collapsed in exhausted defeat on the stairs while water trickled around them.

"I can't believe this!" Kelsey yelled and banged the door with her fist. Suddenly, voices on the other side cried excitedly. The door was thrust open. More water poured in as two bright flashlights glared into the faces of Crystal and the others who were quaking in terror.

"Crystal," a familiar voice called, "is that you?"

She was puzzled, momentarily dazed. Then recognition brought a rush of relief. "Alan?"

"If I'd known this was going to be a swimming party," Alan joked, "I'd have brought my water wings." She threw her arms around him. The strained concern on his face was only partly disguised by a tight smile. He held her for several seconds. Then when she finally released him he asked, "Who're your friends here?"

"They're hurt. We need to get them to the hospital right away," Crystal cried.

In less than five minutes Alan, now joined by the larger Calvin, helped the tired party to the top floor. After a quick look around Calvin gave the "all clear" signal and everyone scurried to a large off-road vehicle.

"Where did this come from?" Kelsey marveled at the giant van.

"An anthropologist that works with one of our villages drove in to offer help," Alan said. "We took him up on it and borrowed these wheels." He gave the driver's seat to Calvin and began to check the escapees for injuries.

The woman had a concussion, a broken leg and a deep cut on her right arm. The man's chest was abraded and his shirt torn off revealing a painfully dislocated shoulder. All had bleeding hands and rope burns. George was still short of breath and his pulse and blood pressure were dangerously high. Kelsey and Crystal suffered minor rope burns and numerous but not serious cuts and bruises.

"What can we do for them?" Crystal asked.

"Well," Alan sighed, "George needs to be monitored and the woman should be x-rayed and watched. Calvin, can you—"

"I'm way ahead of you." Calvin picked up the radio mike. "This is Red Cross One—" For several minutes he called out to the airwaves.

Alan looked intently at Crystal. "I can't believe you did that."

"How did you know where—"

Alan smiled. "It didn't take much to figure out after they told me you three had gone. So when the guy came by with the truck, well, we just took off."

Finally, Calvin called, "A British emergency field camp has a helicopter about two miles away and the storm is easing enough to get out safely."

ON THE DARK BUMPY trip the woman kept trying to fall asleep. "What's your husband's name?" Crystal asked to keep her awake.

"Glen, his name is Glen, and I'm—"

At that moment the man's body jerked and he yelped abruptly as Alan put the dislocated shoulder back in place.

The woman, glanced over at the suffering man and breathlessly in pain from her own injuries, finished her sentence. "—Patsy."

Within minutes they arrived at a small clearing where a large helicopter sat with slowly turning rotors. Patsy, Glen and George were helped onto the aircraft while quick goodbyes were said. Glen, groggy from the pain medication Alan had given him, still managed to speak haltingly to Crystal and Kelsey. "I don't think I've ever—met a real—hero before. God certainly knew—what he was doing—when he sent you. Thank you."

Hero? Crystal raised her eyebrows at the label. "No, once we heard you were being held there, we just had to come," Crystal observed. "I don't believe we ever thought about it; we just did it." Kelsey nodded in agreement.

"Anyway, we're—very—grateful," he murmured as fatigue and medication overtook him.

JUST BARELY PEEKING OVER the horizon, the sun greeted the rescuers driving back to the makeshift hospital camp. Kelsey and Crystal climbed out along with the others.

"What a night!" Kelsey heaved a deep breath.

"Yes, but you know, it doesn't seem real in the daylight."

At that moment Kelsey took a misstep and groaned. "It seems real enough to me, and quite frankly, I've had about all the real I can stand for awhile. I'm going to find a cot or something and sleep for about two days!"

A few of the team came out to greet them. "Welcome back. Where've you been?"

"We just went to see a few friends to make sure they were okay in the storm," Kelsey grinned wearily. "You know, good neighbor stuff."

"I know it left y'all in a bind but we'll explain after a few hours' sleep." Crystal followed Kelsey into a small tent that had two cots in it.

"I don't know whose these are and I don't care." Kelsey collapsed onto one. Crystal, her mind still racing from the night's rescue, located a piece of paper to jot a few notes down for her journal.

Day 26— Nearly time to return home. Last night we rescued some Americans from a prison. It was touch and go. Think the angels must have been holding onto our ropes. They called us heroes. Terrified, cold and wet in the pitch-black darkness with no clue? Some heroes. But Daddy, you were right. This night I will never forget.

Finally, intense fatigue took over from the adrenaline rush of the night. Crystal's head touched the cot and even in the midst of the noisy, waking camp she was instantly asleep.

WITHIN TWO DAYS THE river had calmed somewhat and the move back to the original camp had begun.

"Look! The river didn't come up this far after all!" Happy shouts accompanied busy hands as they gathered up storm-strewn supplies and began righting benches and tables. Some tin had blown off the roof of the main shelter but even the bell was still in place, quiet now in the aftermath.

"It seems we have our work cut out for us just the same," Crystal observed.

"Actually, that's not completely true." Alan came up behind her, standing very near but without touching.

Crystal turned and faced him, not backing away. "What did you say?" she asked with a soft and receptive demeanor.

"The mission group wants you to head back tonight so you can make your flight day after tomorrow." He held her gaze, smiling with his kind eyes.

Crystal dropped her chin. "I guess it's time to click my heels and go back to Kansas, eh?" Through the silence between the two of them, Crystal's mind raced. *What am I going back to though? There's so much for me here.* She looked up and smiled at Alan.

"You know you can stay if you want. I'll ride over with you and we'll make the arrangements with the mission folks." Though his eyes didn't plead, a subtle hopefulness seeped through his offer. He grasped her arms gently. They stood there for several seconds.

Suddenly, Calvin interrupted. "Crystal, hey, in the confusion of the storm and all I forgot. Alan did you tell her?"

Alan continued to hold her gaze. "No, I didn't."

"Well, this radio message came in during the storm while you were gone. Some guy—Dave, Darrel, uh—"

"Duke?" She turned to look at him. Alan released his hold. "What was the message?"

"Something about waiting for you to come home."

"Thanks, Calvin," Alan said tersely. Calvin shrugged innocently then walked off.

She turned back to Alan, her face beaming. "Alan! He called me? During the storm? Did he say anything else?"

"No, the signal broke up," he replied dully. "That was all."

"He's waiting!" She clasped her hands in delight and relief. "Oh, you don't know how it's been. I love him so much, and then the fight, then I came here, and you made me feel so—" She stopped suddenly in mid-sentence then looked at him accusingly. "Why didn't you tell me about the message?"

"We've been busy," he hedged. "It slipped my mind."

She continued to stare.

"Okay," he blurted out, "you do good work. I needed the help. Besides, you still don't have a job or any real prospects back there. I thought I was doing you a favor." His volume increased. "The guy's a jerk anyway, treating you like that." He dropped his eyes and softened his voice to an intimate tone. "I would never—"

As realization pulled Crystal back from her anger she took his hand in both of hers. "Alan—" She hesitated. "I'll miss this place, and you."

He scowled briefly and looked away.

She tiptoed slightly and kissed the tall man on the cheek. "But I have a home to go to, people who love me." She stepped back and looked into his face for signs of understanding. No emotion at all showed in his rigid countenance. She lingered a few seconds more then stepped away. "I have to go pack."

Alan said nothing and his expression never changed as he watched her leave. Finally he turned and walked slowly toward the hospital tent. "People here love you, too," he muttered under his breath.

Kelsey, standing just out of sight, shook her head and sighed sympathetically.

CHAPTER 34

"Mrs. Harper, you have to tell me when her plane comes in," Duke pleaded. "I'm going to meet her."

"And just why would you do that?" Her sternness put him off for a second then resolve took over.

"So I can tell her I've been an idiot and that I don't ever want to be without her again."

"What makes you think she wants to see you?"

"I just pray that she does."

Ann scrutinized him for several more seconds then sighed. "She'll be flying into Atlanta at 9:20 p.m. We were planning to drive there to pick her up. You'll be sure to meet her at her gate? We can't reach her now to change plans."

"Yes, ma'am. I will."

"Well, okay, but take our car. I don't trust that old wreck of yours."

"Yes, ma'am."

GEORGE'S TRUCK HAD BEEN retrieved after the floodwaters went down and Kelsey prepared to drive Crystal to catch the mission shuttle to the main airport.

"C'mon, kid, get in. You had to come in riding coach but the trip out is first class." Kelsey pushed open the door for Crystal who had already thrown her duffel bag into the back.

"Have you seen Alan?"

"No, he pulled out of here early this morning," Kelsey said.

"Well, okay." Crystal looked around slowly surveying one last time the now familiar activity of the hospital compound then she climbed into the truck and pulled the door solidly shut. "I've told everyone else goodbye. I guess I'll just go."

ON THE WAY THE two women chatted much as they had during their evenings together while sharing sleeping quarters. As they neared the landing strip Kelsey turned to Crystal and asked solemnly, "Did you ever find what you came here for?"

She thought for a second. "Yes, I did," she answered. "First, I don't have to wonder anymore what I'd do in a tough situation."

"Yeah?"

"Yeah—bring rope and flashlights." Crystal and Kelsey both laughed. Then Crystal continued. "But I've learned something else."

"And what's that?"

"That God really is working through me. Only the Holy Spirit could have carried me that night. I'm no hero but I can do great things through Him."

They rode on in thoughtful silence. When the runway was finally in sight Kelsey spoke soberly. "You know you'll be missed."

Crystal nodded.

Kelsey stopped the truck next to the makeshift terminal and turned off the motor. They both got out and Kelsey helped Crystal with her bag.

"Tell George I'm glad to hear he's doing better. And those other people, if you hear from them, tell them I wish them well." Kelsey came around the truck and hugged her. Crystal whispered softly, "And please, tell Alan that he will forever be a part of my memories of this time."

Kelsey released her. Crystal noticed tears in her eyes but she gruffly turned away and climbed back into the truck. Crystal, shedding a few tears herself, smiled warmly as she waved goodbye. After watching the truck disappear into the trees she finally picked up her bag and strode resolutely toward the landing area, greeting the others who were arriving.

NINE HOURS AND TWO plane changes later Crystal arrived at the international concourse at Atlanta's Hartsfield Airport. Waiting for her bags before going through customs, she walked to a coffee stand. She turned around, stirring the contents of the cup in her hand, and looked up. Surprised, she saw what she thought were two familiar faces on the escalator moving away from her.

"Patsy! Glen!" she called loudly, waving her arm.

Patsy turned around and shrieked, "Glen, it's her! From that night!" She waved vigorously, nearly losing her balance.

Glen, too, waved then yelled, "We're late for our plane now but we got your number from the hospital. We'll call. Thank you again." They were quickly whisked out of sight by the airline courtesy representative.

Crystal stood in stunned silence for more than a minute. The night of the rescue replayed itself in her head. Then she headed toward customs. She fidgeted impatiently while her bags were checked. Her walk picked up speed as she hurried for the terminal. Topping the escalator, she looked up in surprise, her eyes opened wide. In front of her stood Duke with a bouquet of roses in his arms and a hopeful look on his face. She dropped her bag and threw her arms around him. He lifted her off the ground in an enthusiastic embrace.

"What are you doing here? Where are Mom and Dad?" She spoke excitedly between kisses. "I'm so happy you came." Travelers going by smiled with the soft look of reminiscence on their faces.

At last, Duke sobered and looked her full in the face. "Please forgive me. I'm sorry I wigged out. It's just that I was so—so—"

"—Scared?" Crystal volunteered.

He pulled back in surprise. "What? How did you—"

"My mother shared a little wisdom with me before I left. I wanted to see you to tell you I understood. But then I couldn't find you and I thought, well, I didn't know if..." The sadness and desperation of that moment hit her like a wave. Suddenly she blurted, "They asked me to stay and for a while

I thought I might. But then you called and I had to come here and see you, to see your face, to know—"

"What? That I'm a class-A jerk and a complete fool?" He grinned then kissed her briefly again.

"No, that's not it." Her words came out in serious, measured tones. "I had to know where I really—" She paused. "—was wanted."

He touched her face tenderly and kissed her softly, lovingly. As he held her close he put his cheek to hers and whispered, "Here, right here, where you're loved."

Her tears flowed freely as joy and relief filled her.

Finally he released her. "Look," he began as he took her hand, "we've got a lot to talk about, important things, but I promised your mother I'd have you back before one. And if it's all the same to you, I'd like to stay on her good side."

Both laughing as the tension eased, they held each other again in a reassuring embrace before heading out of the terminal.

AT 10 A.M. CRYSTAL awoke to whispers outside her door.

"Do you think she's awake yet?"

"It's late. She slept a long time."

"I know you've missed her but that's a long, hard trip. I'm sure she's exhausted."

"Can't I wake her up?"

"No, you can't."

As the fogginess of jetlag and exhaustion faded a little Crystal recognized her mother's firm admonition among the whispers. Rousing slowly, she looked around the room half expecting to see the sunlight radiating through tent fabric and Kelsey with her mosquito net wrapped around her. *I might as well get up. No one around here is going to let me sleep anymore anyway.*

She dragged out of the bed and put on her robe Pausing long enough to make a face at herself in the mirror while she ran a brush through her sleep-tangled hair, she finally opened the door. Surprised, she found no one outside and headed across the hall to the bathroom. However when she came out and made her way to the top of the stairs, she looked down at a huge "WELCOME HOME CRYSTAL" sign and four expectant faces.

"Miss Crystal!" Joey blurted out first, so excited he nearly fell out of his wheelchair.

She raced down the stairs, greeting each in turn. Her father, she held close. "You were right, Daddy," she whispered in his ear. "I wrote it all down. I want to remember every minute."

As she hugged her mother, she said, "Thank you, Mama, for everything."

Then she spoke to Phil. "Hello. Did they get you up, too?"

"No," Phil chuckled, "Joey started agitating to come over here about five this morning. We've been up awhile. Welcome home."

Ann took her daughter's hands and smiled tearfully. "We're just glad to have you back safe." Finally releasing her hold on Crystal, she sniffed a bit as she called to the others. "Everyone c'mon. A cold breakfast isn't much of a welcome."

Crystal grinned to herself while her mother, as usual, directed everyone to assigned seats and duties. In that familiar moment the jungle seemed a distant, perhaps even fictional, memory.

"Come sit by me, Miss Crystal." Joey's insistent voice broke the reverie and she joined the others at the table.

As they ate and Crystal answered questions about her trip, she suddenly stopped to ask, "Is there any coffee?"

Her mother looked at her in surprise. "You don't drink coffee."

"I do now, Mama. Things change." Crystal explained the long hours and the trips up into the hills, the living conditions and the constant presence of the soldiers. Her animated descriptions kept everyone around the table enthralled.

A knock at the door interrupted. "Hello, can I come in?"

Crystal's eyes brightened. "Duke, yes, come on." She stood to greet him. He kissed her lightly on the lips, ignoring the audience in the room. Ann quickly looked over at Phil who smiled his approval.

Crystal's father cleared his throat then stood at his seat. "Here Daniel, take my place. I'm done and I can get a chair from the hall. Ann, any of those muffins left?" Crystal's mother rose without speaking and brought the muffins and a pot of fresh coffee.

"Crystal's come back to us a changed woman," Ann commented. "She drinks coffee now."

"Well, that's the least of it, I guess. What about that prison break?" Duke offered innocently while

Crystal winced. "Wasn't that awesome!" All eyes immediately riveted on her.

"Uhm, I was saving that for later," she explained uncomfortably.

"Then let me tell it, please!" Duke jumped in, graphically relating the whole story as she had told it to him, an unmistakable look of pride emanating from his face. The listeners at the table alternated between awestruck silence and terrified gasps. At the end he leaned over to take her hand. Looking her admiringly in the face, he boasted, "And to think I was worried about this one. The Marines will probably want her to come train their special operations people after this." His jocularity overlaid his still fragile relief at her safe return.

"Miss Crystal, are you really a hero?" Joey's rapt look brought a chuckle to everyone.

Crystal's laugh, though, was a little uncomfortable. "I don't know Joey. Some of the people I met down there are much bigger heroes than I am. They rescue people from hunger, disease and despair day in and day out for years at a time and folks like us never hear about it." She drifted to that place for a moment, picturing Kelsey, George and Calvin, and then Alan. Soon, though, she blinked back to the present and made eye contact with Duke who was still holding her hand and smiling at her.

CHAPTER 35

"Debby, I can't even explain what it was like," Crystal bubbled to her close friend. "You'll have to come over soon and I'll tell you everything."

"Great," Debby teased. "Now I can tell everyone that I know the Albert Schweitzer of Central America."

"C'mon. This was a very important experience for me."

"I know, I know, and I do want to hear all about it but that wasn't the reason I called."

"Well, what is it?"

"Do you remember Kathy in our graduating class? Well, she works for a private school somewhere outside Atlanta. She called me in a panic about some new project they're doing. Where she teaches, they're all these smart kids and they want to integrate special education into their school. Something about learning by teaching and peer stuff. I didn't get it all. Anyway, they're looking for someone to put this program together and get it off the ground for them."

"That's amazing!" Crystal exclaimed. "What a concept. Things are certainly up in the air here. It may be worth looking into."

"A good professional opportunity, right?"

"Yes, it is."

"And didn't you tell me that a certain man was going to school in Atlanta in the fall?"

Crystal blushed even in the comparative privacy of the phone conversation.

THAT EVENING CRYSTAL WAS sitting on the porch swing when Duke drove in. He walked up the steps and, noting her pensive mood, eased down quietly beside her. For a moment the two sat without speaking, just moving back and forth in the slow, steady sway of the old swing. Finally Crystal broke the silence.

"I really don't know much about you."

"What do you want to know?" he offered jovially.

"Where did the name Duke come from, and is that what you'd rather be called?"

"My dad loved John Wayne movies. That's what he called me. You, though—" He smiled and kissed her on the cheek. "—can call me whatever you like."

"No, it's important to respect how someone wants to be addressed."

"Why so philosophical?" He reached over and gently turned her face toward him. "This doesn't have anything to do with names, does it?"

"Duke, what I've experienced, what I've seen and been through, I'm not like I was before."

"What are you getting at?"

"When I lost my job and then you ducked out suddenly everything that told me who I was had gone. So I went into a foreign country, into situations that I never dreamed of, met remarkable people, saw—" She stopped and looked at him square in the eye. "Duke, for the first time I see a future that I choose not one that's been handed to me."

"Okay." He responded in a cautiously measured tone. Crystal could see in his eyes the struggle between curiosity and concern. "Now what are you trying to make me see that I'm missing?"

"You're leaving for school in a few weeks and I don't want an every-other-weekend relationship. Not now, not with things the way they are. If two people want to ever have anything as a couple I believe they should be together—to build, dream, plan—together."

He looked down at her hand in his on the swing. "What can I say to—"

She interrupted. "Duke, I've got a chance at a job in the Atlanta area. It's developing a new program at a private school. There's a lot of responsibility but it's also very creative, a great opportunity."

He half stood, eyes brightened, and reached both arms toward her. "Crystal, that's wonderful," he interjected enthusiastically.

Crystal gently refused his embrace. "No, let me finish. Look, I know it's short notice but I have to report to work in two weeks and if you still want, uh, well, I'd like to—"

"Get married?" He perked up and smiled at her, relief and joy radiating from his face. "I thought you'd never ask."

He stood quickly and pulled her up to him, squeezing her in a hug so tight that she squealed. "Duke, you're squashing all the air out of me."

He released her instantly, chagrined, but only briefly. She slid her arms around him and softly brushed her lips on first one cheek then the other. Coming back to center, she looked up into his face. Though they stood with eyes fixed on each other for many seconds, neither wavered.

With no more reasons to turn away in doubt or fear, they pressed together—lips, bodies and souls—now certain that God had indeed brought them together.

Crystal pulled back and smiled at him expectantly.

Duke grinned and studied her without speaking.

"Well?" she asked.

"I'm just trying to imagine what you'll look like first thing in the morning," he teased.

"Duke!" she giggled. "Rule number one of married life: Never look at a woman first thing in the morning."

"CRYSTAL!" ANN SHRIEKED. "PLAN a wedding in two weeks? You can't do this!" While Crystal's mother fluttered out of the room in exasperation her father wrapped his arms around her.

"I'll take care of your mother," he said. "Don't worry about her. I know you've probably already decided how you want everything to be."

"Actually, Daddy, I haven't," Crystal said. "That's the crazy thing. I never would have done anything like this before. I'm wearing new clothes here."

"Well, the look becomes you," he observed as he kissed her on the forehead.

"GOODNESS, IT TOOK YOU two long enough," Debby laughed when Crystal gave her the news. "You were beginning to be the longest-running soap opera of the season!"

"There isn't time to send out invitations so I'm calling everybody. You're coming, aren't you?"

"Of course. I kind of feel like I had a hand in this one."

"Great! See you there."

"SO YOU AND MS. Right are finally gonna' do it." Grunt laughed and slapped Duke on the back. "Camira'll blow a gasket. She was countin' on you bein' available."

"She'll just have to get over it," Duke chuckled.

Grunt stopped laughing. "Oh, and while we're on the subject, I got somethin' to tell you."

"Wait." Duke eyed his friend. "No. Not you? And Mama?"

The big man blushed through his whiskers. "Yeah, well, she kinda' grew on me after the hospital thing, and I ain't gettin' any younger."

"Who'd ever have believed it?" Duke grinned from ear to ear. "Hey, why don't you two hook up with us and we'll make it a double?"

"I guess, just as long as you don't want to do the honeymoon together. I ain't into sharing." Both men laughed out loud.

FRIDAY MORNING, HER WEDDING day, Crystal awoke before sunrise. She lay in bed, the events of the past year playing in the dark room like a private slide show. Phil, the children, Casper Penmartin, Duke, Grunt's rescue. Then the newscast about her job, Duke's proposal and the fight, her trip to Guatemala, Alan, the flood. After all that Atlanta and a new job seemed tame. She propped her head up on one hand and looked out the window at the sun beginning to rise. Soon she heard her mother clanging around downstairs and she got out of bed to join her.

The two women sat alone in the kitchen.

"Mama, I have to tell you how great you've been about this wedding. You've really put everything together in a hurry."

"Oh, not by myself. Phil's offering to have the reception at his diner was the biggest help. You know what it takes to have a wedding—a frock, flowers, food and family."

"Where did that expression come from? I've heard it all my life and never have known."

Ann smiled wistfully. "Your grandmother used to say it every time somebody got married. She said if any one of those things was missing the marriage was sure to fail."

The two women laughed together.

"Well, with Duke's parents gone I hope you and Daddy can be family for him. He hasn't had that in awhile. I'd like today to be special for him, too."

Ann poured Crystal a cup of coffee and set it in front of her. "We will, honey. He's a fine young man.

We're glad to see you two together. Y'all remind me of your dad and me when we were married."

"You two are great together," Crystal beamed sincerely. "What's the secret?"

"That's easy. Don't hold anything back. Live each day together as if there might never be another one." Ann took her daughter's hand across the table. "I only wish for you the happiness your father and I have known."

TWO HOURS BEFORE THE wedding, Crystal and her mother arrived at the church. While Ann was doing Crystal's hair, various friends came and went. Debby stopped by with hugs and tears. Even Joey poked his head in.

"Hey, Miss Crystal, me and my dad'll be on the third row. Be sure to look for us."

She spun around abruptly, jerking her hair loose from her mother's hand.

"What did you say, Joey?"

"I got 'dopted. Now Phil and me can be together always. The judge said we're a family and I can call him Dad if I want to." Joey beamed as he shared his news. "Gotta' go. See ya'."

"See ya', Joey." His whirlwind visit left both the women laughing. Ann observed, "It's a good thing they finally let Phil have that boy."

"Yeah, now Phil won't have to get one of those mail order brides," Crystal giggled.

ON THE FRONT LAWN and now beginning to trickle into the church, a diverse group of guests took their seats. The bride's side held a goodly proportion of the members of the church, people who had known Crystal most, if not all, of her life. In spite of the heat the women, all in elegant dresses, sat next to starched and suited men.

The groom's side also held its share of well-wishers. Sprinkled among conventionally appointed guests were men and women with tattoos and garish hairstyles. Most had on jeans and many strode down the carpeted aisle in heavy black boots.

A generous number of stares went in both directions.

Dr. Reasons moved up and down the aisle shaking hands on each side. He was his usual warm, gracious self but when he came to Reggie with her green hair and facial tattoos even he appeared to be taken aback for an instant. He quickly recovered, though, and welcomed her.

Outside a full one-third of the parking lot was occupied by motorcycles, some older, vintage models, quite a few with custom paint jobs, and all appointed with brightly polished chrome and studded leather accessories. The rest of the lot held all makes of vehicles from Lincolns to pick-up trucks. Arriving last was a large Harley-Davidson. On it rode a tall, stout man with a silvering beard to mid-chest. Riding with him was a shorter woman with ample curves and wavy brown hair.

A now fully-restored Indian pulled in behind the Harley. "Well, Grunt, it's amazing what a clean shirt will do for a man. And is that a haircut I see, too? Eugenia! What have you done to him?"

"Don't push it kid."

"Duke, I'm so glad you included Albert and me in this celebration," she said.

"I still don't know why we couldn't do this outside at Watt and May's," Grunt grumbled.

Mama kissed Grunt, causing him to crack a smile. "I know you're nervous, sweetheart, but it means a lot to me to get married in a church. Thank you for understanding."

"I gotta' run in and talk to Crystal a few minutes," Duke said. "See ya' inside."

PREPARATIONS IN THE BRIDE'S dressing room were starting to come together as the procession of friends and family ceased. However, in just a scant few minutes another pair of heads peeked in on Crystal.

"Patsy and Glen! Come in!" Crystal stood up, completely surprised at the appearance of the two, and once again pulling free of Ann's hair styling attempts.

"Crystal!" Ann chided.

"Mama, these are the people I told you about," she explained excitedly and hugged them both. "How did you— Where did—"

"Well, there are problems with the house and our son seems to have left for parts unknown so we're heading to Florida to stay with Glen's sister for a few months and re-group," Patsy said. "The man, George, from the Red Cross unit got your address for us after we left the hospital. Looking at the map, we noticed we'd pass within an hour of your town, and here we are."

"But how did you know we were at the church?"

"A young man at the gas station knew you and told us about it."

"Please do come in. But I'm afraid there won't be much time to talk. I'm getting married— Wait! You two have to stay."

"No, we couldn't intrude. That's a time for family and close friends."

"Patsy, it doesn't get any closer than executing a prison break in a foreign country together." Crystal laughed and Patsy and Glen joined in.

"Well, the guy's sure getting one tough, resourceful young lady," Glen commented.

Patsy turned to Ann. "We feel so fortunate to be here. This daughter of yours was a godsend. If she and her friends hadn't come along when they did, we might have—"

"Hello. Can the groom come in for a second?" The newly clean-shaven bridegroom peeked in the door. "I mean, I know it's bad luck and everything but I wanted to show you— Oops, I see you have company. I'll come back."

"No, come in. You have to meet—" As Crystal turned, her eyes opened wide in surprise. "Daniel Davis! Where's your—"

Patsy jerked her head around and blinked in stunned silence. Then she found her voice. "Son? Is it—is it you?" Immediately she rushed at Duke and threw her arms around him. Tears streamed down her face. She held him as if she would never let him go. Glen joined them, also overcome with the moment.

"Mom? Dad? How— I thought—" Duke's voice trailed off as he froze in disbelief.

Ann and Crystal both stood with mouths poised to speak but no words came out.

Then Duke blurted, "I thought you were dead." Incredulous, he looked back and forth from one to the other. "They told me your group—all dead—"

"I believe God had a lot to do with it. But actually—" He nodded toward Crystal. "—He had a little help."

Duke looked in Crystal's direction. "What?"

"Duke, these are the people. The prison. The flood."

Consternation began to replace amazement on his face. "Why didn't you tell me?"

"I didn't know," Crystal said. "Everything happened so fast. They needed a hospital. Nobody got around to asking last names."

Glen placed a hand on Duke's shoulder. "Son, it's an amazing story but this young woman and her friends came along when we thought there was no one. Now it looks like she's done the same for you."

"I—I have to sit down." Patsy loosened her hold on Duke but he supported her as she eased into a chair. Ann also, her face pale with surprise, plopped herself down onto the small loveseat next to the window.

Glen was the only one who seemed able to continue. "They told us you had left, Son. How?"

"I took the Indian."

"It runs? We thought it had been stolen."

Still in a daze of disbelief, Duke answered distractedly, "Yeah. Ran good until the wreck."

"Wreck?" Patsy perked up again. "What wreck?"

Duke touched her shoulder. "I'm okay now. This is all that shows." He pointed to the scar on his jaw.

Crystal at last recovered from her shock. "Look, y'all need to talk. We have to postpone the wedding."

"No, no," Glen and Patsy said in unison.

Glen continued, "We've missed three years of major events of our son's life. We're not going to ruin this one." He smiled at Duke. "Besides, she's got our vote." He took both of Crystal's hands. "Thank you—for us and for our son."

Ann studied the three, Glen, Patsy and Duke. "Why don't you all sit awhile and get reacquainted? We've got some time yet. I'll go check on things."

"Yes," Crystal said. "That's perfect. Mama, go ahead." She gestured Ann out of the room then spoke to Patsy and Glen. "Here, make yourselves comfortable."

DUKE BEGAN THE THOUSAND-QUESTION conversation that would fill in the huge gaps in their lives. "I'd like to know where you two have been the last three years and why you didn't let anybody know you were alive. And how did you and Crystal meet up?"

Crystal sat with them, also hearing for the first time Glen and Patsy's story of hiding from the military, being captured and then living in prison. Recounting three years moved the clock rapidly.

IN THE SANCTUARY, REV. Reasons announced to the guests, "The groom's parents have been out of the country for some time and have just this minute arrived. We'd like to give the family the opportunity to talk together on this important occasion. I ask your patience. How about if we invite each guest to tell us your name and how you came to know Crystal and Duke?" His congenial smile grew strained as hands went up on the groom's side first.

After thirty minutes, he sent Ann back to the bride's dressing room. She knocked politely. "Excuse me but we're running out of things to do out here. I hate to interrupt but if we don't start soon I'm afraid Dr. Reasons is going to try to organize a group sing and, well, it won't be pretty."

Everyone exchanged glances then chuckles. Glen spoke first. "You're right. Duke, we have the rest of our lives to catch up now." He took Patsy's hand. "C'mon, we need to get out of here and let these two get married." He guided her out the door after one more quick hug for her son and then Crystal.

Ann excused herself as well. "I'll go rescue the Reverend and make sure everything's ready."

When the two were alone, Duke moved close to face Crystal and took both her hands in his. He released one hand long enough to brush an escaped strand of hair from her cheek.

He chuckled a moment causing her to give him a questioning look. "Now I know why I survived that wreck."

"Why?"

"So I could be around to look after my parents when they got old."

She smiled with him. "Feels pretty good to say that now, doesn't it?" She looked at his face and saw peace, something she had never seen there before.

"Why did you shave off your beard?" she asked.

"I figured this was the face you first fell in love with. It just seemed like the thing to do for today."

"Hmm, I remember. You know, like this, Duke fits you. Maybe I'll have to get used to calling you that after all." She raised her eyebrows. "Grunt didn't—"

He laughed. "No, he thinks his beard is his charisma, kind of a Samson thing. Besides, Mama loves it." Crystal laughed with him. He put both arms around her waist and pulled her close.

"No man could have more than I've received today." Looking her directly in the face he spoke softly. "You've given me back my past. Now I can truly pledge you my future." They kissed until they were interrupted by Ann's return with Crystal's bouquet.

Duke hurried out to change clothes while Ann took up Crystal's last-minute hair styling and helped her glide the silky pure white dress over her head.

WITHIN FIFTEEN MINUTES ALL were at last at the front of the church with Reverend Reasons smiling relief. Duke's father had declined Casper Penmartin's offer to step down as best man and sat, instead, in the pew with his wife and Crystal's parents. Debby was in place beside Crystal. Eugenia stood, beaming, behind Debby, while Grunt, somewhat pale and fidgety, flanked Penmartin.

Parked out in front of the church, wildly decorated with paint, streamers and old shoes, sat Crystal's aged Cadillac outfitted with a brand new transmission and, in the trunk, jumper cables and a complete tool kit—just in case.

ABOUT THE AUTHORS

Kyle Grob - From a young age, Kyle had an interest in anything with two wheels. By age 10, he had saved enough money to buy his first dirt bike; that was the beginning of a lifelong passion that developed into *Saved for Something More*. He went on to compete in professional Extreme BMX events. Today, Kyle is a Welding Engineer who designs, rebuilds and customizes cars and motorcycles. He lives in Georgia with his wife, dog and cats.

Sandra McKee - For most of her adult life Sandra has helped people bridge the gap between where they are and where they want to be: as a career coach, a college educator, a professional development author, a riding instructor and as a mentor for women in transition. *Saved for Something More* was yet another bridge—across the abyss that existed between her and son, Kyle, when her marriage ended.

Raised in the South and having lived all her life there, Sandra wanted to tell a story of healing and self-discovery set in her most familiar part of the world. She and her family still live in Georgia where she pursues her passions: teaching college students, writing books and training horses.

Made in the USA
Charleston, SC
02 September 2012